The Traveler

The Amulet of Life

Melissa Toppen

Copyright © 2014 Melissa Toppen

All rights reserved.

This is a work of fiction. Similarities to real people, places, or events are entirely coincidental.

The Traveler:

The Amulet of Life

Written by Melissa Toppen

TABLE OF CONTENTS

CHAPTER ONE
CHAPTER TWO
CHAPTER THREE
CHAPTER FOUR
CHAPTER FIVE
CHAPTER SIX
CHAPTER SEVEN
CHAPTER EIGHT
CHAPTER NINE
CHAPTER TEN
CHAPTER ELEVEN
CHAPTER TWELVE
CHAPTER THIRTEEN
CHAPTER FOURTEEN
CHAPTER FIFTEEN
CHAPTER SIXTEEN
CHAPTER SEVENTEEN
CHAPTER EIGHTEEN
CHAPTER NINETEEN
CHAPTER TWENTY
CHAPTER TWENTY-ONE
CHAPTER TWENTY-TWO
CHAPTER TWENTY-THREE
CHAPTER TWENTY-FOUR
CHAPTER TWENTY-FIVE
CHAPTER TWENTY-SIX

MELISSA TOPPEN

THE TRAVELER: THE AMULET OF LIFE

Chapter One

"Please take whatever you want, just don't hurt my family." I hear my mother plead. I shoot up, disoriented and confused. I don't know what's happening but the feeling in the pit of my stomach tells me it's not good.

"Please...." I hear my mother whimper once more. It takes me a minute to figure out that I am actually awake. Shaking off my disorientation, I try to process what is happening.

"Don't hurt her." I hear my father say.

I know I should stay put, hide even but I can't sit still. I tip toe to my door and crack it open just enough that I can see into the hall. I don't see anything but I can hear muffled voices, including a man's voice that I don't recognize.

I open my door a little wider, enough that I

can squeeze through it. I walk as quietly as possible down the hall. When I reach the end where the hall opens up to the foyer, our living room to the right, I stop.

"Is there anyone else here?" I hear the man ask.

"No." My mother chokes out, clearly terrified from the tremendous shake in her voice.

I want to help her but I can't make my feet move. That's when I hear it. A loud gun shot followed by a thud.

My mom's body lands just close enough to the hall that I can see her hair and the pool of blood that is quickly forming around her head.

I choke back a scream but again cannot will myself to move. I know she's dead. I can't process it but I know.

Another loud gunshot followed by another thud. I know it's my father this time even though I cannot see into the room.

I quickly make my way back down the hall. My heart is beating so hard and fast I can hear it thudding in my ears.

Please let Myra be okay is all I can think as I

pass my bedroom and proceed to the last door at the end of the hall. Her door is wide open and the room is empty.

My stomach twists in knots. Where is she? Certainly they wouldn't hurt her. She's only twelve.

I search her room, under her bed, the closet. She's no where to be found. Just as I am about to sneak across the hall to my parent's room, I hear her scream.

"Mom, dad! No!" I hear her cry out but her screams are quickly silenced when the third gunshot fires.

"Search the house, make sure there is no one else." I hear another man's voice say.

I scramble to the window and try desperately to pry it open. My dad had been saying for months he was going to fix this window but he still hadn't gotten around to it.

I can't get it open and the quickly approaching footsteps coming down the hall tell me that I am running out of time.

I dive into my sister's closet and pull as many clothes down on top of me as possible, trying my best to cover myself. A ray of light seeps through the crack under the door as the light flicks on and the unknown man steps into the room.

    With each footstep, my heart rate picks up speed. Please don't let him find me, I repeat over and over in my head. I sit completely still, crouched in the corner of the closet under a pile of my sister's clothes.

    This can't be happening. I am desperate to get to my family but I know I can't help them if they find me so I stay put.

    My hands are shaking uncontrollably. I try so hard to quiet my breathing. I know he's close. And then the door opens.

    At first I think he doesn't see me but then I feel something grab my head and suddenly I am being dragged out of my sister's room and down the hall by my hair.

    I twist and kick, trying to break free of his hold on me but it's useless. Realization sets in when he stops, dropping me next to the body of my little sister. This is it. My entire family is dead and I'm next.

    I hear the gun cock and the cool metal against my temple. I'm not ready to die. I have experienced so little in my fourteen years on this earth. I am shaking so hard as I wait for him to pull the trigger. I wait for death but it never comes.

I feel myself being lifted and shoved to the side. It is then that I finally open my eyes. Everything happens so quickly that I can barely process it.

The two men are laying not three feet from me, either unconscious or dead, neither one moving. Standing directly over them is a man.

He is stunning, god like even. Tall, lean, with dark brown hair and perfect features. Then his eyes meet mine........

I shoot up in my bed gasping for air. I have had this same nightmare countless times but the effect it has on me never weakens.

Each time I wake up to the sad realization that it's not just a bad dream but my reality.

My recollection of the events that took place that night four years ago are scattered and sometimes the pieces don't fit together, but I guess that's how your mind copes with things like this.

THE TRAVELER: THE AMULET OF LIFE

It's in my dreams that I remember it all. Eventually the dream will fade and until the next, I am left with only one image. Bright green eyes staring back at me.

The dream never gets past that point and I can't remember what happened after that. It's like the moment his eyes met mine, everything went blank and the next thing I knew I was sitting at the police station.

They kept asking me over and over again what happened and how I managed to escape. I tried telling them someone was there, someone had saved me but they blamed it on my situation. My mind creating something that wasn't real due to stress and shock.

They assured me that when the police arrived they found no one else in the house and no sign that anyone else had been there.

Eventually I started to believe them. After all, the two men had vanished, leaving police to believe that they had spared me and left on their own free will.

Within hours my grandparents were at my side and I have been with them ever since. After the funerals, I packed up what little I had left of my old life in Chicago and started over on my grandparent's farm in Tennessee.

It's been four years and I still feel like any minute they are going to walk through the door and this will have all been some crazy nightmare that never actually happened.

It's hard to accept when your worst fear becomes your reality.

Then there's my angel. Whether he was real or I simply made him up, he changed me that night.

I remember the way my surroundings seemed to warp around him. The pull between us so strong that I felt like my body was going to rip apart and break into a million pieces.

I want to believe that he was just my mind playing tricks on me but deep down I know there's more.

It's like I can feel him. I don't know how to explain it but I can still sense his presence. As if he found me that night and has not left my side since then.

I lay back down, trying my best to push all of this to the back of my mind. It's still dark out and I really need to go back to sleep. I don't get nearly enough with the nightmares that consume me and some days I feel numb, like I'm in a fog. Eventually I feel myself starting to drift.

It is there, in the state between awake and asleep that I see them the clearest; bright green eyes burning into mine. Claiming me, for what, I don't know.

****

Standing in front of the mirror that hangs on the back of my bedroom door, I search for some sign of the girl I used to know.

For so long now I have aired on the side of caution, afraid to take any risks or venture from the comfort of my grandparent's farm.

I used to have so much spirit. I had fire in my veins, my mom used to say. But I see no remains of the person I was before. The flames that once burned so brightly have been extinguished, the ashes the only evidence that it was ever there.

I tie my long brown hair back into a ponytail and don't bother with make up. It's not something I wear often and honestly I don't think the animals care much what I look like.

It's funny how what I used to view as important now holds nothing for me. It's in our vanity that we lose sight of what actually matters.

I remember when I was younger, I wanted nothing more than to look like my mother. She was always so beautiful. Tall and thin with long blonde hair and bright blue eyes.

It's when I take the time to really study myself that I can see her in me. I am built just like her but a few inches shorter. I have my father's hair color and his dark eyes but other than that, I am all her.

I usually don't spend much time looking in the mirror. Truth be told, it's hard for me to look at myself knowing the people that created me, the people I see when I look at myself, are no longer here.

"Today is a new day. Today everything will change." I say aloud. Each day I try to find new hope. Something to help me heal. Something to help me feel alive again.

After joining my grandparents for breakfast, I head out to the barn to visit Sasha and Bennett, two of my grandpa's horses. I was never a fan of animals or the country. Growing up in Chicago, I was used to city living, but I have grown to love the animals on the farm. I find comfort in caring for them, especially the horses, though I have never been able to bring myself to ride one.

"Hey girl." I say to Sasha, running my hands down her long white coat. She is a beautiful horse and my favorite to talk to.

I have spent many days in the stall with her, brushing her and talking to her. Sometimes I feel like she can understand what I am saying, the pain I feel. I know that's probably crazy but no matter how alone I seem, I never really feel it.

The farm is therapeutic. There are acres and acres of land for as far as the eye can see. I have ventured most of it, but today I feel adventurous and decide to walk Sasha out to the woods that surround the end of the property.

It is the first time that I have visited this part of the farm and it takes me nearly a half an hour to finally reach the creek that lies beyond the woods. I tie Sasha off to a nearby tree and sit down just feet from the water. It's peaceful out here and I feel a sense of calm that is foreign to me.

It's mid-July and the weather could not be

more perfect. I lay down stretching out my body and peer up through the trees where the sun is shining through. The sound of the birds chirping and the water flowing down the creek is enough to lull me to sleep.

When I wake up, it's getting dark. I must have slept for hours. The only light provided is from the setting sun and because of the trees, that isn't much.

Instantly I feel a sense of panic, knowing I'm not really sure how to get back to the house. I'm thankful to have brought Sasha with me. I quickly untie her and we start to make our way back.

We aren't walking long when the sun sets completely and the trees become so thick that they block out what little light had been provided by the moon.

I'm terrified, hyper-aware of every little noise around me but I continue forward, my hand out in front of me to prevent myself from running into anything.

I am about to give up hope when I see a light just a few feet ahead of me. I can't tell what's causing it but I'm thankful to be able to see anything at all.

I speed up, eager to make it to the light as quickly as possible. But it seems the closer I get to it, the further away it moves.

Before I know it, we have reached the end of the woods and I can see the clearing ahead where my grandparent's large white farmhouse sits and just like that, the light is gone.

I search frantically for it's source. Did I imagine it? I strain my eyes into the woods but it's pitch black.

Deciding not to press my luck, I break into a light run, Sasha trotting next to me. A rush of relief flows through me when I see the porch light shining brightly from the house.

My grandparents are probably worried sick. I never stay out after dark. I take a moment to appreciate the white paint chipped two story house that stands in front of me.

It was built by my great, great grandpa over a hundred years ago and while you can tell it's an old house, my grandpa has done well with the up keep and it is a pretty nice home for the most part.

A giant white barn sits off to the right and I quickly make my way over to it and put Sasha in her stall.

My grandparents don't have the usual farm animals. Just a couple of horses and some chickens. My grandpa makes his living from his corn and bean fields, which make up most of the property.

Throw in a couple stray cats and an old Beagle named Rusty and that's all that makes up the farm that I call home.

As I lock up the barn and make my way towards the house, I can't help but feel like I am being watched. I glance back in the direction of the woods but everything is so dark I can't see anything.

A small light at the end of the field catches my eye and without thinking, I walk towards it.

Like with the light in the woods, the closer I get, the further away it seems. I have walked several feet away from the house when the light dies out again.

I hear the rustle of footsteps somewhere in front of me and my heart begins to pound. I should be scared. I should run like hell into the safety of my house, but I can't bring myself to move.

"Who's there?" I call out into the darkness, not really expecting an answer. And when one doesn't come, I really do start to believe that I am losing my mind.

I hear rustling directly behind me this time and scream when something brushes my leg.

"Rusty, what are you doing all the way out here?" I reach down and pat the beagle on his head.

Deciding it must have been him that I heard, I quickly make my way to the front porch, Rusty at my heels.

"Dear heavens girl, where have you been?" My grandma breathes out in relief when I step inside.

"You must be starving. Go wash up and have a seat and I will bring you some dinner." She instructs me.

Without hesitation, I do as she says. I didn't realize it until now but I am starving.

I make my way into the kitchen and have a seat at the four person wood table that sits in the corner of the room.

The kitchen is exactly how you would

imagine. White linoleum floors, light wood cabinets, and white counter tops make up the small space.

There are a few pictures of roosters and chickens that cover the walls that wear a flowery wallpaper.

It's not my taste at all but it's comfortable and I have come to appreciate the simplicity of this house.

My grandma sets a plate of chicken and dumplings in front of me and instructs me to eat up.

Once finished, I make my way to the sink to wash my plate. I miss the finer things in life that I had at my parent's house. Air conditioning and a dishwasher being the two things I miss the most.

I glance out of the window and for a minute, I swear I see someone leaning against the barn watching me.

I blink, trying to register if I am really seeing someone or if once again my mind is playing tricks on me. When I open my eyes, there's no one there.

I can't control the tremble that runs through me or the uneasiness that settles in the pit of my stomach.

I quickly finish cleaning my dishes and make my way into the living room that sits on the other side of the foyer.

My grandpa is in his recliner, an old brown beat up chair that he practically lives in, reading a book I don't recognize.

My grandma is sitting on the edge of the couch finishing up yet another afghan. She has tried to convince me on several occasions to learn how to crochet but it's just not for me.

I cross the small living room and take a seat on the opposite end of the couch. Just like the rest of the furniture, it is old and beat up, with the ugliest floral pattern I have ever seen.

I usually avoid this room, as my grandparents are of the generation where you hang every picture you have ever received of your family on the walls.

Since my dad was there only child, there are a few dozen of him growing up and several more after he married my mom. There are pictures of me and my sister, of our family together.

I look away and focus on the old box T.V. in front of me.

Bewitched is one of my grandma's favorites and I have come to enjoy it myself. I love the thought of someone being able to just wiggle their nose and make things happen. After watching two episodes, my grandparents head upstairs to bed and I follow.

There are only three bedrooms in the house and as much as I hate it, only one bathroom.

My room sits at the end of the hall, past my grandparent's and my dad's old room, at the back of the house. I love my room. It's like being in a completely different house. My grandparents allowed me to redecorate it when I moved in with them.

What once was an old room used for storage is now my sanctuary. The hard wood floor is covered with a large black shag rug. The walls that were once paneled, are now a dark beige with a couple framed pieces of art hanging on them.

I have a full size canopy bed that sits on the back wall, a window on each side of it, and a large dresser and vanity that sit on the opposite wall.

Other than that, the room is rather empty. I didn't bring much with me from Chicago. All my belongings seemed to be tainted by the murder of my family, so other than my clothes I left most of it behind.

Some days I wish I would have brought my television, others I am glad that I don't have it as a distraction.

It's as I lay in bed replaying the days events that it seems to sink in. The light that led me from the woods, it didn't just miraculously appear so where did it come from? I sensed I wasn't alone out there and now I am really starting to believe I wasn't.

But who could it have been? There aren't any neighbors for miles and the closest town is twenty minutes away. It's not like people just happen to be in the area, there is nothing here.

And then I swear I saw someone standing next to the barn, or at least I think I saw someone.

I'm starting to feel like I really am losing all sense of what is real in this world. I can't even trust my own eyes anymore.

Am I going crazy?

MELISSA TOPPEN

Chapter Two

  I have visited the creek several more times over the last few days. It has quickly become my favorite spot. I always take Sasha or Bennett with me. I don't know why but I feel better if I am not alone. I love it out here but that is not the only reason I continue to return.

  I am drawn to this place for some unknown reason. A part of me feels like the events that happened the first time I came here has something to do with it.

  I am desperate for answers and with each day that passes the only conclusion I can come to is that I have absolutely lost my mind.

  But it's in that moment, when I think that I have no other explanation, that I see him. He's standing on the other side of the creek at least twenty feet from me. I can't make out his face but I know it's him, my angel. At first I think I am seeing things again, but he seems so real.

My heart is beating rapidly and I feel my hands starting to shake, but I don't look away. I am fearful that the moment I lose sight of him, he will disappear.

Without really thinking, I stand and take a few steps forward until I am standing just at the edge of the water. He mirrors my actions until just the five feet width of the creek separates us.

He's tall, I would guess about six one, with broad shoulders and a lean muscular frame. His hair is short, dark and messy. He doesn't look up, keeping his head tilted down so that I can't get a clear shot of his face.

For a moment I am fearful that I got it all wrong and that this is some stranger that has come here to hurt me. Panic rises like bile in my throat but I don't back down. I have to see his face.

"Who are you?" I blurt out, not recognizing my own voice.

He doesn't respond but slowly raises his face to meet mine. The second our eyes meet, I feel the ground move beneath me. I struggle to find my balance. My mind whirls and my knees are shaking so hard I wonder how I am still standing.

Nothing could have prepared for me for what I would feel looking into those piercing green eyes again.

"You were there, in Chicago. It was you wasn't it?" He doesn't respond. "I knew you were real, I knew I didn't make you up. Who are you? How did you find me?" I hit him with question after question without giving him a chance to answer.

He eyes me curiously and then finally speaks. "Tate." He says in a voice that is deep and smooth and spreads fire through my veins.

"I'm sorry?" I question him, not really sure what he said.

"Tate, my name is Tate Harper." He says again, this time a little louder.

"Tate Harper." I say the name aloud, liking how it sounds on my tongue.

His look of ease changes to one of concern. "I shouldn't be here. I'm sorry, I have to go." He says, taking a few steps backwards.

"Please don't leave." I cry out, afraid that if he walks away now I will never know what really happened the night my family was murdered.

I felt a pull to him that night and I have felt some sense of that ever since then. Now with him standing in front of me, the pull is greater than ever. I have to know what this is.

"I'm putting you in danger by being here. I really must go." He says again, but makes no attempt to leave.

"Putting me in danger how? You saved my life! It was you, wasn't it? In Chicago?"

"Yes." He says simply, but doesn't elaborate.

"I need you to tell me what happened that night. What happened to the men that murdered my family? You know don't you?" I ask, stepping into the creek and walking towards him.

The water rushes up to my knees soaking my pants and shoes but I don't care. All I know, is I need to be near him.

He makes no attempt to distance himself from me as I step directly in front of him and sit down next to his feet.

To my surprise, he takes a seat next to me.

His hand brushes mine for the briefest moment and I feel like I just touched an electrical fence. The shock so great, I can feel it in my toes. I gasp and pull my hand away, terrified by the sudden fire coursing through me.

He takes no notice of my reaction and adjusts himself so that his legs are stretched out in front of him.

I don't know why but with him next to me, I feel safer than I ever have. His presence alone brings me a peace I don't quite understand.

"I was staying in Chicago for a while. I decided to take a walk when I heard the shots being fired. I knew something was wrong and I wanted to help. When I got inside your family was already...." He breaks off, not finishing his sentence.

"One of the men had a gun to your head and was about to pull the trigger. I pushed you out of the way and knocked them unconscious. You had passed out, so I called the police and took the men away somewhere where they could never hurt anyone ever again." He says, with such protectiveness in his voice that my heart swells.

"Did you kill them?" I ask, my voice barely a

whisper.

"It is not in my nature to kill, but let's just say I know some people who don't share the same values. I am not sure of their fate, but rest assured they are never coming back." He says with a small smile playing on his lips.

He doesn't strike me as a violent vindictive person, but I can tell he's pleased that they have been taken care of.

"Did you know I was here?" I ask, not being able to chalk this up to coincidence.

"Yes, I have been checking in on you, making sure you're safe. I'm sorry if that's strange. I feel very protective of you."

"You said that you weren't supposed to be here, that you are putting me in danger. What did you mean by that?" I ask.

"I can't explain it, I'm sorry. I'm not supposed to be here but I can't stay away."

"I can keep a secret. After all you did save my life." I say, taking his hand in mine.

This time I am prepared for the rush that seethes through me and I brace myself so to not show it on my face. Surely he can feel it too.

"I trust you." He whispers, his face just inches from mine. My breathing becomes labored and my heart feels like it will beat out of my chest at any moment, but I can't break the connection.

His eyes burn deeply into mine and for the briefest moment, I feel like he can see into my soul. Like he can see what I am feeling inside. Feelings that I will most definitely need to sort through later, as I don't understand them myself.

Just when I feel like everything is about to explode between us, he breaks the connection and turns to face the water again.

I can't help the disappointment I feel but a part of me is grateful that I have a moment to get my emotions in check.

"The light in the woods, the person next to the barn, that was you wasn't it?" I ask, noticing for the first time the shake in my voice.

He nods but doesn't say more. He really is my angel but who is he?

It scares me that I know nothing about him and yet I am not the least bit bothered by the fact that he's been watching me, helping me without my knowledge.

I'm just about to ask him if he's helped me other times but a rustling noise in the distance stops me.

He stands abruptly pulling me to my feet. "Cally, I need you to get Bennett and go straight home, do you understand me?" He says as he grips my shoulders with both of his hands.

"What..... but why?" I stutter out, confused by his sudden persistence.

"Please go. I promise I will find you again. Hurry you must go now." He says, taking my hand and pulling me across the creek to where Bennett is tied to a nearby tree. He unties him quickly and hands me the strap.

I turn to leave, confused and a little hurt, when he grabs my arm and spins me around, pulling me into his arms. Before I even have time to process what is happening he has pulled away and is urging me to walk away.

I take two steps before I turn around. He's gone. There's no sign of him anywhere. How did he get away so quickly?

Deciding the best thing I can do is to do what he asked, I quickly make my way back towards the house.

The walk back is quick and honestly I feel a little disoriented. By the time I reach the house, I have all but convinced myself this was all just some crazy dream.

There is so much mystery surrounding Tate Harper. I don't even know him and yet I feel like he was destined to find me. Like we were made to be one.

I know it sounds crazy but when I look into his eyes, I can see my future. The same green eyes that have consumed my dreams for four years are no longer just a dream, but a staggering reality. A reality where happiness may actually exist.

As I lay in bed, I try to rationalize what happened. I should be fearful of this strange man who has been watching me.

There is something very strong between us. I know he feels it too. It's like an unknown force is pushing us together and I know without a doubt that I could never put up a fight against it. How could I when I want to be near him so badly?

There may be a lot of unknown surrounding Tate but one thing I know for sure is, that life will never be the same again.

MELISSA TOPPEN

Chapter Three

It's been weeks since my encounter with Tate Harper. I have returned to the creek everyday since then just hoping he will show himself again. It sounds crazy, I know but I just keep waiting.

I have been sitting here by the creek bed for hours. I swear I keep hearing noises and I jump to see if it's him, but no such luck.

Normally I wouldn't pay any mind to the sounds. I have grown accustomed to the noise of the trees as the wind blows through them, the sound of a squirrel running across a branch, the deer grazing. It's only because I want so badly to see him, that I am over thinking each noise as it comes.

As nightfall approaches, I decide it's best to

head back. It's strange how four years ago I was creeped out by anything relating to nature. Now I have come to appreciate the beauty of it all.

So many other things have changed too. I find myself questioning if I am even a resemblance of the person I once was.

I can't help but feel like the girl I used to be, died that night in Chicago. Not physically of course, but mentally and emotionally.

So many things that mattered to me before, suddenly don't matter anymore. I used to love going to school. Experiencing the social aspects of the environment. I thrived on being the center of attention and always had to be the best at everything. Not that I ever was, but I sure tried to be.

I lived for football games, school dances, being a cheerleader, and student council. I was an all around over achiever. Looking back now, I can't help but think I was just another spoiled brat who didn't know how lucky she was until everything was taken away from her.

All that changed in one night. I no longer cared about friends or school. I protested so much in fact, that my grandmother agreed to home school me for my last three years of high school. It was dreadfully boring but I would have done anything not to have to face the world again.

In fact, I have done very little outside the life on this farm. I don't have any friends. I don't think I have ever even talked to someone that is close to my age since moving here. I live in my safe bubble with my grandparents, scared of the world around me.

Still to this day, I have done nothing but help my grandpa on the farm. I have never had a real job. The thought of college lost it's appeal long ago. I feel guilty that I lived when they died. Because the life I live, really isn't a life at all.

I used to be active and know how to have fun. Now my once athletic build has given way to a smaller thinner frame.

It was a good year after I came here that I actually starting really eating. For the longest time I felt like if I gave into the simple pleasures in life, like food, that I was betraying my family.

I didn't deserve to enjoy anything. It was all too unfair. Eventually I came to grips with the reality, which is my mom and dad would never think that. They would want me to be healthy and happy. All the things that I gave away, thinking it was a betrayal to them.

I guess that's why I am so drawn to Tate. He stirs a life in me that I haven't felt in a very long time. He makes me want to live, want to be happy. Even just the tiniest thought of him brings a smile to my face. How strange it is to feel this way about someone I do not know.

My grandparents have been wonderful through all this, even though I know they have been suffering too. I try to remind myself that I am all they have left of their only child. Because of this, I do my best to plaster on a fake smile and make them believe that I am okay.

Truth is, I'm not okay. I'm lost and broken. No words can describe what seeing your entire family lying dead in front of you will do to a person. Sometimes the nightmares are so bad that I will go days without sleep. Afraid that if I close my eyes I won't be able to escape their horror.

As I make my way up the front steps, I notice my grandparent's car is not here. I totally forgot about bingo night. I love that they have little things that make them happy, but I hate being in this house alone. There aren't any neighbors for miles and I am terrified that someone will break in.

These fears, of course, stem from my past

but it doesn't make it any easier to deal with. I don't have the luxury of saying, "Oh those things would never happen to me." They did happen to me, and I live the same hell everyday because of it.

Even though I am hungry, I run up the stairs as fast as I can and run to my room, shutting the door and locking it behind me. This is the only way I feel even remotely safe when I am home alone.

The house isn't huge but there are a ton of entry points and there is no way I can keep an eye on all of them at the same time. It seems easier to guard just one entrance.

I push my dresser in front of the door and lay down on my bed. My grandparents have come to learn to knock when they get home so I know I can move the dresser. While I know they hate that I do it, they never complain.

I envy their strength and courage through this whole ordeal. They really are amazing people. I have learned so much about them these last few years.

My grandpa will sit outside on the porch swing with me and tell me stories of how they fell in love and what life was like with my dad as a child.

They are in their their late sixties but you would guess them much younger. I guess it's life on the farm. It keeps them active and in shape.

My grandma is a petite woman. Skinny with white hair that hangs to her butt and she always wears it in a bun.

My grandpa towers over her, standing well over six feet. He always wears his salt and pepper hair in the same comb over. I used to tease him relentlessly about his hairstyle.

They are so cute together and have been married for over fifty years, which is almost unheard of in this day and age. People marry and get divorced like it's their job.

Sometimes I just sit back and watch them. Its heartwarming to see how much they truly love and care for one another.

I can't help but wonder if I will ever find that. The one person that I can't live without. The one person that makes me whole. My mind instantly wonders to Tate.

I know it's impossible to think that he could be it for me when I don't even know him. But something changes in the air when we are together. I have felt it both times I have been in his presence.

It's like the earth is pushing me to him and there is nothing I can do about it. There's no rationalizing it or talking myself out of it. I know it's true.

The electricity that surges between us is pure magic. I can't ever imagine experiencing that with another person and I can't believe that it is something that happens everyday.

If it were, more people would stay together, fight for what they have. I can't ever imagine walking away from Tate. Then again, I don't even know the man so to say this would be a bit premature. Not to mention the fact that I will probably never see him again.

The thought leaves me devastated. What if I never see him again? That's all I can think as I lay in bed, curled into a ball. My anxiety is through the roof and every sound makes me jump, but my only real concern is that never seeing him again would be worse than any fate I could face otherwise.

Just as I feel like I am about to crawl out of my skin, the familiar panic creeping up the back of my neck, I feel a calmness settle in the air.

Something shifts and I am no longer scared,

anxious, or worried. I feel calm, relaxed, at peace. The feeling is almost eery and I don't know why.

I sit up and look around my room. My grandparents aren't home yet. If they were, they would have already let me know, knowing how much I hate being alone. But in this moment, I don't feel alone. I feel whole.

I stand up, pacing my room trying to rationalize the way I'm feeling. Everyday I feel like I am losing it more and more.

Am I imagining things? The encounter with Tate, was that all in my mind? The way the atmosphere seems to shift on a dime, am I imagining that too?

I walk to my window and glance out towards the barn. It's completely dark, with the exception of the small light in front of it. I squint trying to see but my eyes can't break through the darkness of the night.

Just as I'm about to return to my bed, something catches the corner of my eye. I turn, peering back out the window and then I see it.

A small light shining at the edge of the field. Tate! Without thinking, I shove my dresser out from in front of my door and take off in a sprint through the house and then outside.

I am panting by the time I reach the barn, and I can no longer spot the light I had seen earlier.

I am about to venture out there regardless, but suddenly the calmness I once felt is gone, replaced by the panic and fear of being alone in the darkness.

I turn and run back up to the house, returning to my safe haven. My hands are trembling uncontrollably and I can't stop the tears that have begun to spill down my cheeks.

I really am crazy. I don't know how else to explain what's happening to me. Nothing makes sense to me and I don't know what is real and what's not anymore.

I curl up in my bed and let go. Sobbing so hard I find myself struggling to catch my breath. I need a breakdown. I need to let it all out, but the pain is so overwhelming that I feel like my insides are turning out.

After some time, I manage to calm myself. Finding a focal point on my ceiling, a glow in the dark star that is attached by tape.

There has to be more to life than this.

Waiting, wondering, never really knowing if the man I can't stop thinking about even exists.

I know I want there to be more, but how do I find it? How do I walk away from everything that I know and actually start my life?

I don't think that I am ready for that. Truth is, I don't know if I ever will be.

****

Weeks go by as if no time passes at all. Things rarely change and I take comfort in the consistency. There is also the downside, which is of course the boredom that comes along with knowing what each and every day will hold.

Today is no exception, my same old routine. Once I have fed the animals I decide to take Rusty for a walk. Not that he really needs it, he has free room to run on the farm, but today I feel like his company.

As we make our way away from the house, I choose a different course than the one I usually take. Instead of walking through the fields, I make my way up the dirt driveway that leads to the road. It's long and winding with trees blocking any real view.

I don't know why, but I have the overwhelming feeling that this is the path I need to take today. As if something were guiding me.

As I reach where the driveway meets the road, I hesitate before stepping onto the pavement. But the moment I do, freedom surges through my veins like a drug and I break into a run, Rusty struggling to keep up behind me.

For so long I have feared leaving the comfort of the farm land, but now I am loving the feeling.

Like the walls that held me in suddenly have fallen away and I feel free. Free from all restraints. It takes me a while to realize I no longer recognize my surroundings. I feel like I should be scared, worried at least, but I am none of those things. It feels exhilarating.

As much as I want to keep going, I know I need to head back. Rusty has slowed to a walk several feet behind me and I know that I will be lucky if he makes the trip back. He's not as young as he once was and I certainly don't want to push his limits.

As we round the curve in the road just before my grandparent's driveway, I feel the air shift. I know he's here before I even see him.

I look up and am not surprised when his beautiful eyes meet mine. He's standing just a few feet in front of me but I feel like our bodies are pressed firmly together and I am finding it difficult to catch my breath.

Something tells me this has nothing to do with my run and everything to do with the effect this man has on me.

"Hi." I manage to choke out breathlessly. He tilts his head to one side. A small smile turning up the corners of his mouth.

"Why do I get the feeling you are trying to convince yourself if I'm really here?" He asks, looking more than a little amused.

"Because I am." I answer truthfully. I have wondered several times over the past four years if I have simply just made him up in my head. Something to distract me, comfort me in some way.

"Well I can assure you." He says, stepping forward until he's standing directly in front of me. "That I really am here." He finishes, reaching up and gently brushing my cheek with the tips of his fingers.

The contact stirs fire deep within me and it takes everything I have not to buckle under the heat.

"It's like you're a ghost. One minute you're standing right in front of me, the next 'poof' you're gone."

"Yes, I do see where my behavior may seem a bit out of sorts. I'm sorry about that. I guess you can say I have a lot going on right now." He pauses and then gently takes my hand.

"May I walk with you?"

"Yes." Is all I can manage.

I embrace his hand in mine as we slowly make our way up the drive way. The walk down seemed like it took forever. The walk back has gone by in a flash. I guess that's what happens when you focus on something other than the trip itself.

We don't stop at the house, instead Tate silently leads me to the barn. Rusty calls it quits and collapses on the back porch. I expect us to keep walking to the fields but instead he stops at the barn and slides open the large wood door, taking a step inside.

I follow and wait to find out what we are doing here. He walks straight to Sasha, trailing me behind him. When he stops, he releases my hand and reaches up, trailing his fingers down her long mane.

I want to object the break in contact but can't bring myself to care much when I see how the horse responds to him.

Normally she's not much for strangers, but her reaction to Tate is similar to how she is with me. She seems very at ease with his presence. At least her and I have that in common.

"Horses really are amazing creatures." He says, more to Sasha than to me. "This one has a lot of spirit but she hides behind her fear, a lot like you. I can see why you love her so much."

"How do you know?" I blurt out, not sure if I should be insulted or just plain freaked out that he can read me so well.

"One simply only needs to look deep enough. You wear your fear like a coat. I can see the warmth it offers, but it's only skin deep. Fear is not only part of us, it becomes us. Consuming all that we are until we simply have nothing left."

"You talk as if you know this from experience. Are you afraid?"

"I am." He says, turning his attention to me. His eyes burning deeply into mine. "But the fear I have is not for myself."

"Then who?" My heart rate accelerates from the intensity of the conversation and being in such close proximity to a man that sends heat through my very soul.

"I thought that much was obvious." He whispers, tipping my face upwards with his index finger, leaving our faces just inches apart.

"Why?" I manage to get out, but only as a whisper.

"I can't explain what saving you that night did to me. It altered my entire existence. I can't give you any explanation or answers to the questions I'm sure you have. But I would like to know you, to be your friend, to live in your world."

"There's only one world Tate, and it certainly doesn't belong to me." I can feel his breath on my cheek, smell that sweet scent that radiates from his body.

My legs are trembling but I hold my stance. I can't imagine it gets any better than being here like this with this man.

"If that's what you choose to believe. But this..." He trails off, gesturing around him. "This is your world. Where you choose to spend your days and nights. A world that I am drawn to, one that I can't stay away from. Tell me, do you feel it to? The shift in air, the way the wind seems to sing around us when we're together. This...." He says, grazing my cheek with the back of his hand, sending a shock down my spine.

"It's indescribable isn't it?"

I nod, losing any ability to speak in that moment. I'm not sure if I am scared by how fast things seem to be moving or if it's because I do feel it too and more importantly I want to keep feeling it.

"Come, I want to show you something." He says, taking my hand once more and leading me from the barn, to the center of a bean field that has only begun sprouting.

I almost protest because my grandpa does not like anyone to walk on the fields once they have been planted. I always take the small paths that cut through the fields making extra sure I don't step where anything is planted.

He stops just a few feet in and looks up to the sky. "You see that there?" He asks, pointing up to the sky which has started to darken with the rising of the moon.

I can't see what he's pointing at so I struggle to match his line of sight, hoping to catch a glimpse of what it is he wants me to see.

"No there." He says, adjusting my head a little more to the left with a gentle guiding hand.

I can see a few stars but most are still hidden by the dim light still shining in the sky. Then I see it, a small speck that burns the shade of fire.

At first I think it's a star, then no, it looks more like a comet. Truthfully, I don't know what I'm looking at. "What is it?" I finally ask.

"A red star." He answers simply.

"Okay, so it's a star that's red?" I ask, not sure if it's actually a question.

"Well to put it simply, yes. But it's so much more than that. A red star is very much like other stars, only it's life has begun to fade out causing it to burn at a much lower temperature than your average star."

"Okay....." I stretch out, gesturing for him to make a point. While I think it is quite intriguing, I never knew red stars even existed, it still doesn't change the fact that he's showing me this for a reason, and I want to know why.

"It is clear that the human life is much like the life of the stars. Burning hot and bright in the first few years of life and then slowly over time losing their fire. I sometimes wonder, if I were given the choice between this life and the life of a star, which I would choose. Burning brightly for thousands of years, free to sail the universe, or this. Life, and all it's beauty and it's pain." He pauses before continuing.

"I think I would choose life. What a lonely existence to be a star. Forced to live in a universe with no real connection to anyone or anything."

"I wish I could say I agree with that choice. But when the pain outweighs the beauty, maybe the nothingness would be a welcome thought."

"You think so?" He eyes me questioningly.

"You would have to live a life of pain to know that it is no life at all. We aren't living, not really. We are empty souls, faced to brave the world with no real sense of self. Knowing only fear. Would you really choose that life for yourself?"

"Yes." He says, turning his position so that he is standing in front of me, our bodies so close together I can feel his chest rise and fall as he breathes.

"If I knew I would have you in my life, there would be no question." He tilts my chin gently upwards and slowly leans forward.

He stops just shy of my lips, as if silently asking for permission. I grant it by pushing up on my tip toes and pressing my lips to his.

The fire engulfs me with a force that causes my entire body to tremble.

My heart feels like it is in overdrive and I don't even know if I am actually breathing or not.
None of that matters. All that matters is this. His arms around me, his lips on mine.

When our lips finally part, we are both breathless and honestly I feel a bit woozy. Tate must sense this too because he gently lowers me to the ground and sits next to me, stretching out onto his back, he resumes looking at the stars.

I mirror his actions. The sky that just minutes before only had a couple stars is now littered with them. That's one thing I love about the country, how clearly you can see the stars at night. In Chicago, you were lucky to spot a couple, but out here they are endless.

We lay in silence. Words don't seem to hold any meaning appropriate at this moment. The feelings speak for themselves.

For the first time in a very long time, I think, just maybe, I would choose this life after all.

THE TRAVELER: THE AMULET OF LIFE

Chapter Four

As hard as I try, I can't shake the feeling that Tate is hiding something from me. We have spent every waking moment together for the last four days, and while I cherish the time I have with him, I am left each night with a sinking feeling that none of this is going to last.

There is something about him I can't quite put my finger on. Something different, special even. I've tried to question him but he is always so cryptic. Talking as if we live in two different worlds.

I can't explain the feelings that come over me in his presence. The calm that takes over my body. I want to believe that it's all in my mind. That I am making something out of nothing. But something tells me not to be so sure.

I try not to dwell too much on what I can't explain and simply enjoy the moments while they last.

As we walk through the fields hand in hand, I find myself staring at him. Committing every inch of his face to my memory. I want to remember him this way, always.

He glances at me and smiles, his beautiful straight teeth almost sparkle in the sunlight and I can't help the smile that crosses my face as well.

"What?" He asks innocently.

"I'm just trying to figure out how on earth god created such a perfect creature." I say, mockingly but I mean it seriously.

"What makes you think god had anything to do with it?" He asks, giving me a wink.

I can't help the giggle that escapes my lips or the butterflies that rush through my stomach. Such a small gesture but it still makes me weak in the knees.

"You're right, I suppose I should give the credit to your parents." I say, noticing the hint of sadness that crosses his face but it's gone within seconds.

I continue on, pretending not to notice the sudden change in the air. "Tell me about them. Where do they live? Do you see them often?"

He takes a deep breath as if deciding on what to say. "My parents died a very long time ago." He says, stopping just at the edge of the woods.

"I'm sorry." I say, trying to keep the sudden well of tears at bay. I don't know why it bothers me so much. People die everyday. But knowing how it feels to lose the people you love, my heart breaks for anyone that has suffered that kind of loss.

"How?" I ask.

"Like I said, it was a very long time ago. My dad died of a heart attack. My mom died three years later, cancer. They stopped taking care of themselves after..." He trails off, leaving me confused but hesitant to push for more.

"After what?" I ask, giving his hand a squeeze.

"After they lost a child." He says, abandoning his spot next to me and making his way into the woods. He moves so quickly I struggle to keep up, tripping over branches that litter the ground.

I finally catch up to him and by this point I am a little breathless but I'm not giving up that easily.

"I didn't know you had any siblings." I say, trying to sound casual but failing miserably.

"I don't." He says, glancing towards me and then continuing on through the woods.

We walk in silence for what seems like an eternity. My mind is trying to process what he is telling me but it doesn't make sense.

His parents gave up after they lost their child and yet he had no siblings. How is this possible? Surely there is a reasonable explanation.

He slows as we reach the edge of the creek bed. I open my mouth to speak but he cuts me off, holding his hand up beside him gesturing for me not to speak. I try to follow his gaze to the other side of the woods but I can see nothing through the trees.

"What is...." I whisper, but he cuts me off before I can finish.

"Shhhh." He whispers back, holding his

finger to his lips.

"We need to go." He says abruptly, grabbing my hand and spinning me so I'm facing the opposite direction.

He takes off walking at a very quick pace with me struggling to keep up.

"Tate what are you doing?" I ask, frustrated and confused. I have seen him behave oddly before but this is a little extreme.

"Keeping you safe." He says sternly and quickens his pace, practically dragging me from the woods and into the fields.

I start to resist him. Digging my heels into the ground and pulling backwards, so his only option is to stop or leave without me.

Eventually he gives into my tantrum. Stopping abruptly he turns to face me. His eyes are dark and cold and his expression reads the same.

Suddenly I feel very guilty for acting like a child. I should have just went with him and asked questions later. It's too late now and I brace myself sure that he is about to give me hell.

But he doesn't. Instead his features soften

and he breathes out loudly, running his hands through his messy brown hair.

"Tate, what is going on?" I ask exasperated.

"It's a warning..... Callista please, if you care for me at all you will come with me." He pleads, his eyes burning deeply into mine.

I want to say no, ask what he's talking about, but something in his eyes tells me that right now I need to trust him.

"Okay." I say, my voice barely a whisper.

The calm that I feel in Tate's presence has shifted and I can feel the fear creeping in. He's afraid. I can tell this not by his actions but by his very soul. I can feel him. I don't know how to explain it but I know it without question.

He says just being with me gives him a peace that he has never known. This must be why I feel such a calmness when he's around, and why I feel his fear now. It's not just that he affects me, he's connected to me.

In some unexplainable way, I think I have always known this. We aren't just drawn together, we are connected to one another, pushed together by a force well beyond our control. I guess this is how it feels when your soul finds it's other half.

By the time we reach the back porch, I am panting heavily and collapse on the back step that leads to the door, my legs no longer able to support my weight.

"What... What is going on?" I breathe, struggling to get the words out.

He crouches down, resting his elbows on my knees.

"Cally I have to go away for a while....."

"What! You're leaving?" I cut him off.

"It's only temporary. I have to take care of something." He says.

"Please don't be upset. Look at me." He says, lifting my chin with the back of his hand, forcing me to look into his eyes.

I can see his pain, better yet I can feel it. And in this moment I feel like the world is shattering beneath my feet.

I want to be better than this, stronger, but for some unknown reason I can't stomach it. I'm more than a little confused by what is happening and truthfully I'm scared.

Scared to be without him. He takes away the pain, the nightmares, the guilt. When I'm with him I feel free.

"I don't want to go." He admits, his face apologetic.

"Then don't."

"It's not that simple."

"Then explain it to me... because right now not one thing makes sense to me. What happened in the woods Tate? What are you running from?" My tears and words are flowing freely now and dammit I want some answers.

"You are simply going to have to trust me when I tell you that some things are better left alone. I need you to promise me something." I don't respond but gesture for him to continue.

"Promise me that you won't stray too far from the house."

"What, why?" I question him. My confusion probably written all over my face.

"Just do as I ask and if you see a tall, young man with white hair and black eyes....Don't trust a word he says." He says, pressing his lips to mine silencing me before I can even process a word.

The calmness returns as his lips claim mine but that's not all I feel. Love.....

Just as the feeling leaks through me, it's gone, and so is Tate. I stand looking frantically for him.

How could he have vanished so quickly?

Yet another unanswered question. What is it about this man that causes me to question everything I once thought reality? It scares me, I mean really scares me. But more than anything, right here, right now, I feel helpless. I feel alone.

Not confused or angry like I think I should be. In this moment, it doesn't matter that there is still so much I don't understand. All that matters is that he is gone and once again I feel dead.

****

Days bleed into weeks with the loneliness that once haunted me returning full force. It seems so strange that just weeks ago this was the very existence I lived everyday.

How could I live such a life? One where the world holds no beauty or happiness but simply darkness and fear.

I throw on my hooded sweatshirt and head downstairs for breakfast. With fall quickly approaching, the mornings have become much colder and I am spending less and less time outside or with Bennett and Sasha.

When I make my way into the kitchen, my grandfather stands from the table and gestures for me to take a seat. This is not typical behavior and makes my stomach twist into knots as I pull out the chair directly across from him and sit.

"Is everything okay?" I ask, unsure of why it appears as though he's been waiting for me to come down so he can talk to me.

He sits quietly for a moment, and for the first time in a long time, I take a minute to study his features.

I notice he looks much older than I realized and the thought scares me a bit. I have to remind myself that my grandparents won't be around forever.

Where will that leave me? The thought makes me more than a little uneasy and my stomach lurches as my grandma sits a plate of bacon and eggs in front of me. I'm not hungry at all, my nerves wearing thin and the anxiety that hangs in the air feels like a knife to my throat. Forcing me to hold my position still and wait.

"A man came looking for you this morning." He finally says, concern and confusion ruffling his wrinkled face.

"What? Who?" I manage to choke out completely at a loss for who would come here looking for me. I don't even know anyone and Tate would never just stop by, he would wait for me to show myself.

"He said his name is Braize. A very strange looking young man. He was asking a lot of questions that honestly made very little sense."

"Questions?" I ask, confused but wanting him to continue.

Braize. I have never known anyone by that name before. The thought that someone is looking for me sends more than just panic rushing through my veins.

Could it be someone that was associated with my families death in Chicago? Someone coming back to finish the job?

"He wanted to know if you left the property often and where you usually go. When I asked him what his business was here he simply brushed me off and insisted I tell him what he wanted to know. I didn't, instead I demanded he leave, but before I could shut the door he said something, something that I really don't understand."

"Now Richard, you are just scaring her. She probably has no idea who this person even is. This is all non sense if you ask me." My grandma interrupts.

"No Nancy, something is going on here, and I intend to find out what it is. Tell me Cally, do you know someone by the name of Tate?"

My heart quickens at the mention of his name. I have obviously not told my grandparents about Tate, or the fact that he feared I was in some type of danger and had to leave.

I don't know why I felt the need to keep them in the dark where he was concerned. Our relationship is very strange and there are so many questions I have no answers too.

I didn't need to add my grandparents grilling me with curiosity to the mix. How could I tell them that he was there that night and that he found me all these years later? Even that sounds odd to me.

That's when it hits me. "The man, did he have white hair?" I ask my grandfather, finally piecing together that Tate's warning actually may have meant something.

"How do you know that?" My grandfather asks, eying me curiously.

"A friend of mine warned me about him. He's dangerous. If he comes here again, you must not answer the door... Promise me!" I plead with so much intensity it causes my grandma to drop the plate she is washing into the sink.

It pings around a couple times before the foundation finally gives way and it shatters, the noise echoing through the kitchen.

"Are you in some kind of trouble dear?" My grandma asks, making her way from the sink to sit in the chair between me and my grandpa.

"No, I just....." I can't finish my sentence, not really sure how much I should tell them and if any of it would make sense.

"I really don't know okay?" I breathe out, exasperated and honestly a bit irritated.

"Look, I can't really explain it. I know this seems strange but can you please just trust me on this. Whatever you do just do not let that man into the house."

I don't know what's going on here but remembering the helplessness in Tate's eyes, the severity of his warning, I have to trust him. Even if it makes absolutely no sense.

"Wait, what did he say to you? He must have mentioned Tate."

"He said that he saw you wandering in the woods talking to yourself and that when he tried to see if you needed help you just kept calling him Tate." My grandpa says, a look of sheer concern crossing his face.

I can feel the heat rush to my face and the tears are spilling down my cheeks before I even realize they have formed.

"Honey you're scaring us." My grandma chimes in. "Is there something you're not telling us? You said a friend told you, what friend? I don't mean to sound shocked that you have someone other than us in your life but dear, you never leave the farm."

"Tate." I say, watching my grandpa's eyes widen in concern.

"I know this doesn't make any sense but please just trust me. I can't really give you an explanation and I'm sorry for that but I'm fine, everything is fine." I say, not sure if I am trying to convince myself or them.

"I think we should schedule a visit with Dr. Peterson." She says, and I feel like she has just punched me in the stomach.

Dr. Peterson is the psychiatrist I visited for two years after I moved here and while she is a wonderful person to talk to, the fact that they are suggesting this means only one thing.

"I'm not crazy!" I exclaim, rising from the table and shoving my chair backwards.

"We don't think you're crazy Callista, but you sound a lot like you did after.... well after that night. It might help you to start seeing her again." My grandpa says, gesturing for me to sit back down.

I don't. Instead, I turn on my heel and quickly exit the room, leaving my grandparents behind me confused and probably a little hurt, but I don't care.

I can't explain to them something I don't understand myself and honestly this is the conclusion I knew they would jump to.

I can't say I blame them much. I was a mess

for a very long time and had trouble grasping what was reality and what my mind was simply creating to help me cope with such a tragedy.

I have questioned myself many times since then but Braize showing up, only confirms to me that I am not crazy.

Not only that, but he knows about me, at least enough to know how to play my grandparents towards the "something is wrong with her" idea.

What's his angle? Who is he and why is Tate running from him?

My mind is racing as I make my way out the back and without thinking, through the fields and into the woods.

I know Tate told me not to wander, but I have been out here a thousand times with no interference from anyone, and I can't just stay cooped up inside all day. Not with grandparents that think I have officially lost my marbles.

What if they are right? I sit at the creek bed tossing handfuls of rocks into the water. I watch the ripple that each one causes and follow it with my eyes until they have all disappeared.

Then I hear another plop in the water and

another ripple has formed. I frantically search the creek bed suddenly very fearful. I'm not alone....

Deciding that I should not have come here, I rise from the ground and turn quickly but before I can take more than one step, I run smack into something hard and lose my footing, falling backwards. Hands grab me around my forearms and stop me before I hit the ground.

The force of the electricity surging through my veins gives away what I ran into or who for that matter.

I hesitantly look up to find Tate staring wildly at me.

"What were you thinking coming all the way out here by yourself?" He asks, anger lacing his voice.

I want to throw my arms around him and pull him close to me but I stay rooted to the spot. He is clearly upset with me and for the life of me I can't figure out why. So I went a little further from the house than he would have liked. Last time I checked he's not my father.

"Perhaps if you tell me why I shouldn't be out here I might be a little more apt to submit to such ridiculous demands. What would you have me do, stayed boarded up in my room all day?"

"If it means you will be safe, then yes." He breathes, his features softening a bit.

"I've asked too much of you without giving you any explanation, I'm sorry." He says, taking my hand and pulling me into his arms.

I nuzzle my face in his chest and breathe in the warm manly scent that radiates from his body. It's moments like these that I feel most alive. Moments that assure me that I am not crazy and that this really is happening, no matter how strange it all seems.

When he finally releases me, I step back, letting my eyes wander the length of his tall, lean body.

He's dressed casually in jeans and a black v-neck t-shirt. His brown hair is messier than usual and that only makes him more attractive.

I reach up, trailing my finger from his temple, down his cheek, and along his jaw line. His green eyes burn like fire when they finally meet mine and I inhale sharply, fully grasping the power this beautiful man has over me.

He takes my hand, placing a small kiss on the palm before releasing it and letting it fall back to my side.

"We really should get you back to the house." He says, turning to walk away but not actually moving until he's sure I am by his side.

The walk back is in silence and I catch myself watching him rather than paying attention to where I'm going.

I trip over a branch and fall forward but once again, Tate catches me before I hit the ground.

"Watch where you're going angel." He laughs and then takes my hand, leading me out of the woods, to the edge of the field.

"This is where I must leave you." He says, turning to face me.

"That's it? I haven't seen you in weeks and you're just going to walk away again, just like that?" I ask, not trying to keep the hurt from my voice.

"I'll be back soon. But right now I think it would be best if you soothed things over with your grandparents. They are the only family you have left and despite the fact that they hurt you, they really just want what's best for you."

"How do you know all this?" I eye him curiously, confused that he seems to know what took place just an hour prior.

"Let's just add it to the mystery box shall we?" He says, laughing lightly to himself.

"If we keep going, before too long it will be overflowing." I bite back, a little harshly.

I don't want to be this way with him. Angry and insulted that he feels like he can't just tell me things straight up instead of leaving me in the dark.

"Touche Ms. Price. Perhaps one day......." He trails off, not finishing his sentence.

"So you know about Braize then?" I ask, sure that he does.

"Yes." He responds, looking off into the distance.

"He's making sure you're not with me and while I am not comfortable with any interaction between the two of you, I can't believe that he would harm you in any way unless he was provoked to do so." He eyes me apologetic.

"I am not taking any chances where you are concerned."

"Tate, you can't just keep leaving me in the dark. If I am in some kind of danger, if you are, I think I deserve to know why."

I can't for the life of me fathom why someone would be out to hurt us or keep us apart but then again I don't know anything so how could I understand it?

"I know." He breathes out, running his hands through his hair.

I reach up drawing my hand around the back of his neck and pulling him down to me. Our faces now just inches apart, I study his eyes, sure that if I stare hard enough I can read his soul.

I can feel the anxiousness coursing through him start to melt away.

Hesitantly I place my lips to his and revel in the intensity that surges through me like a lightening bolt.

Wrapping his arms around my waist, he pulls me to him until there is no space between us. Until we feel like one. Our bodies and souls connected in a way that leaves me feeling weak from the power.

He breaks away all too soon, tucking a stray strand of hair that has fallen from my pony tail, behind my ear, and trailing a light kiss along my jaw line.

"I will see you soon, I promise." He breathes into my neck as he pulls me tightly to him once more.

He releases me and steps backwards, staring deeply into my eyes as if trying to gauge my reaction to yet another mysterious encounter that leaves all too many questions gaping open.

I open my mouth to speak but the words don't come. I want to tell him to stay, that we can face anything together. Instead I stand, rooted to the ground and watch him walk away.

MELISSA TOPPEN

Chapter Five

I have managed to smooth things over somewhat with my grandparents, though I fear they still believe that something is wrong with me.

I love that they care but wish that they could just trust me when I tell them that everything is fine.

They have dropped the matter for now, but I am confident it will resurface again in the near future. My grandma isn't big on leaving things unresolved and I am sure the questions and doubts are still there, festering below the surface.

At least I have today. I know they won't hound me about anything. It is after all, my eighteenth birthday.

I haven't really celebrated birthdays since I

lost my family, but my grandma tries every year to do something special for me. Today is sure to be no exception.

I can't help but feel like I am missing out on some really important milestones in my life. I can imagine how other people my age spend their birthdays, and my guess is that it isn't hiding out on their grandparent's farm.

They are, no doubt, out celebrating with friends. The thought leaves me envious of what others have, that I do not.

I wish things had turned out differently for me. I wish I could enjoy this time in my life. A time where I should be applying for colleges and hanging out with all of my friends and maybe even have a boyfriend or two.

Instead I am stuck in a life that offers me nothing but safety and a small amount of peace of mind.

True, these are things I need, but not what I want. I want to live life to the fullest, experience everything this world has to offer. Instead my fear wins out and I am left with only this.

As much as I wish for things to be different, I can't say I would change the fact that all of this led me to Tate, or him to me, depending on the perspective.

If my life had turned out differently, then we may never have found one another and that is a thought I can't begin to accept. Is it possible to live a full life when the other half of your soul is not with you?

"Cally, can you come downstairs please?" My grandma calls through my door.

No doubt it's time to open this years birthday present, and I am sure there is some over the top cake that needs eating.

I don't respond, instead I run a quick brush through my long hair and tie it up in a ponytail.

"You're eighteen now Cally. Today is the day that everything could change." I say to myself in the mirror.

I look better than I have in a long time. The dark circles under my eyes have faded and my face seems brighter somehow.

I know I have only one person to thank for not only the physical changes, but the emotional changes as well.

When I reach the bottom of the stairs, I

falter. Standing in the foyer is none other than Tate Harper.

My heart does a flip flop at the sight of him. He's dressed in a black sweater and jeans, wearing a very sweet smile.

"Happy Birthday Angel." He says as I step off the staircase and stand just a foot in front of him.

My grandparents are purposely making themselves busy in the kitchen so I take advantage of the moment alone to ask him what he's doing here.

"I wanted to meet your family." He says casually, as if it's no big deal. I can't help the smile that crosses my face. He's never reached out to me like this before. He's always so secretive, as if no one can know about us.

"Besides, I thought it would help if they see that I actually do exist. Might help ease their minds." He says, giving my hand a squeeze.

"Would you two care to join us in the kitchen?" My grandpa says from behind us, causing me to jump a little.

We follow him in and take our seats at the table. I make the decision to sit on the opposite end of where Tate is sitting.

As much as I want to be close to him, I don't want to give my grandparents more to question.

My grandpa takes the seat to my left and I notice that he's eying me curiously. No doubt wondering what the heck is going on here.

My grandma sits paper plates and plastic silverware in front of us and then heads back to the counter to retrieve my cake.

We sit in silence as she cuts and serves each of us a piece and then she finally breaks the silence, joining us at the table.

"So Tate, how long have you and Cally known each other?"

"We actually met back in Chicago. I just recently relocated to the area. Imagine my surprise when I go for a walk and find myself at the creek that runs behind your property, staring at none other, than this beautiful girl here." He says, gesturing towards me.

I can feel the heat rush to my cheeks and know I must be blushing crimson.

"What a small world." My grandma says.

"So where are you living then?"

"Here and there." He says casually. "I typically don't stay in one place for long, but I think I might stick around here for a while." He says, staring intently at me.

A violent shudder runs through me, causing every hair on my body to rise.

"What do you do for a living?" My grandpa chimes into the conversation. Leave it to him to gauge Tate's ability to provide for me, should our friendship become more.

"I travel. Help people." He responds, not really giving a clear answer but giving them enough that my grandpa seems to form his own conclusion and not push for more information.

I, myself, am left wondering what exactly that entails and if that is really what he does.

"Tell us about your family dear." My grandma says, finally taking a bite of her cake.

As if we were all waiting for someone to start eating, once she does, we all do. The cake, of course, is divine. My grandma is a wonderful baker and today she made my favorite, red velvet cake with cream cheese icing.

Tate responds with a vague answer about his family not living around here. The conversation stays light and casual and by the end I have learned no more about the mysterious man sitting across from me.

My grandparents seem to approve. I see no tell tale signs that he has raised any red flags with them.

As my grandma clears the table, we make our way outside, sitting on the front porch swing side by side.

Finally alone, I jump at the chance to speak to Tate freely. But before I get a word out, he speaks first.

"I hope you don't mind that I came here. Honestly, I just wanted to spend some time with you. You know the way normal people do. Plus...... I have something for you." He says, reaching into his pocket.

He pulls out a beautiful silver chain bracelet and lays it in the palm of my hand. I hold it up examining the charm that hangs from it.

It's a silver cross with angel wings that extend from the top of it. It's stunning and I have no words.

"It was my mothers. I want you to have it. That way no matter where we find ourselves, you will always have a piece of me with you."

You don't give away something that belonged to your deceased mother to just anyone. To me, this is a confirmation. He is just as consumed by me as I am by him.

"Thank you." My voice comes out only a whisper. "Will you put it on?" I ask, holding the chain out to him.

With steady hands, he drapes the bracelet around my wrist and clasps it, his fingers lingering on the back of my hand just long enough for me to notice it's intentional contact.

Just the briefest touch sends shivers down my spine and causes every nerve ending to stand to attention. I can't imagine that I will ever get used to the way my body responds to his touch.

We sit there for hours. Just me and Tate, on the old porch swing. It's odd how casual our conversation flowed and how very normal it all seemed.

He told me about his childhood and where he grew up, all about his family, which I learned have all passed.

The sadness that caused me was overwhelming. He really is alone in this world.

Sometimes I have trouble separating my feelings from his, and I can't help but wonder if he can feel me as well.

Can he feel the way my heart speeds up when he smiles? The way my knees shake and my body quivers when he holds my hand? More importantly, can he feel my heart? Does he know that I am falling in love with him?

The thought scares me more than I care to admit. Not loving him so much, but the fear of losing him once I let myself fully accept the magnitude of my feelings for him.

The way he speaks so freely of his past makes me even more curious about his life today. Why can he discuss things like his childhood so detailed and non cryptic but when the conversation turns to the present day he shuts down and nothing makes sense?

This only leaves me more confused and more intrigued by him.

As the sun begins to set, he slowly rises to his feet without warning.

"I need to go." He states, turning to take my hand and pull me to my feet.

"Can't you stay?" I ask, knowing that he

won't, but wishing that he would.

"If I had a choice I would never leave your side again." He says, meeting my eyes.

"You do have a choice. You can choose not to leave." I say, holding on to hope that he will change his mind.

"I wish it were that simple angel." He says, leaning down and placing a gentle kiss on my lips.

"Happy Birthday Cally." He whispers in my ear and then turns to leave.

"Tate!" I call, just as he reaches the bottom step of the porch.

"When will I see you again?"

"Soon...... But my sweet girl, I am always with you." He says with a wink, and then disappears into the quickening darkness.

I sit there for quite sometime before I finally realize what I need to do. If he's not going to give me answers, I'm going to find them on my own.

I run upstairs and fire up the old computer my grandparents had gotten for me when I first moved here.

It's used and beat up and runs on dial up

internet, which is so slow it takes at least ten minutes to load a page, but it's enough to do the trick.

Once the search engine finally loads, I type in the only information I know about him. Tate Harper, 24, Chicago.

It takes a good five minutes for the results to load and honestly there is not as much as I had hoped.

I may live out in the middle of no where with next to no technology, but I grew up in today's world and I know that you can find out just about anything you want about someone on the internet.

I filter through the results, most of which are dead ends. Just as I am about to give up, I find a link that has a list of every Tate Harper in the United States.

There aren't many and most are clearly not him but then I come across one that has me believing that finally I have found him.

I click on the link next to his name and have to reread the information in front of me at least five times before it finally sinks in. Tate Jonathan Harper, 24 years old, Chicago Illinois, Deceased.

I am convinced that I have the wrong person. Until another link leads me to a news article. One that has a picture. I wait for it to load expecting to see a stranger. Instead, I see beautiful green eyes staring back at me.

My mind starts to go fuzzy and for a moment, I feel like I am in the twilight zone. I know what I am seeing but I don't believe my own eyes. I read on, hoping to find some explanation.

Tate Harper, 24, of Chicago, was found brutally beaten in the 900 block of Lancaster. His body was discovered at approximately 1:22 in the morning on September 2nd by a bar owner who called 911.

Police responded and Harper was transported to County General where he was pronounced dead from severe head trauma.

It is unclear what transpired and police currently have not named any suspects but a full investigation is underway. Harper, a recent graduate of Northern Kentucky University, was only in town for a few days to visit his family before he was set to leave for New York, a family friend reported.

Funeral arrangements have not been announced at this time.

I stare at the computer screen in complete disbelief. I know what I am seeing but I also know that there is no way it can be true. He was sitting right next to me only an hour before.

I can still feel the warmth of his body, the power of his touch. He is very much alive.

I reach down and toy with the bracelet he gave me. A cross with angel wings.....

He saves my life, shows up years later and seems to know everything about me. He appears and disappears without warning. I can feel him. I can feel the way the earth shifts around him.

Could it be true? Did he really die? Is he here now, in some form other than life?

I can't keep up with all the possibilities swirling around in my mind. I power off the computer and collapse on top of my bed, not even bothering to remove my clothes or shoes.

I find my star on the ceiling and focus on it, trying desperately to calm myself.

There has to be a reasonable explanation. Some kind of mix up no doubt. I will see Tate soon and when I do, he will clear all this up for me. This is what I tell myself but deep down I know that is not the case.

As crazy as this all seems, I have known all along that there was something very different about him.

How he refers to my world and his world like they are two completely different places. Like we don't exist in the same universe, even when we are standing side by side.

Just as my panic and confusion start to boil over, a calmness clears the air and I know that he is near.

Not with me, but close enough that I can feel his very presence.

"It's all right angel." I hear his voice but not with my ears.

I can hear him in my mind. I don't know if this is really happening or if I am simply between dream and reality.

It's here, in this moment that I realize, it must be true. And by some design of fate, we have found each other, despite the world that separates us.

One of the living, and one of the dead.

THE TRAVELER: THE AMULET OF LIFE

Chapter Six

With all my new found information, I am finding it hard to focus on anything but Tate and the circumstances that surround us. I have waited days to get the opportunity to speak to him and my patience is starting to wear thin.

"Tate I need you...." I whisper to the night sky as I lay on the ground at the edge of the field, staring up at the sky.

As if that is all it would ever take, he appears at my side. Laying down next to me, he takes my hand and places a soft kiss across each of my fingers.

"Is everything okay angel?" He asks, closing his hand around mine.

Such a simple act, yet it is one that sends

my body into a flustered ball of emotions.

"Tell me the truth." I manage to get out, my eyes not leaving the sky. I hold my breath, willing him to let me in.

"What truth can I tell you that you haven't already figured out on your own?" He asks, turning on his side and propping up on his elbow, so that he is looking down at me.

I chance a look at his face, and regret it the moment I do. Everything melts away, and suddenly nothing else really matters, just that he is here with me.

I try to refocus and not let him distract me from my purpose. I need to hear him say it. I need to hear him tell me that he is no longer among the living.

"Tell me.........." I breathe, focusing on his eyes. Letting myself revel in the fire that penetrates me to my very core. "Are you real?"

His sweet laughter breaks a little of the tension I feel, but doesn't take it away entirely.

"I'm right here with you aren't I? Do you feel this?" He asks, releasing my hand and placing it on his chest.

The steady rhythm of his heart makes me sigh out in relief. At least I have that much to hold on to.

"I am real Cally. As real as you are. I am a human soul, just as you are. How we exist in this world is irrelevant."

"Maybe you feel that way because you know with me what you're getting. I can't say the same."

"I see....." He says, resuming his position on his back. He breathes out heavily and drops his arms to his sides. "Can you promise me something?"

"Anything..." I respond without hesitation.

"Promise me that what I am about to tell you, won't change us. I am still me, and you are still you. How all this has come to be does not change that we are connected on a level that neither of us truly understands."

"I promise." I whisper.

"I'm a traveler Cally." He states, as if I know what that's supposed to mean.

"Okay. And what exactly is a traveler?" I ask.

"I don't know how to explain it to you in a way that will truly make sense. You have to experience my world in order to understand it. You are bound by this world, your mind has not yet expanded to everything that actually exists around you, sometimes in plain sight, others hidden from view....... I died Cally, and yet I exist in human form. This is the path I have chosen, though I never understood why. Until I found you." He exhales loudly and I can feel his tension mounting as he waits for me to react.

"You chose this path over what?" I manage to get out.

"At first I felt stuck in between two worlds. I wasn't ready to leave this one but I also couldn't watch the world around me, knowing I could not be a part of it."

"I found myself as what you would refer to as an angel. I can't really explain all that it entails, but I can tell you after a few years I grew restless and could not find peace with my existence."

"I was granted the right of a traveler. Able to take any form and travel all space and time. Most of my kind exist in other universes, other forms, but for whatever reason, I could not pull myself from this world. Drawn here by reasons unknown to me. For a while I wandered aimlessly and eventually I found a purpose in helping those in need."

"Like you did for me that night." I interrupt, piecing together the pieces of a very difficult puzzle.

"Yes, like the night I found you. I never expected that what was drawing me here was a beautiful young girl who seems to possess the part of my soul I had lost long ago, or never really found for that matter."

"After that, I never strayed too far from where you were. Making sure you were safe became my sole purpose on this earth. I never intended on making any contact with you. But the older you became, the more I could feel you sense my presence. Eventually the urge to reveal myself to you took over and once it did, there was no going back."

"Is this why you believe that I... that we are in some sort of danger?" I ask, sitting up and crossing my legs in front of me. He mirrors my actions, resting his hand gently on my knee as he continues.

"It is frowned upon to form connections to the living. The lines become very blurred and things get complicated. They knew I was getting too close. That's why he sent Braize."

"To keep an eye on us, make sure that the lines remain intact. I tried throwing him off my trail, but as a servant of god, he is not so easily fooled."

"Now that you know the truth, the risk becomes even greater. They will try to pull us apart, intervene somehow. That's why I have been leaving. Trying to find others like me to see if there is a way....." He trails off, taking my hand and shifting his position so that he is facing me.

"A way that we can be together in this life." He finishes.

"Is that even possible? I mean, I'm alive and you're........not." I say, apologetic.

"No but I have chosen human form. Which means physically I exist just as you do. Outside the form we take, we are all souls, we are all the same." He says, reaching up and gently caressing my cheek.

"Talk to me Cally, tell me what you're thinking." He pleads, his eyes penetrating mine so deeply I wonder how he can not just read my thoughts as they form.

"It's a lot to process." I admit. "I knew there

was something different about you, I just couldn't put my finger on it. This is all so confusing....." I trail off, distracted by the thumping of my heart, the blood rushing through my veins.

I can feel each breath as it enters and leaves my body, all my senses hyper aware. My entire body on edge.

"I don't care what you are Tate. All I know is that I can't live without you." I finally say and I mean it wholeheartedly.

Nothing in this world matters more to me than this man and what he makes me feel.

"I don't know if this will work Cally, or if it's even possible, but I have to believe that me being drawn here by you, this...." He gestures to the connection between us. "There's a reason for it all."

"Then where do we go from here?" I manage to get out, though I notice the quiver in each word as I say them.

"I don't know." He answers honestly.

"You have to be upfront with me Tate. No more secrets. I can't protect myself... you.... us, if I don't know what I am dealing with. You said that things will get more complicated, that they will try to keep us apart. How?"

"I'm not sure. Braize has been tracking me, keep an eye on things. I can't see him interfering anymore than that for the time being. I know I have kept this a secret for far too long, but I was so scared that you would want nothing to do with me once you knew the truth. I couldn't bare that." He says, leaning in and resting his forehead to mine.

We remain that way for a few minutes, both of us silent. Lost in our own minds. I finally break the silence, not actually intending to.

"I love you." The words are out before I even realize what I have said.

"Angel" He whispers. "You have held my heart from the moment I laid eyes on you. This belongs to you." He says, placing my hand over his chest.

"My soul belongs to you. My very existence is yours. And I love you, my sweet girl." He says, placing his lips gently to mine.

The fire that courses when we touch waves through me like an inferno. My skin prickles as he deepens the kiss. Claiming me, owning me. I give into the feeling, the power. Let it take me away.

Away to a place where nothing matters but this. The love that flows through us. The sheer power when our bodies touch.

I don't know how limited our time is and I can't waste away precious minutes obsessing over the things I simply can not change, let alone understand.

He pulls me into his lap with such ease that, for a moment, I am caught off guard by his strength.

Eventually he breaks away. "I should go." He says, lifting me by the waist and setting me to my feet.

I look at him, with what I am sure is disbelief, and he laughs, realizing that this is the first time that he has not tried to hide who he is.

"You're very strong." I observe, as he rises to his feet next to me.

"Power of the mind." He says, as if it's no big deal. "Physically I am no stronger than the average human, but with my mind, I can do most anything."

"Show me." I challenge him, just hoping to get a glimpse at the power this man possesses.

Suddenly the wind swirls, trapping us inside it's walls. He wraps his arms around my waist and pulls me close to him as he shuts out the rest of the world. Leaving us standing in the center of a small cyclone.

I laugh out, amazed and in disbelief. Without warning, the wind stops suddenly, as if someone flipped a switch. The sudden change catches me off balance and makes it clear why he had embraced me before he let the veil fall.

"Amazing." I breathe out, pushing the hair out of my face that had been blown loose by the wind.

"Yes angel, that is exactly what you are." He says, leaning down and placing a kiss to my forehead.

I close my eyes and lose myself in his touch. The wind blows, whipping my hair behind me, and when I open my eyes.... he's gone.

MELISSA TOPPEN

Chapter Seven

"Close your eyes." Tate says as we sit facing each other in the loft over the barn.

I do as he says, taking his hands in mine. "Brace yourself angel, this is going to seem very strange to you at first."

I hold my breath, both scared and excited by what he's up to. Suddenly, I am no longer sitting with Tate, but standing in a backyard.

I don't recognize my surroundings, but a young boy's laughter draws my attention to the back of a house.

"Come on mommy, you have to hurry." The boy says impatiently, pulling his mother by the hand.

He's young, maybe six or seven, with brown hair and beautiful green eyes, a carefree, excited smile plastered across his face. His mother laughs freely behind him.

"Slow down Tate, I'm sure whatever it is will not be gone by the time we get there." She is beautiful, an angel.

I wonder how she could be anything but. She's tall and slender with hair as dark as night, that hangs to her waist.

"Look mommy. There, look there." The young boy says, pointing to the fence line.

His mom crouches down and reaches out, picking up something I can't see.

"Can I keep it mommy? Can I please?" He pleads.

The woman turns. I can now see she's holding a small baby kitten in the palm of her hand.

"Poor thing, must have lost her mommy." She says. "Come quickly, we need to find a bottle so we can feed her."

"It's a girl!?" The little boy exclaims. "Can I keep her mommy?"

The woman crouches down so that she is eye level with her son.

"Yes, but you must promise me that you will take care of her. She will be your responsibility. What should we call her?"

"Ummm." The little boy rubs his head trying to decide.

"Cally, her name is Cally."

"What a beautiful name. What made you think of it?" She asks.

"I can feel it mommy. That's what her name is meant to be." He says, smiling widely and skipping back up to the house. His mother following behind him, Cally in her hands.

When I open my eyes, Tate is staring back at me intently.

"What was that?" I question, trying to regain a sense of my surroundings.

"A memory." He says, smiling.

"That was your mother?"

"Yes, and the very first love of my life, my kitten Cally. Seems I was drawn to you much earlier than I even remembered myself."

"That was amazing, how were you able to show me that?"

"I told you angel, power of the mind." He says smiling. I see it is the same smile the little boy wore.

"Show me something else." I insist, excited by this insight into a man I still know very little about.

"What do you want to see?" He asks. I immediately know but am hesitant at the same time.

"Show me the night you died...." I say, meeting his eyes and seeing the surprised look that crosses his beautiful face.

"I don't think that's such a good idea." He pauses, taking a deep breath.

"That is a place I have yet to travel and I don't think I could bare to relive the memory." I can feel the tension, the anxiety the surges through him and into me.

"Then tell me." I compromise.

"There's really not much to tell." He says, shifting his position to make himself more comfortable.

"I had only been home a couple of days. I was spending some time with my mom and dad. I had accepted a position in New York interning at a law firm. I was set to attend law school that next fall and needed some hands on experience."

"I knew my time with my family would be limited, so I made an impromptu visit to surprise them. I caught up with some of my old friends at a local bar my last night there and we spent the night drinking, catching up. It was an uneventful night and after a few beers I decided to head home."

"I wasn't in any shape to drive, so I walked the back way. I was cutting down a small alley between two buildings not five minutes from my parent's house when it happened."

"I don't remember much. Just something hitting me in the back of the head, then everything going black. When I woke up, I was standing in the hospital. I asked a nurse how I got there but she acted as if she couldn't hear me."

"I stepped directly in front of her and asked again. This time she looked up but not at me, more like through me, like I didn't exist. The chart in her hand had my name on it. When I turned to see what she was looking at, I saw my body sprawled out on a bed in an operating room." He shivers at the memory. "That's all I know."

"So you have no idea who did it to you or why?" I ask.

"It wasn't long after that, I realized I wasn't meant to stay in the in between. It's hard to explain, but once you have made the choice to leave this world, all parts of your past seem to fade away. You know who you are but your life seems less important somehow, a small part to a much larger picture. It wasn't until I retook my human form, that the memories of my former existence started to resurface. By that time, it no longer mattered who or why, it just simply was."

"Does everyone become an angel?" I ask. He immediately picks up on my intention behind the question. I am asking about my family.

"No..... Everyone must choose their own path. Some become travelers without ever leaving this earth. They form a new independent soul and eventually realize they can materialize into reality appearing human, free to explore all space and time. Some simply choose to remain here and exist in the in between. Some become angels, other demons."

"Each soul must choose their path based on the life they lived here. I know you want to know about your family but I can't tell you where they are, any more than I can tell you where you will end up once you leave this life."

"I'm sorry, of course you can't tell me that. I just think it would be easier to live if I knew that they were okay, happy...." I break off, choking back the knot beginning to form in my throat.

"I know angel. But the things that separate our worlds, the specifics, are off limits. There are rules, I am bound by my knowledge. It's part of my place. I lost the right to know certain things when I made my choice. There's too much risk involved, too many people seeking the answers of what life beyond death holds. They would never take that chance."

"I understand my world, my existence, but all others have been erased. I know I was an angel at one point, and I know I needed a different path, but the specifics of that time are blank. I have no recollection of the fifteen years prior to this life." He says, studying my reaction.

"Don't over think it Cal, not everything needs to have an explanation." He says, sensing my worry and unease.

We are raised to live this life, never really sure as to what is in store for us beyond. Some people spend their lives determined to know what awaits them next. Others, like me, simply accept that there may or may not be something after. Life is just life. At least that's what I used to believe.

"What's going to happen to us Tate?" I ask, suddenly fearful that we truly have no control in a life that we call ours.

"I wish I knew angel." He says, pulling me close to his side. "I wish I knew...."

Hearing this from him. Knowing that life holds no guarantees and that this may be the last time I am ever with him, sends a fear through me greater than I have ever felt before.

Not even when I was staring death in the face did I feel this type of fear. Knowing that more exists and not being able to share it with Tate is a fate damned to hell.

I can feel his fear mingled with mine. I know he's scared too and yet here he is. Breaking all the rules and risking his very freedom just to be able to sit here and hold me in his arms.

This thought alone causes my heart to swell and my pulse to quicken. Will I ever know sacrifice like this? Risking my very existence to be with the one I love? But isn't that what I am doing?

    A life without Tate is more than I could ever bare. Now that I have tasted him, felt the power of our connection, the beating of our two hearts as one, I could never face a world knowing he's not here to share it with me.

    I knew there was more to life than what I had been living. Tate has opened me up to a world I didn't even know existed. But the only world I care about, is the one he is in.

****

    I'm walking down a dark alley, I feel scared but I'm not sure of what. The unknown? I wander aimlessly not sure which direction to take when I hit a fork in the road.

    Looking left I see flowers, sunshine, happiness. The other is dark, cold, and yet I am drawn towards it.

    A voice is telling me to go left but my body seems to have taken control and turns right. The further down I walk, the darker my surroundings become. A shining light at the end gives me a ray of hope and I quicken my pace.

"Cally stop!" I hear my mother cry out to me. I turn to see her standing just feet from me.

"Mom!" I try to reach out to her but an invisible wall is between us and I can't reach her.

"Mom, I'm scared. I don't know what to do."

"Turn around darling. There is nothing for you here."

"I can't. I don't have a choice. Mom please, help me."

"He's coming. Go. Run Callista! Run!"

Without hesitation, I take off in a sprint. Further and further into the darkness, until I can see nothing at all. Only the blackness that surrounds me.

"Help me!" I scream out. Laughter vibrates all around me. I turn around and around trying to find it's source but I can't see a thing.

"Why are you doing this?" I plead.

"You chose your path. This is your fate." A

man's voice calls out.

Suddenly the floor drops below me and I am falling. I look up, desperate to find something to grab on to but then stop abruptly, floating in mid air.

A light shines brightly from below and I can see that I am in some sort of tunnel.

"Cally....." I hear Tate call to me. I turn.

Behind me he is floating not a foot away. I reach to him but like before, an invisible wall holds us apart.

"I'm sorry. Cally I'm so sorry."

Then he's gone and my feet are back on solid land.

"Tate." I scream into the blackness. "Tate......."

I shoot up soaking wet and panting.

"Cally, Cally, it's okay I'm here. It was just a dream." Tate's voice soothes me as he holds me in his arms. It takes me a minute to calm down and realize that I am safe in my room.

"What are you doing here?" I pant out, still trying to convince myself that I am awake.

"I told you, I'm never far away. When you dream I can sense their meaning. I could feel your fear." He says, pulling me into his lap and cradling me.

I nuzzle my head into his chest and relax in the comfort of his arms.

"It wasn't just a nightmare." I say. "It was a warning Tate. I don't know how I know, but I do."

"I know, I could feel the interference. The outside source forcing it's way into your dream. We are pushing the limits. The warnings will only get worse. Eventually they will act on them. I just haven't figured a way out of all this yet."

"I'm scared." I admit, hugging myself tighter to him.

"I know angel.... so am I." His admittance only makes me more uneasy.

He seems so powerful, so sure of everything. But this is one thing he isn't sure of and that terrifies me.

What if they take him away from me? How would I survive?

"Stay with me." I plead.

****

I try to hang on to sleep for a moment longer, but the sunlight blazing through my window pulls me from my haze. It feels like any other morning, like nothing has changed. But memories of last night come billowing in and I am left with the simple acceptance that nothing will ever be the same again.

Tate held me for as long as I can remember. I'm not sure how long he stayed once I fell asleep, but guessing from how peacefully I slept, I would say he was here most of the night.

Tate is not only showing me how to love. He's showing me how to let go, how to be okay, and most importantly how to live again.

I close my eyes and I can see his face, I can smell him, I can taste him. All my senses are connected to him now. It's moments like this, that I swear he is right behind me.

"Good morning angel." He says over my shoulder, causing me to jump and scream out at the same time.

"It's okay, it's me. I'm sorry baby, I didn't mean to scare you." He laughs a little, causing me to break into laughter myself.

"Don't do that!" I squeal. "You scared me to death!" He grabs my wrist and locates my pulse.

"Nope still alive." He jokes, pulling me into his arms and wrapping them around me.

I hold tightly to him, too afraid the moment I let go, he will disappear, and right now I really need him.

"Can you stay with me today?"

"I wouldn't dream of leaving your side angel. Did you have anything in mind?"

"I want to leave the farm." I blurt out, before really thinking about it. "Just for the day. Can you take me somewhere, anywhere? Just away from here."

"I would take you to the ends of the earth if it's what you desired." He says, releasing his hold on me.

"Go get dressed. If you're wanting to get away for a while, there's someplace I would like you to see." He says.

****

"Come here." Tate says, scooping me into his arms and carrying me up the side of the mountain. We have been walking for hours, it must be midday by now, and my body is starting to protest. "Were almost there."

I wrap my arms tightly around his neck and enjoy being in his arms. I don't have to feel guilty that I am too heavy or that he is growing tired, his body is controlled by his mind, and his mind knows no limits from what I can tell.

"We're here." He says after a few moments, gently lowering me to my feet.

"Close your eyes." I do as he asks. He places his hands on my hips and turns me in place until I am facing away from him. His chest firmly against my back, his arms wrapped around my waist, his chin resting on my shoulder.

"Open your eyes angel." He whispers into my ear.

"Wow." I say, before I can even process the beauty of what I am seeing. The world is stretched out below. Miles and miles of grass and mountains all laid out before us.

"This is amazing." I breathe, feeling light headed more from the man than from the altitude.

"This is my favorite place. Anytime I just need to get away, to lose myself in the beauty of it all, this is where I come. I have sat on this very mountain for hours upon hours dreaming of what it would be like to know you, to hold you in my arms. What it would be like if you were mine."

"Is it everything you dreamed?" I ask, turning to face him. No matter how beautiful the view, it doesn't compare to the masterpiece standing in front of me.

"It's more angel." He says, pulling me into his arms. "Much, much more."

THE TRAVELER: THE AMULET OF LIFE

Chapter Eight

TATE

The days with Cally fly by and I can't help but feel like I have finally found my place in this world. Every touch, every moment, becomes more precious than the last.

I know I have put us both in an impossible situation but I can't regret my decision to be with her, to love her.

I wish I wasn't so selfish. Maybe then I would have been able to walk away from her without her ever even knowing I existed.

But I am selfish and I can't stay away from her. I know it's what's best, what's right but I simply can not survive without her.

Her nightmares, warnings really, have

grown increasingly stronger. I know they will be here soon which is why I am not all surprised when I feel that we are no longer alone in Cally's room.

"I wondered how long it would take you. Your mind tricks can only work so much magic Braize." I say, turning to face the young man standing next to the window. Much to close to Cally for my own comfort.

"Is that so, lost my touch have I?" He replies coolly, his white hair gleaming by the moonlight.

"Maybe we should test that theory." He says, reaching down and placing his index finger across her forehead. Instantly she is withering in pain, arms flying, legs kicking.

"Tate! Please Tate! Nooooooo!" She screams through the dream. The sound is earth shattering and I can't take seeing her in such pain even if it is only a nightmare.

Her screams rip through me like a blade, cutting me from root to tip. I can tolerate it no longer.

"Get your hands off her." I warn, fully intending to use physical force if I need to. "This is between me and you."

"It is for now." He says, breaking his

contact with her. Immediately her body starts to relax and her dream becomes peaceful again.

He takes two steps towards me, his black eyes give nothing away. He's taller than me, but not by much. Of course we both know that none of that matters.

I have the body of a human, him of an angel. I am more solid matter than him but to the blind eye we would appear in the same league.

I'm stronger than he is, I can feel it. Sense his unease. His overcompensation with words. But that still doesn't mean I am willing to take the risk.

I shift, disappearing from the bedroom, and reappearing just outside the house. Braize follows me and I am thankful to have him away from Cally.

Angels are extensions of god, all that is holy. It is not in their nature, or mine, to do harm. But when it comes to separation of the world of existences, they will go to great lengths to protect what they view as right.

"So Tate Harper, the famous Traveler, fallen in love with a human. Tisk, tisk.... One of the strongest minds to have ever crossed into our world. What a shame to throw it all away on something that you will only lose in the end.... Tell me..." He says, stepping towards me, his long black coat trailing behind him. "Was it worth it?"

"I would do it all over again if I knew that I could hold her in my arms, even for one day." I shoot back without hesitation.

"Ah, would you now? Well, the time has come to choose. Will it be you or will it be her? Maybe we should make it interesting and ruin you both."

"He would never let you harm a defenseless human and you know it." I retort back, the anger rising like bile in my throat.

"Even if that human threatened the very thing we fight to protect.....Hmm I wouldn't be so sure Mr. Harper. How sure are you?" He says, closing his eyes with a smile.

Her screams rip through the night, radiating every nerve in my body until I can contain myself no longer.

"NO!" I command, throwing him into the air without even touching him.

"Leave her out of this!" He lands on his feet, skidding to a stop, dirt flying up behind him.

"Now now, do you really want to cross that line?" He laughs and before I can react, I am being thrown backwards against the house, held in place by golden ropes he materializes out of thin air.

He takes one step, gliding through the air, and lands directly in front of me.

"There is an easy solution. Walk away Tate, walk away and all this just... Disappears." He says, making a vanishing gesture with his hands. The rope extends, coiling around my neck, cutting off my ability to speak with words.

"Why are you doing this? Do you really believe either of us would do anything to jeopardize the world as it is? We just want to be together." I speak with my mind, willing him to feel the emotion, the honesty behind it.

He barks out a laugh, shaking his head. A piercing siren starts blaring in my ears, drowning out all ability to think, to speak, or to defend myself. I'm trapped, helpless.

"If I can do this to you.... Imagine what I could do to her. I could end her and you know it." He says, tilting his head to one side.

He drops the bindings and I topple forward to the earth, the ropes vanishing. The white noise stops as quickly as it started and my mind begins to clear.

"You can make it all go away. You can keep her safe."

I rise to my feet standing toe to toe with the only thing I know I can't stop. It's inevitable. Even if I defeat Braize today, more will come in his place.

The only thing I can do now is decide what is more important. Cally's safety or my own selfish need to be with her.

"Give me one day." I sigh, admitting defeat. "One day to be with her, to say goodbye. I know you can give me that."

"You have one day Mr. Harper, I suggest you make it worth while. And rest assured I will be keeping tabs, making sure that you aren't up to anything. If you so much as try to contact her after this day, I will end you both." He gives one final warning and then vanishes.

I collapse to my knees, unable to find the strength to stand anymore. The thought of being without Cally, of saying goodbye to her, is more pain than I can bare. But I know there has to be another way.

I will do as they ask..... for now. But I will never stop trying, never stop fighting to find a way for us to be together again. I can only hope that she will understand, that she will let me go.

For as much as I love her, I know she loves me the same. It isn't just about my wants, my needs, not anymore.

It is just as much about her as it is me and I know that in just a few hours time, I am going to have to break the heart of the only person I have ever truly loved.

This is something I must do, no matter what the cost. I must keep her safe. I must protect her until there is a way..... I will find a way.

****

I wake with a start and the overwhelming feeling that something is off. I search the room frantically for Tate and immediately relax when I see him, sitting in the arm chair in the corner of my bedroom.

"Hi." I manage to get out through a yawn.

"Good morning angel." He says, leaning

down and placing a kiss to my forehead, reaching me so quickly, I swear I blink and he's there.

He sits on the edge of my bed staring at me. He doesn't blink, he doesn't speak, he just stares. For a moment, I feel the weird urge to smile, like he's mentally photographing me.

"What are you doing?" I finally break the awkwardness that seems to be growing between us.

"I just want to remember everything about you. The way you crinkle your forehead when you're concentrating too hard, the way your eyes brighten when I touch you like this." He says, trailing his finger lightly across my cheek leaving a trail of fire long after his hand is gone.

"I love every line of your face, every freckle." He says, tapping on the tip of my nose.

"The example of pure beauty. I just want to remember you this way. Happy, alive, here with me."

"Why do you need to remember me, I'm not going anywhere? I will always be with you." I reassure him, taking his hands in mine as we sit facing each other on my bed.

"You never know what the future holds, I

just want to make sure I cherish you while I can." He says, breaking his eyes away from mine. I can feel the wall, the stone that is separating his feelings from mine.

"I can't feel you." I say, turning his eyes to face me once more. "Tate why can't I feel you?"

"Feel me?" He questions, as I realize I have never shared this information with him before.

"I can feel you, your emotions. When they shift, I sense it. I feel what you feel. When you're afraid, I'm afraid, when you're at peace, so am I. You must know this, you're shutting me out right now, I can feel it."

"I'm not purposely shutting you out. You're over thinking things again angel." He says, running his hands through the end of my hair.

"Don't insult my intelligence. I'm not stupid and I'm not blind." I say, pushing his hand away.

"Tell me the truth Tate. What is going on and what are you hiding from me?"

"This isn't how I wanted to spend today." He says exasperated.

"I just want to be with you. Please can you give me that?" He pleads.

The look in his eyes makes me want to give in, melt at his request but my mind won't rest until I know he's being honest with me.

"You promised..... You promised me no more secrets. We are in this together, remember?" I plead back, holding his face in my hands as I look deeply into his eyes.

It is there that I can see it. The fear, the grief. He's scared, he's heartbroken, but most importantly he's lost.

"What happened?" I whisper to him.

"Braize." It's all he has to say.

"Did he finally show?" I ask, knowing that he was expecting him.

"He did...."

"Well, are you going to tell me what happened?" I ask, a little irritated that I have to continue to ask questions when he should just be telling me.

"Can we talk about it tomorrow?" He asks, and I am a little thrown off by his request. What power does tomorrow hold over today?

"I promise to tell you everything, but right now, today, I just want to be with you. I don't want to think about Braize or what the future holds. I just want to hold you in my arms and focus on nothing but that."

"Okay." I finally cave, not feeling up to the battle that is sure to ensue if I continue to push the issue when he simply does not want to discuss it.

Besides, he makes a good point. We should enjoy each day as it comes. Otherwise they win. What is the point of being together if we can't truly be together, body, mind, and soul?

For today we have that. And each day after, as long as we can hold on. To each other, to our love, to the path we have chosen together.

****

"Do you really have to go?" I ask Tate as we stand outside the back of my grandparent's house.

We spent such an amazing day together and I really don't want it to be over. But more so, I don't want to be away from him.

I know I will see him again tomorrow. But

he has stayed with me the last few nights and I can't express the level of peace he brings me. The level of comfort I feel just by knowing he's with me.

"I'm sorry angel, but I must. We both know that the more time we spend together, the more attention we draw from unwanted individuals."

"Will we ever just get to be together?" I ask, nuzzling into his chest and wrapping my arms around him.

I know he says he's only leaving for the night, but deep down I can't help but get the feeling that this is somehow goodbye.

The feeling rips my insides apart and I have spent most of the day trying to figure out if I really could survive in his absence.

"One day angel. I promise you, I will do everything in my power to make it possible." He says into my hair, before pulling me from his arms to stare into my eyes.

I concentrate hard, trying to feel him, get a sense of what he is hiding from me.

As much as he says it's nothing, I know better. He may have formed a wall to shut me out but he can't hide what lies behind his eyes.

I can read him, even if I can't feel him. And he gives too much away. Something has happened and he's not telling me what. He's keeping me in the dark, even though he promised he wouldn't.

A part of me feels angry, the other knows he is only doing what he feels is right to protect me.

"I love you Callista Price. More than you will ever know. Promise me that no matter what happens you will continue to fight, for yourself, for us."

"You're starting to scare me Tate. Why are you talking like this? Wherever you are, I will be. It's the only way." I say, not able to contain the tears that have begun to well in my eyes.

"Where you are, I will be." He breathes.

"If not in body then in soul. You own my heart angel. Nothing will ever change that." He says, pulling me to him once more and kissing me forcefully.

I embrace the passion that surges through me. The sheer emotion brought on by the force of this man's love for me. The same love that I feel for him.

He breaks away too soon, resting his forehead to mine. "I love you." He whispers.

I close my eyes inhaling his scent, breathing in his love, his soul.

Before I can open them again, I feel the overwhelming emptiness that tells me that I am alone.

MELISSA TOPPEN

Chapter Nine

TATE

I stand at the edge of the field looking up at Cally's bedroom window. I know I need to leave, walk away, but I haven't yet found the strength to make my legs move.

I am stuck, glued to the very ground I stand upon. Leaving her has already proven to be the most difficult thing I have ever done and I haven't even left yet.

I hate the way I left things with her. That I didn't tell her I was leaving her for the foreseeable future. She would have only tried to stop me and this is hard enough without having to witness her heart break, even though it is sure to happen when she realizes what I've done.

I spent most of the night mapping out my plans. I'm not going to just step to the side and live my life without her. I vowed to find a way for us to be together and I fully intend to do just that. I don't know how or when, but I know deep down that I will, I have to.

I've decided upon finding others of my kind. I know a couple that are around. We are linked so finding them should be the easy part.

It's finding someone who is willing to help me that will be the problem. Surely this has happened before, there must be someone that knows something, anything, that will assist me in my quest.

I close my eyes and am now standing over her, watching her sleep peacefully in her bed. My angel. The one thing that makes existence worth while. The only thing that makes me feel whole.

I sit the note I wrote her on her bedside table. I don't even want to imagine the pain she will feel when she reads it. When she realizes that I lied to her, that I broke my promise.

"I love you." I whisper to her, placing my lips gently to her forehead, very careful not to wake her.

I inhale deeply, memorizing her scent. I am sure most days this will be the only thing that keeps me going. Remembering her like this. Sweet and beautiful. The other half of my own soul. My partner in this life and every life following.

****

My first stop is New York City. Nicholas, a traveler like myself, frequents these parts and with any luck I shouldn't have too much trouble locating him.

He is the only one of my kind that I have ever taken the time to know. When I first chose this life, I wandered aimlessly, not really sure how to live this type of existence.

I met Nicholas in New York a year in and I guess you could say he showed me the ropes. Or at least his version of them.

I didn't crave the type of life he had chosen but it worked for him. We lost touch not long after some angels appeared to scare some sense into him..

Scared me is what they did. I vowed then

and there to never make waves with the powers that be. This was, of course, before Callista Price.

Standing in the middle of Times Square, I close my eyes and focus. Within minutes I know exactly where he is.

Challitos is a little dive bar on the corner of Fifth Avenue. I shouldn't be surprised that this is where I would find him.

He's always been a bit of a free spirit, a go by the seat of your pants kind of soul. He's more for making his own rules then following ones that are set for him. Because of this, I know that if he can help me, he will.

I spot him at the edge of the bar, talking to a very attractive young girl. Just like him to be scouting out fresh meat.

Interactions with humans, mortals as they are called, is completely acceptable as long as it is in short spurts and no real connections are formed.

Nicholas has never lost the playboy side that he carried with him as a human. He has always loved women and I can tell watching him now that some things really do never change.

"I see you're still at it." I joke from behind

him.

He swivels on his bar stool, turning to face me. His sky blue eyes are almost white and remind me too much of a husky dog. His hair is black, shoulder length, slicked back away from his face. Tattered jeans partnered with a tightly pressed button up collared shirt, he wears the part well.

"Well, well, Tate Harper, to what do I owe the pleasure?" He asks, in his thick Australian accent, shaking my hand and smiling widely.

Standing from his stool he pats me on the shoulder. "Love, could you give us a minute?" He turns his attention to his catch of the night.

I gotta hand it to him, he knows how to pick them. Innocent and easy to persuade, not to mention stunningly beautiful. She nods, her blonde hair flowing behind her as she walks away.

"Hey Joe, get my friend here a drink and I'll take another." He orders the bartender, pointing to his glass.

The bartender nods and returns within seconds with two glasses of scotch on the rocks.

"Cheers." Nicholas says, clinking his glass to mine and draining the contents. I hesitate for only a second before following suit. It is the first time I

have drank in this form and the liquid soothes my raw throat and aching heart but just a tiny bit.

I have not indulged in many of the perks of this existence. Choosing to take human form, allows you all the privileges of being human, with the exception of actually belonging to this world. Belonging to a human that inhabits it.

Cally's face flashes in my mind and I hold up my glass signaling for another.

"So, you just gonna stand here and leave me guessing all night? Spill Harper." Nicholas says, resuming his seat and gesturing for me to take the one next to him.

"I need your help." I admit, trying to play it casual.

The last thing I need is to come across desperate and well, human. Nicholas would never respond to that. Lucky for me, I have had enough interactions with him to understand this and take the sure fire route.

"I'm breaking all the rules here, thought you might want in."

"Do tell....." Nicholas says with a smirk as the bartender sits two more drinks in front of us.

"Let's just say they are not too happy with me right now. I'm trying to find a way around their control. A way to be human again, or at least live like I am. Without the bounds, the restrictions."

"Now why would you want to go and do something like that? Look around brother, we've got the world at our feet. Able to be human again but with many added benefits.... Unless...." He breaks off, picking up on the obvious that I have not yet stated.

"You didn't." He laughs. "Well how about that. Tate Harper has gone and fallen in love with a mortal. Good god man and I thought I was at the top of their shit list."

"Can you help me or not?" I bark out, not wanting to waste my time with his typical banter.

"I can't help you mate." He says, draining yet another glass of scotch.

"But I might know someone who can." He holds up his hand signaling the bartender and asks him for paper and a pen when he approaches us. He scribbles something down, folding the paper and handing it to me.

"What's this?" I ask, taking the paper and unfolding it. Scrawled across the middle in perfect form reads:

Emily Bennett

7459 Westminster Bridge Road,

Lambeth, London.

"Be careful with that one, bit of a wild card she is. A demon, and a real bitch if you ask me. She is always looking for ways to stick it to the man, so to speak. If anyone can help you, it is her."

"But I must warn you mate, once you cross that bridge, there's no going back. You know as well as I that teaming up with anyone of her kind is the ultimate betrayal. They won't take this lightly."

"Thank you." I say, standing. I extend my hand and he takes it, giving it a shake.

"I hope you know what you're getting yourself into. Is it really worth it?"

"She's worth a billion years burning in hell." I say in complete honesty.

"Well good luck to you. And Tate..." He says, as I turn to leave.

"Be careful. Demons are not creatures you want to cross. If you go to her, be sure it's what you really want." He says, tipping his head to me.

"Thanks Nicholas." I say, turning my back to him and exiting the bar. As soon as the night air hits me, I feel a sense of revived hope. Maybe just maybe, this could be the solution to everything.

I close my eyes and focus on the address he gave me. When I open them, I am standing in the middle of a brick laid road.

It's dark and the city is mostly deserted. In front of me is a little shop with 'Incantation' screen printed across the glass door leading inside.

Reaching for the door, I pull. It's locked. One thought and the door swings open. I let myself in, knowing before I even inspect the place that I am alone.

I can sense any presence, especially that of a demon. They feed off of fear and anger and such feelings tend to consume you in their presence. It's not something that could be easily masked.

I lock the door behind me and take in my surroundings. I find myself standing in the middle of what appears to be a shop dedicated solely for witchcraft and dark magic.

I guess I shouldn't be surprised. Placing temptation in the middle of a city, willing people to the dark side. It's a shame humans are so easily persuaded by evil.

To my left is a glass counter with various trinkets and pieces of jewelry. On the right, candles, potion mixes, and other non sense that is clearly only out to draw a crowd mainly on curiosity alone.

None of that stuff actually works. The back of the store is lined with bookshelves from floor to ceiling covering every aspect of magic you would care to know, including spell books and other various 'how to' guides.

I can't help but laugh at the ridiculousness of it all. However, I'm smart enough to know that magic does exist, especially dark magic.

It can be used to consume even the purest of souls. Dooming them to an eternity of damnation.

I don't know when she will choose to show herself. I can only hope that once she does, she is the key to finding what I need.

I know I shouldn't be here. Nicholas is right, once I cross this bridge there really is no going back. But what would I have to go back to if I can't be with Cally?

The thought of her alone gives me strength, courage. I have to do this, for me, for her. For the very thing that we want more than anything in this world. A life together. It seems so simple and yet it is anything but.

I can only hope that when I return, if I make it through this, that she is waiting for me. That she can forgive me for leaving her the way I did.

I know I am in store for a long journey. I can only hope that at the end I will have found something, anything, that will give me the one thing I desire above all else.

Until then, I wait......

****

I wake with a start feeling the overwhelming presence of loneliness. I know he's not here but I search for him anyways, only to confirm what I already knew.

I sit up, stretching my legs out and over the side of the bed. I am finding it more difficult than usual to get up and face the day.

Just as I am about to hoist myself up, I see

it. A cream colored envelope with *Cally* scrawled across the front, sitting on my bed side table.

With shaky hands I reach for it. I know who it's from and I am terrified by what it may say.

I sit for a moment, just staring at it. The loneliness, the absence of his presence. And now this?

All signs point to what I already know to be true. He's gone. I rip the envelope open at the seam and remove the pages from inside. Slowly I unfold it and it's contents rip my world apart.

My dearest Cally,

If you are reading this letter then that means you already know what I am about to say. Such a clever, brilliant mind. I could never get anything past you. But first let me say that I love you, and while this may be goodbye for now, it certainly is not goodbye forever.

You have changed my world in ways I never could have expected and while leaving you is the hardest thing I have ever had to do, I know it is what's best for you, for us. In the long run anyways.

Please forgive me that I did not say goodbye to you in person the way I should have. Having to face you and say those words was not something I could bare.

To see the pain that I am sure is written all over your face right now would have ripped me apart and I simply could not stand to see you hurt the way you are hurting now. Though I know that I will feel your pain and that alone will haunt me until I am with you once more. Words can not express the magnitude of my love for you. You feel it when we're near. I would die a thousands deaths for you.

What I am about to tell you must never be repeated, though I know that goes without saying but just to be safe. If anyone starts asking questions DO NOT give them any information, it will only put me and us at greater risk.

As you know, Braize found me. You were right yesterday when you said that I was hiding something from you, I was.

I'm sorry to have broken my promise. I kept you in the dark after you specifically asked me not to and for that I will forever be sorry. But please try to understand that for the first time in all of this, I felt like I couldn't keep you safe. This is so much bigger than us Cally. This is existence itself fighting against us.

I have gone in search for a way for us to be

together the way we dream we can be. I'm not sure where my journey will take me or whose paths I may cross but I promise you that I will fight with everything I have to return to you... one day.

I am heading to New York to track down an old friend of mine. One that will hopefully be the lead that I need. At least something to get me started.

I am afraid that for whatever reason, I will not find my way back to you. That you will have to forever endure the pain of my absence. Please know that I will do anything in my power to ensure that does not happen.

You are my world. The other half of my soul. No man, or object, no matter how powerful, can take that away. We are destined to complete one and another. I will find you again and when I do, I will never let you go.

I love you angel. Please keep yourself safe. I dream of the day that I will see you again.

Until then..

All my love, Tate

The tears are flowing so hard and fast that I can not contain the sob the escapes my lips as I crash to my knees on the floor.

He broke his promise... He left me here, alone. Anger and pain surge through me like blood through my veins.

I need to get out of here. I need to leave. But where do I go, how will I survive anywhere without him?

It devastates me to know that I rely so heavily on him. What will happen to me if he really doesn't come back?

Managing to calm the storm raging within, I stand to my feet with new purpose. He needs me. I can help him, I know I can.

Why couldn't he have taken me with him? Instead he leaves me here, trapped and defenseless.

I'm done being an empty shell, floating through this life with no real meaning or purpose.

Being with Tate is the only thing that has made me feel alive in years. I have to find him. But my hands tremble and my stomach rolls at the thought of leaving.

Where do I go? I have no idea where to find him and even if I did, travel by plane or a car would never suffice. He would always be ten steps ahead of me.

There has to be a way. I have to try. I can't just stand by and chance that he may never return. I have to make sure he does.

****

It's taken me two days and three different buses but I am finally here, standing in the heart of New York City.

A place I have ever only seen in pictures and on the television. It's magical. Going from a solitary life on the farm to a city like this is enough to scare the average person.

Me, I'm quivering like a child, wishing every minute that I had just waited for him like he had asked. I have no idea where to go. I don't know anyone.

I'm standing in a city with millions of people and yet I have never felt more alone.

I wander the streets aimlessly searching for anything that may give me a hint as to where he is.

Thus far I have shared a connection with Tate that I still don't fully grasp. Little things that pull me, guide me. Deep down I truly believe that if I try hard enough I can find him.

By the time the sun begins to set, I am tired, and desperately hungry. I look up trying to figure out where I am. The street sign to my left reads Fifth Avenue. I make my way further down the street spotting a little diner on the corner.

Relieved, I run inside and slide into one of the booths in the corner. It's a small place. Reminds me of the diner in 'Back to the Future' and I love that it gives me something comfortable, something familiar, to hang on to.

I skim the menu but nothing sounds overly appealing. Seems strange that only moments before I was starving and now my stomach is turning and my appetite has disappeared. I settle on something simple and set the menu back down on the corner of the table.

Within minutes, a chubby red head in a pin striped uniform, complete with white apron, approaches me to take my order.

Once she has what she needs, she disappears and I am left with only my thoughts and a gaping hole in my heart.

I have already burnt through half of the

money that my grandparents gave me just to get here.

I lied to them, told them I wanted to go to Chicago to visit my families graves. At first they insisted on coming with me but backed off when I was very adamant that this was a trip I needed to take alone.

I think part of them hopes it's the first step to me getting back out into the world, so they didn't want to put up too much of a fight.

Instead, they gave me as much money as they could spare and sent me off. I brought with me only one backpack, stuffed full with a couple of outfits and some snacks for the trip.

The waitress reappears, bringing my ice tea and salad that I ordered.

She asks me if I need anything else and when I don't respond, she just walks away. Truth is, as soon as I felt it I stopped hearing her.

Nothing mattered but the pull, the force. Telling me that something or someone is close.

It isn't until the door swings open and he steps in, that I know who he is. The friend that Tate had come to find.

I don't know how I know but I do. Like there

is a voice that is guiding me, telling me that I am right.

His build and height are very similar to Tate's, probably close to the same age, but that is where the similarities end.

He's dressed in jeans and a black sweater, his black hair slicked back away from his handsome face.

He looks in my direction and my pulse quickens. Does he sense me the way I do him? When his eyes meet mine, it sends a shiver down my spine.

He has the eeriest eyes I have ever seen. So blue they almost seem all white. Suddenly I am very nervous. I can sense his danger but for whatever reason, I am not afraid of him.

At first I think he notices the same charge I do, but then he turns away and sits at the bar in the center of the restaurant, not glancing my way again.

Gathering my barrings, I stand and make my way over to him. My food and drink left abandoned and untouched. What mattered moments ago, no longer does.

I don't care that I am hungry or alone. All I

care about is finding Tate and if this man is somehow involved, I have to know.

I scoot onto the bar stool directly to his left. He doesn't acknowledge my presence at first, instead just studies his menu.

Finally I think he notices he is being watched and he turns to face me.

"Can I help you love?" He croons out in a very attractive Australian accent.

"I.. I... Um..." I stumble over my words, not able to form a sentence.

"Cat got your tongue there does it?" He asks with a laugh, but continues to stare at me intently.

Finally I find my voice, but there is an obvious shake in each word as it comes out.

"Tate Harper, you know him?" I don't miss the way his features tighten or the way his eyebrows shoot up in surprise. It's the tell tale sign that I got it right.

My inner cheerleader is doing back flips but the rest of me is not so sure I should be celebrating just yet.

"Well I'll be...." He says, eying me up and

down.

"So you're the girl. Now I can see what's got him so out of his mind. You're gorgeous love." He says, making me blush but that doesn't break my focus.

"Where is he?" I breathe, not wanting to waste precious time with chit chat.

"Where he is, you aren't going love. No business in a place like that. Emily Bennett would eat you alive, pretty innocent thing like you." He says, nodding towards me.

"Please....... Please, you have to help me." I plead. "He's all I have."

"Now don't look at me like that. I am only doing right by Tate. He would never forgive me if I told you where he is. It's too dangerous, especially for a mortal. Demons are nothing to play around with."

"Demons!" I gasp, trying to keep my voice low enough as to not be overheard by the other patrons in the restaurant.

"What is he doing with demons?" I ask, lowering to a whisper.

"He's throwing caution to the wind.

Grasping at anything that will help him find a way to be with you. To seek help, to break the rules, you must find someone who does not follow them. I simply pointed him in the right direction." He says, taking a sip of coffee.

"Then you can tell me where to go." I insist. I know this man is my only hope and I am not giving up.

I can't turn back now. Not when I am so close to closing the gap between us.

He stands, tossing a couple dollars onto the counter as he turns to leave. I follow directly behind him as he makes his way outside.

"Are you going to help me or not?" I snap, my patience wearing very thin.

"London." He says over his shoulder, but keeps walking.

"London! What is he doing in London? I will never be able to get there....." I call out after him.

"Please..." I plead, stopping in the middle of the sidewalk and choking back the sobs that are threatening to escape.

"Oh bloody hell." He yells out, throwing his hands in the air and turning to face me.

"You seriously want to do this? Walk into literally, hell on earth, for what? By the time you reach him, he is sure to be long gone."

"I have to try. Wouldn't you? If it meant finding the one person you can't live without? Wouldn't you at least try?" I beg him, willing him to feel the power of what Tate means to me.

"Please."

He runs his hand through his hair as if considering my words.

"I guess I would." He finally responds as I hurry to where he is standing.

"Then help me. You must know a way to find him, please."

"I will take you where I sent him, no further. Let me be clear, once we are there, my part is done. I will walk away without any remorse."

"Deal!" I exclaim, wrapping him in a tight hug before I even realize what I'm doing.

His body tenses and I can feel the ripple of hard muscle under my grip. I drop my arms quickly.

"Sorry." I say, backing away from him. "So how do we get there? I don't have much money."

He laughs lightly. "Love, the way we travel, you don't need money. Come with me." He says, leading me down a dark alleyway between two large buildings.

"I'm Nicholas by the way, thought we should be properly introduced before we break every rule in the book." He says, laughing at himself.

"Cally." I manage to get out, trying to keep up with his long strides.

He stops abruptly, turning to face me.

"This is going to be quite uncomfortable for you Cally. Wrap your arms around my waist. That's it." He says, as I do as he instructs.

"Now hold on tight. Whatever you do, do not let go of me."

I start to respond but suddenly the world is being ripped out from under me. Shapes and colors pass but I can't make out anything that I am seeing.

I feel like my body is being stretched, pulled to it's furthest limits and I am finding it difficult to breathe. I clasp Nicholas tightly.

Before I know it, my feet are back on solid

ground. I gasp for breath, inhaling deeply. My stomach twists from the sudden change in motion and I stumble to the side unable to get my balance.

"Easy there love." Nicholas says, grabbing me by the shoulders and steadying me.

"Where are we?" I ask, looking around. Nothing is familiar to me but I feel the pull, Tate has been here.

"London." I answer my own question. "But how?"

"Travel." He answers simply. "We focus on where we want to go and then." He gestures around us. "We appear there."

"Amazing...." I breathe out, still reeling from the sensation that is shaking through my body. I am still having trouble grasping the reality of any of this.

The powers, the other beings. It's all so surreal.

"Well here we are... Incantation. Awful place. This is where I leave you. I'm sorry but even I know my bounds and this is not a war that I want a part of. Ask for Emily." He says, as I turn to face the small shop to my left.

It's an eery place. I can feel the darkness radiating from it.

"Good luck love…. Oh and Cally." He says, as I turn to face him. "Be careful." With that he vanishes and I am left alone.

Alone, facing god knows what. I stand on the sidewalk, rooted to the spot. I know the moment I walk in that door, everything will change. The world I know will no longer exist.

Instead it will be replaced by a world that I am still not able to comprehend. A world until days ago, I never even knew existed.

THE TRAVELER: THE AMULET OF LIFE

Chapter Ten

It takes everything I have to take the five steps to the door of the tiny shop. It's glass, framed with a thick, dark wood. *Incantation* scrawled across the front in red lettering.

What a strange little place. It's not very inviting and I can't see why people would want to shop here.

It's late or well early, I'm not sure which. I have never been much on keeping up on the different time zones. I have a hard enough time remembering the ones in the States, let alone half way across the world.

I take in the town. I am surrounded by multiple buildings and little shops, some similar to this one but with a lighter feel to them.

A cool breeze sends a shiver to my feet. Rubbing my arms, I step closer to the door, trying to shield myself from the cold.

I peel off my book bag and set it on the sidewalk next to me. Leaning down, I unzip it and retrieve a black hooded sweatshirt. Slipping it over my head, I snuggle into it's warmth.

Closing up the bag, I stand, sliding it onto my shoulders, and freeze. Standing not a foot from me, staring through me with yellow eyes, gleaming with just a hint of red around the edges, is a woman. I stand motionless afraid to even breathe.

Fear and sadness radiate through my very soul. She cocks her head to one side, examining me. I avoid eye contact and try to focus on leveling my breathing.

She no doubt can sense my unease but I am not going to show her the effect she is having on me. That being in her very presence seems to be ripping me into pieces and the pain is making it hard to stand on my own two legs.

"Such a pretty little thing." She breathes, leaning in and inhaling deeply.

"Ahh... a pure soul." She rasps out directly

next to my ear.

Her breath on my neck gives me the feeling of a hundred spiders crawling all over my body. The thought alone causes me to shake.

"What can I do for you love?" She asks, taking a step backwards with a large smile.

Clearly it satisfies her to know she can affect me. Only then do I really look in her direction.

She's tall and thin, with dark skin, and hair as black as night that hangs to her waist. Her black trench coat is tied tightly around her.

In a normal world I would go as far to call her pretty, but the eyes, they tell me what she really is. She doesn't appear much older than myself but I am sure has lived in some existence or another for many years.

She smiles again, as if she is amused by me. "Not much of a talker..... Let's see what we can do about that. Come..." She says, unlocking the door to the shop and ushering me inside.

My mind resists but my body betrays me as I duck into the dimly lit store. It's cluttered and dusty and smells of incense and moth balls. That alone is enough to make my stomach turn.

There's an uneasiness in being here, a darkness.

When the door closes behind me and I hear the click of the lock, I jump. My body on high alert.

I stand with my back against the counter at the front of the store so that I can keep her in my line of sight.

She makes her way over to a wall of books in the back. Scanning her finger along a row near the middle, she pauses, before deciding on a book and pulling it off the shelf.

She makes her way towards me but doesn't approach me directly. Instead, she sets the book on a table filled with candles in the middle of the room.

Without saying a word, at least twenty candles jump to life. I muffle a shriek as the action takes me by surprise.

She looks up at me, her expression blank, unreadable and then turns her attention back to the book.

I watch in silence, as she whispers something I can't hear. The book opens, shuffles through a couple hundred pages before dropping open about midway through the contents.

"Let's see here...." She croons out, skimming the page with her finger. "Ah yes, this is it."

My curiosity wins out and my feet are moving before I even realize it. I cross the distance between us as carefully and quietly as possible. She knows I am here but I don't want to draw any unwanted attention to myself.

Once I reach the table, she walks away without a word. Disappearing behind a large crimson curtain that acts as a door on the far left wall.

I stare at the curtain, making sure she is really gone. Glancing down I immediately gasp. In large old style lettering, the heading reads: The Traveler. Not only does she know why I am here but she is showing me an insight into Tate's very existence.

The Traveler

A traveler is a soul free in existence. The ultimate expression of free will in an intelligent being. Travelers are the fifth most powerful supernatural beings in existence.

Choosing a life free to explore all time, space, and parallel universes. A traveler can take on any form of the existence they choose. Appearing to belong no matter what the environment. Physically they are natural holograms in solid form possessing powers that are almost limitless and only bound by their mind, which acts as their source of power.

Travelers most commonly begin as Angels that were once human, leaving God to travel the universe to discover their own path and purpose. This is typically permissible as God gives all beings free will. Ones that also hold the ability to return as an angel if they so choose.

Travelers are known to explore and can share interactions with mortal beings. Such interactions are tolerated as long as the true self of the Traveler is not revealed. Such revelations are not tolerated in the universe.

Though not permitted, a Traveler can conceive children with a human. The child would be born to their environment but would live as an immortal.

The soul of a Traveler is infinite, however a Traveler may be stripped of their light and energy if the destruction they can materialize is too great. Forced to take on biological form, they become demons.

I read the same lines over and over again, finally realizing the magnitude of what faces Tate. What he has risked just to be with me.

My heart aches for him. If I focus hard enough, I can still smell his scent, feel the warmth of his arms around me. It only makes me feel stronger about my decision to be here.

Suddenly the pages of the book begin turning by themselves. Rapidly at first and then slowing, coming to a stop near the end of the book. I eagerly scan the page. In the middle is a picture of a large pendant. A cross, twined with snakes, a red stone in the center.

The Amulet of Life

The amulet of life is a powerful magical object said to hold the ability to return human life to any existence. The origin of the object is unknown but is believed to be made of very dark magic.

Allowing the person that so chooses, to return to their life before death. However by doing so, damning themselves to an eternity of darkness upon completion of the new life.

The whereabouts of the amulet are unknown.

It remains to be seen if it actually exists.

"There is another way." The woman rasps behind me, startling me.

I hadn't seen her re-enter the room and her sudden presence leaves me shaken.

"What do you mean, another way?" I ask, turning to face her.

I have to be brave, strong. She can't hurt me if I don't let her. I stare straight into her eyes and while that simple action leaves me feeling helpless and full of despair, I don't break my focus.

"The transfer of life." She says, retrieving the book and returning it to the shelf.

"Transfer of life?" I question, as she glides past me and kneels down behind a glass counter top filled with jewelry and other small items that I can't make out.

She slides open the back of the case and begins rummaging through the jewelry.

"Ah, here it is." She says, retrieving a small gold ring and holding it up as she makes her way back to me.

"A mortal can give life to someone no longer of the living, thus merging their two souls.

Binding them for eternity." She says, taking my hand and placing the ring in my palm, closing my fingers around it. Her touch is like ice, sending an uncomfortable ache through my arm.

I uncoil my fingers and stare at the tiny object in my hand. It's nothing but a standard gold band. I eye her questioningly.

"What is this?"

"That, my dear, is your key to the amulet." She hisses.

"And this." She says, reaching behind her and retrieving a locket from the counter, "Is your map."

"I.... I don't understand." I stutter out, confused.

"The locket will show you the way. You must focus on what you desire. When you open it, it will take you to where you need to be. Once you are there, you must read the inscription on the inside of the ring to gain admittance."

"Why are you helping me?" I ask . Not that I am entirely certain that she is helping me but what else can I believe?

What other options do I have? Sit back and

let Tate throw everything away for me. I can't do that, I won't. He means too much. He means everything.

She doesn't answer my question. Instead, she walks to the door and holds it open, gesturing for me to leave.

There is so much more I still want to know but am afraid to push my luck. I don't hesitate. Slipping the ring on my finger and the locket around my neck, I quickly make my way out the door and into the cool morning air.

The door snaps shut behind me and the fresh morning air clears my mind. Cleanses me of the darkness I was consumed by just moments ago.

I can only assume that she is the demon, though I never asked, and she never confirmed, I could feel the darkness radiate from deep within her.

I have no other leads, no way of knowing what Tate's next move is. My only option is to find the amulet. That is where I will find him.

I have no idea what's in store for me and I am scared. But the fear of what may happen to me is far outweighed by the fear of what will happen to Tate if he gets to the amulet first.

I know what I have to do.

Now it's a race. One that I must win to save us both.

THE TRAVELER: THE AMULET OF LIFE

Chapter Eleven

Finding a deserted alleyway is the easy part. The hard part is figuring out what to do once I'm out of sight to anyone who may stumble across me.

I slide between two small buildings that are separated only by a matter of a couple of feet. Pressing my back to the cool brick, I inhale deeply and try to focus on the information I have learned thus far.

First, there is the amulet of life. A pendant that will give life but at a price.

The other is the transfer of life, in which a human takes the amulet for their own thus willing their life to someone no longer of the living.

What exactly will happen from there, I am unsure.

I never dreamed at the age of eighteen, I would be walking so willingly into deaths arms. But according to Emily, if I take the amulet as my own, I will bind my soul to Tate's, thus guaranteeing that in the afterlife we will be together.

I have to focus on that and not that in the matter of hours, I will be sacrificing my own life for someone that I love, but that I will be gaining the ability to spend an eternity with Tate by my side.

I slip the gold band from my left index finger and hold it up, studying it. At first glance, I thought it just a standard band, but now in the darkness of the alley, it seems anything but.

Squinting, I look closer. It has etching that wraps around the entire ring and gives off the allure of a river, only it's not water flowing through the crevice, but fire.

Flipping it sideways, I look for the inscription that Emily referred to. Sure enough, there are letters scrawled in cursive writing along the inside. I struggle to make out the words:

Upon life give death, upon death give life.

This is my key. The way to the amulet. The only way to save Tate.

It hadn't occurred to me until now that if Tate is searching for the amulet as well, how is it that I hold the map and key?

Certainly there are other ways to find it and yet, something about it doesn't sit right with me. Reaching up, I turn the locket over and over in my hands. It's heavy, too heavy.

I am tempted to open it, but given my instructions, I fear where I may end up if I do.

Focus on what I desire, that's what she said. Right now I desire the amulet. I focus all my energy and thought on that one object.

Envisioning the picture that was scribbled in the book. The cross, the snakes, the fire red crystal directly in the center.

Hesitantly, I reach up and remove the locket from around my neck. I hesitate for only a moment before speaking.

"Take me to the amulet." I say aloud, and then flip the locket open.

I brace myself, holding my breath, but

nothing happens. Trying hard not to break my focus, I open my eyes, glancing down at the locket now lying open in my palm.

    Each side contains a picture, each of a child. I study them closely and then gasp when I realize that one is me.

    I couldn't be more than eight or nine, smiling widely, my long brown hair flowing around my face.

    The other is the same little boy I saw in a memory, Tate. As beautiful as ever, his green eyes full of light, of life. But how.....

    Suddenly the world around me vanishes and the ground is no longer beneath my feet. I have an overwhelming sense of deja vu as I begin falling, fast and far down a dark deep path.

    I struggle to find something to grab onto, anything to slow my descent. My hands grasp nothing but air.

    I've seen this before, experienced it, in a dream. The one where my mom tells me to run. I see her face now in the darkness. The same pained look on her face, the fear in her eyes. I close my eyes tightly, knowing that it is only in my mind.

I continue to fall. My stomach feels like it is in my chest and I struggle to find my breath. Without warning I stop, suspended in the air, held by nothing, and then topple to the ground.

I open my eyes and frantically search my surroundings. I have no clue where I am but it feels good to have solid beneath me once more.

I stand, my legs so shaky they can barely support my weight. I lock my knees, trying to balance myself. It's dark but I can see the sun slowly rising over the top of a large hill.

I reach down, retrieving the locket that had slipped out of my hands when I landed. It remains open but the pictures are no longer there. Instead, they are only silhouettes. One of a man, the other a woman. Closing the locket, I re-clasp it around my neck before glancing around.

I am surrounded by trees and forest. Something about this place is so familiar to me.

I take a couple hesitant steps forward and then stop. I know these woods. The very woods that sit just beyond my grandfather's bean fields.

But how... Why? Why would the locket bring me here?

I turn, making my way in the direction of

the farm house, only to find myself ending up in the opposite direction. As if a force beyond myself is guiding me, no matter which way I turn, I keep ending up in the same place. I keep trying a different route, only to find myself in the same clearing I had just left.

Confused, I search for a sign. Something, anything that will tell me where to go, what to do. My body is weak from lack of food and sleep. Not to mention that twice in the last twelve hours I have found myself transported, leaving my body feeling stretched and out of place.

My mind struggles to keep up, not fully able to comprehend exactly what is happening to me. I know the events but they seem jumbled somehow.

My meeting with Emily was only an hour prior and yet I feel like it has been days, weeks even.

I can feel the panic rise in my chest but I do my best to force it back down. I keep processing this as if it were a dream, something out of reality. But I know it's real.

The rapid beating of my heart, my forced breathing, tell me that this is very much real. My body fully aware of every twitch, every prickle of my skin. My senses on high alert.

Deciding I can stand no longer, I slump to the ground, dropping my back pack behind me. I slide the ring from my finger and read aloud:

"Upon death give life, upon life give death."

Suddenly the earth shifts below me and I quickly realize I am not where I think I am. Its an illusion. A trick, something to lower my guard.

I quickly shuffle to my feet and step back as the ground slides open in front of me revealing a large stone staircase.

Every fiber of my being is telling me to turn back, to run. I can feel the darkness before I even take a step forward. But once again, as if I have no control over my body, my legs begin to move.

With each step, I try to force my body to stop, but as if I am not the one controlling my movements, I continue forward, deeper into the darkness.

It's cold and damp. The only light, a small gleam given off by torches suspended from the stone walls.

Each one I pass extinguishes as another in front of me ignites. I can't still the shake of my hands. I can't regulate my breathing or slow my heart. All I can do is continue down, down, down. It's endless and I wonder if I will ever reach a destination.

Another torch goes out but this time a new one doesn't light. I can see something ahead and feeling like I have regained some control of my body, I quicken my strides.

Once I reach the landing, the source of the light is revealed. I am standing in an open space, a perfect circle of stone walls. Torches lighting each angle of the large space.

In the center, a larger flame seems to burn from nothing at all. I step towards it, my heart rate accelerating as I see it.

There, floating in the middle of the flames, is the amulet. I step forward again until I am so close that the heat of the fire is unbearable.

I reach my hand forward but stop when someone clears their throat behind me. I pull my hand back quickly and search the room.

"I wouldn't do that if I were you." A man says, stepping out of the darkness and into the light of the fire. It is only then that I know exactly who my guest is.

"Braize." I breathe out, recognizing him immediately. It's not everyday that you see someone with such a distinct appearance.

He's tall, lean, and very young, or at least the form he inhabits is. He steps towards me, his white hair gleaming in the light of the fire.

He continues to move until he is standing directly in front of me, his black eyes piercing daggers into mine.

"And I thought Harper was the foolish one." He says, a slow callus grin crossing his perfect pale features.

I want to be offended. I want to bite back with my own words but I can't seem to form any. The control of my body seems to have ceased once more and I am glued to the spot in which I stand.

"Mortals....." He says, throwing his head back with a laugh that cuts through me like knives.

"Such impulsive, silly creatures. I must know Callista, how far did you think this through? Willing to give your life for an immortal soul, such a waste." He says, reaching up and trailing a long white finger along my cheek, sending shivers through my body and leaving a trail of ice from where his flesh met mine.

"It's only life." I manage to get out, but my words are heavy and I don't recognize my own voice.

"Only life?" He snaps back, suddenly angry. His features tightening.

"I want more." I say, meeting his gaze. "I want what you have. Endless life, the possibilities, the adventure, the love." My voice weakens at my last words.

"What is the quote you all so frequently use.... Ah yes. The grass is always greener on the other side. You want this life and in due time you will have it, but not this way. You can't force yourself into an existence where your soul simply does not belong. Why is it so hard to understand that the existence you live now is the very existence that we envy?" He asks, his tone becoming lighter.

"Envy? Why would you envy this life, when you... Well when you're you?" I question him curiously, not grasping what he is getting at.

"The dead envy the living for just that very thing. They are alive and we are not. Not in the biological sense anyways. We all become this one day, in some form or another, but it is this life, your life, that is the most precious. You appreciate things more because you may never see them again. You love deeper because you don't know if there will be a tomorrow. Each day to you is more precious, more important than the one before it, because it could be your last. Because of this everything is more beautiful, everything means so much more. That is the life that is envied. The life that you would so carelessly give away."

"But what is life if you are living it with half a soul? Never knowing your true place in the world, never belonging anywhere? Without Tate, my world holds no beauty. Instead of each day being more precious, each day is pure hell. You have no idea what I am talking about do you?" I ask, basing the question off of the look of complete confusion written all over his face.

"Mortals are sentimental creatures. There is so much more to the world, to the existence, than one soul. We are all part of a much larger picture."

"You say this, but as you do, you know who you are, your place in all of this." I say, gesturing around us.

"Imagine that you shared your soul with

another being. Imagine having that being ripped away from you and being forced to live as half a soul. Would you have as much faith in the master plan if you had no choice but to exist just that way? Broken, lost..... Alone." I say, the pain apparent in my voice.

Each minute that passes, each second, only makes me miss Tate more. The comfort and security of his arms around me. The way my body responds to his every move, every touch.

"Everyone is one. There are no split souls, existences are not shared." He snaps, his agitation returning full force.

It's then that I realize, there is no bargaining with this man, no reasoning with him. If he's determined to stop me, than he will have a fight on his hands.

I will not walk away. Not after I fought so hard to be here. I have to act fast.

Without a word, I reach into the fire, clasping the amulet in my hand. My flesh burns and the pain is so great I struggle to keep my hold.

I pull my hand from the fire quickly and glance down. My flesh is bubbled and charred from the fire. The pain takes over and I topple to my knees. Tears flowing freely down my cheeks but my grasp on the amulet remains in tact.

"Callista what are you doing......DON"T!" He screams, reaching for me as I slip the amulet onto my neck and breathe my last words.

"For the other half of my soul, I give my life. I love you Tate." I whisper, willing him to hear me.

I can feel my chest tighten, my breathing becoming labored as I struggle to fill my lungs. Fire bleeds through my veins and I collapse on the cold dirt floor.

A moment of sheer panic followed by nothing...... but darkness.

THE TRAVELER: THE AMULET OF LIFE

Chapter Twelve

"Callista Marie... Get your butt down here, you're going to miss the bus." My mom's voice rings out, breaking the silence of my sleep.

I pull the covers over my head and snuggle into their warmth.

"Callista!" She screams again and this time I shoot up, awake but very disoriented.

"All right, all right. I'm up!" I holler back, peeling the covers off of me and throwing my legs over the edge of the bed.

As soon as my feet touch the cool hard wood floor, I realize where I am and look around my bedroom. It's the same as I remember it.

Cream colored walls covered with band posters. One wall plastered with pictures of me with my friends and family. A collage I had spent months creating.

I walk to the dresser that sits on the back wall of my room and glance into the vanity. It's me, but not the me that I have become accustomed to seeing. I am younger, happier.

The guilt and pain is no longer visible across my ivory skinned face. I reach up, brushing my hand against my cheek and then giving it a little pinch, as if trying to convince myself that the girl staring back at me is real, that she is me.

"Callista!" My mom's voice calls again, more irritated than before.

I run to the door and rip it open, desperate to find her. The thought of seeing my mom again is both devastating and the thing I have dreamed about since she was taken from me.

It's all I have ever wanted. Suddenly the scenery melts away and instead of standing in my old house, I am standing in the hallway of my high school, pools of teenagers bustling all around me.

"Hey baby girl. I have been looking for you everywhere." Mike says, stepping next to me and sliding his arm tightly around my waist.

"Come on I will walk you to class." He says,

urging me forward. I give no resistance and instead feel a smile light up my face.

"Well you must not have been looking very hard." I joke back, leaning into his touch. One that is so comfortable and yet so foreign to me.

It is then that I realize, that this isn't real, nor is it a dream. It's a memory. One that I have long since forgotten.

How clearly I can now remember the days when life was so simple. When I had eyes for only one boy. The captain of the soccer team and in my opinion, the hottest guy in school.

Looking back now, I know that it wasn't about him or some connection we shared. Instead, it was about the image, the perception I wanted to give other people.

I glance up at Mike and soak in his warm features. His golden hair perfectly spiked. His tight jawline and perfect cheekbones. He is just as handsome as I remember.

Standing a good six inches taller than me, he catches my stare and leans down, placing a kiss to my forehead.

I can feel my heartbeat quicken and the butterflies swim in my stomach. I know this is not what I am feeling but what I felt. No matter how much time has passed, no matter how much has happened, I still appreciate the light that he brought to my life.

He was always so funny and playful. Making me laugh no matter how sour my mood. I missed this. The carefree life I once lived. The one where all bad things were worlds away and I was perfectly content in the bubble I had created for myself.

"Well, here we are." He says, stopping just outside of my Algebra class. "Safe and sound." He says holding my arms out and inspecting me.

"Not a scratch on ya. Am I good or am I good?" He jokes, his lips curling up in an amused smile.

"You never disappoint." I joke back, leaning into him and wrapping my arms around his waist.

He wraps his arms around me and squeezes before releasing me. I watch him walk away and disappear around the corner.

When I cross the threshold of the door, my scenery molds again, and I am now standing in the middle of my living room. I feel the surge of emotion run through me at the sight of my family all gathered around the Christmas tree.

    I want to run to them, embrace them, but alas I am only seeing what has already happened and my body has done all this before.

    My eyes roam the living area. Modern and sleek. My mother's style of course. She was always so particular about where every piece of furniture sat, where every picture was placed.

    The thought of the last time I stood in this living room is enough to make me want to turn and run, but in this reality I have no control but to follow each movement that this version of me makes.

    I walk over next to my sister and plop down a couple feet from the tree. It's early and I can feel the expression on my face telling everyone how much I just want to go back to bed.

    I wish instead of being a spoiled, ungrateful brat, that I could show them the joy that I really felt being with them.

    Myra is bouncing up and down next to me. Clearly much more enthused than I in that moment. Her curly brown hair is a wild mess, her eyes bright and full of excitement.

    She looks so much older than I remember.

For some reason, when I picture her, I see a small helpless child but she wasn't a child anymore. Almost a teenager, she tried desperately to be just like me.

I used to get so angry with her when she would sneak into my room and steal my clothes. She was smaller than me of course, and while my clothes were too big for her, she would wear them anyways.

My mom used to make excuses for her. Always saying that I should cut her some slack, that she just wanted to be like her big sister. I wish I had taken my mother's advice. I wasn't mean to her all the time, just most, as sibling rivalries go. But I loved her dearly.

I can't help but wonder how it would be now. Both of us older, adults. I imagine we would be the best of friends. She would have been someone I could have shared everything with, at least my mom used to say it would be that way, even if I couldn't see it at the time.

I think a part of me was jealous of her. Being the baby of the family, she always seemed to get special privileges and I can't remember a time my mom or dad ever told her no. Add on the fact that she was absolutely adorable and that was enough for me to feel challenged somehow.

Too bad I didn't take the time to appreciate her while she was alive. Things could have been so very different.

"This one is for you dear." My mother says, turning my attention to her, as she takes a seat next to me on the floor and hands me a beautifully wrapped petite box.

I linger on the bow for only a second before I rip it open to reveal the contents. A beautiful cross pendant, one that I had forgotten, lost to my previous life.

I look up into her beautiful bright eyes that hold the light of the heavens. I want so badly to wrap my arms around her and hold her close.

I glance down at the pendant and when I look back up, it is no longer my mother that I see. I am sitting in the middle of my best friend's bedroom floor. Ashley sitting directly across from me, her legs crossed in front of her.

"So girl are you gonna spill or what?" She asks, giving me a look that tells me I don't really have a choice.

"There's nothing to tell." I insist and try to change the subject. "So what's the deal with your parents. Have they told you about the divorce yet?" I ask, knowing they haven't.

Her parents fought constantly and Ashley knew it was only a matter of time. They hadn't shared the same bedroom in over a year. Both convinced that it was the best thing for their daughter if they all remained under the same roof.

Ashley had stumbled across divorce papers one afternoon and had been waiting ever since for someone to come clean and just give it to her straight. This almost always did the trick but not this time. She wasn't going to be so easily distracted.

"Nice try." She laughs out. "You're fourteen Cal, it isn't unheard of for someone our age to have sex with her totally hot boyfriend. I can't believe you didn't tell me!"

"Because it isn't true." I insist. Rumors had been flying ever since homecoming that Mike and I had hooked up at his house after the dance. One guess as to where the rumors started. I guess that's what you get for dating a Senior freshman year.

"If that's your story. I choose to believe the more exciting version." She jokes. Giving me the famous Ashley smile.

I find myself smiling too, not just on the outside. I missed this. The typical girlfriend banter. Just sitting with my friend, catching up on all the gossip and the what's hot right now chit chat.

I forgot how much I loved spending time with people. Laughing, just hanging out. Something I have not been able to do since leaving Chicago.

I can't shake the nagging feeling that all of this is wrong somehow. Me being here, seeing all this. But it doesn't stop me from enjoying the moment.

Just getting a glimpse into the life I used to live is enough to make me miss it more than I ever have before.

The comfort of being in the presence of my best friend vanishes in front of me and I find myself on the back porch of my grandparent's farm house, my dad by my side.

I shift my position from one leg to the next, showing clear signs of agitation.

"I know that you don't want to be here honey. But for your grandparents sake, can you at least pretend? They get to see so little of you." My dad croons out in his soft voice that always had a way of lowering my guard.

As much as I loved my mom, I had always been a daddy's girl.

"Come on, I want to show you something." He says, leaving his spot on the porch and making his way through the yard.

I follow quickly behind him, for the first time noticing how he moves so powerfully, each stride a revealing sign of the confidence he possessed.

"Dad where are we going?" I whine behind him. Growing restless as he continues his pace, making his way through the fields.

"I know it doesn't seem like much." He says, pausing at the edge of the woods. "But this place holds more beauty than you will ever realize. Just listen…." He says, closing his eyes.

I mirror his actions and close mine as well. Focusing on the sounds around me. The peace that comes with the quiet was something I didn't appreciate at the time, but I now understand what he was telling me. To stop and appreciate the beauty of what is in front of me. The sound of the wind wiping through my hair, the birds, the absolute serenity of nature.

I open my eyes again and when I do, he is staring at me. Love and adoration cover his handsome features.

"Life gets hectic and sometimes we forget to just stop and appreciate the beauty around us. I know it may not always seem like it to you, but you and your sister mean everything to me and your mom. I know you think we are too hard on you, but one day when you have children of your own, you will see that we only do these things to protect you." He says, drooping his arm over my shoulders and pulling me to his side.

"I love you Callista, more than you will ever know."

I nuzzle into his side and inhale deeply. In this moment, I can see how everything they ever did was for me, for Myra. I close my eyes and enjoy the feeling of being with my dad, seeing him alive again.

Just as the setting is growing comfortable, I feel the same shift and again find myself in a different place and time.

It's dark, but I can see enough to know that I am back in my old bedroom. The sound of my mother's screams rings through my ears.

Not again, please god, not again. I can't relive this moment.

I try desperately to will myself to stay in bed, but again I have no control over memories. Each second replays exactly as in my nightmares. The screams, the gun shots.

Before I know it, I am in the living room. My eyes squeezed tightly together, waiting.......

MELISSA TOPPEN

Chapter Thirteen

TATE

Having followed a lead to the Southern tip of Italy, I find myself once again at a dead end. I had hoped to be closer to finding answers. The demon that Nicholas had referred me to turned out being just as useless as I had feared.

Speaking only of the Amulet of Life. Something I was already familiar with and had no interest in seeking out. I wasn't looking for a way to be with Cally temporarily.

No, I need something more permanent. Something that can guarantee me an eternity by her side.

I close my eyes and inhale deeply as the sweet smell of the sea envelopes me. For a moment, I feel hope. Even after all I have seen in my existence and how unsuccessful I have been thus far, I know deep down that there is a way to possess the one thing I desire above all else.

The hope drowns out to a feeling of pure dread. Something in the air changes and I can feel it. Something is not right.

I close my eyes again and focus. When I open them, I am standing in front of Cally's house. I can't shake the urgency that I feel as I approach the front door and knock.

I have only met her grandparents once before but it was enough that I don't think they will mind or question the reasoning for my visit.

After what seems like an eternity, the door opens, revealing Cally's grandmother with a look of confusion written all over her face.

"Is Cally here?" I ask, not managing to disguise the rise of panic in my voice.

I can feel the lack of her presence. She's not here, that much is clear. But maybe she can tell me where I can find her.

"No dear, I'm sorry. I thought for sure she would have told you. She left for Chicago five days ago. Said she needed some time to find closure."

She says, her voice trailing off, losing herself in her own thoughts.

"Did she tell you anything else?" I demand, sounding harsher than I intended.

"No....What's this all about? Is everything okay?" She questions me. Her white eyebrows arching up.

"When she gets home, can you please tell her I am looking for her?" I manage to get out, sounding a bit calmer.

"I sure will hon, but truthfully I don't know when that will be." She says, but I don't stick around to hear anymore.

I turn, making my way quickly from the porch, leaving her standing there with a look of utter confusion plastered across her wrinkled face.

She's not here. I asked her to stay, to wait for me. As much as I want to applaud her independence, it doesn't take away from the sheer panic I feel that this may have been the worst thing she could have done.

I quickly make my way down to the edge of the driveway, being sure that I am out of view of the house before I disappear. I focus on one thing, and one thing only.

"Cally." I whisper, closing my eyes. I search for her but nothing sticks. Finally I feel the familiar pull and let myself go.

When I reappear, I am standing in an underground stairwell. Confusion and panic mingle together overwhelming my senses.

I quickly make my way down. The amount of stone steps seems to be never ending and I wonder if I will ever reach the bottom.

As if my prayers are instantly answered, I can see light protruding from the end of the stairwell.

I have no idea what will be awaiting me at the bottom but the only thing that matters in this moment is her. Finding her, making sure she is safe.

Exiting the stairwell into a large round room with dirt floors and stone walls, I find only one focal point. Cally, lying still upon the ground. Her brown air splayed wildly around her.

Her heartbeat is there but only just. The faintest of palpitations still pulsing through it. She's alive, but barely.

I drop to my knees beside her and pull her into my arms. As I do, something drops from her hand, clattering to the floor.

I cradle her closely to me, only glancing down for a fraction of a second when it all makes perfect sense.

She doesn't have much time. The amulet laying not a foot from us tells me exactly what she has done. But why? How?

"The transfer of life." A voice rings out, so powerful it echos off the walls and vibrates through my soul.

I glance up to find Braize hovering over us, his pale skin ablaze, his cheekbones hollow.

"I tried to stop her……." He breaks off, his voice ice cold.

"I don't understand, why would she do this?" I croak out, not able to hide the fear that laces my voice.

"She was under the impression that by giving her life for you, that it would bind your two souls for eternity.... The work of a demon, well played I must say." He says, not trying to hide the humor in his voice.

Fear turns to anger as I slowly lower Cally back to the ground and rise to my feet.

"You did this." I grit out, knowing full well he had the ability to stop her.

"You let her do this. Why? To get back at me? For what? You think that he will let you back? You enabled a human soul to walk into the darkness and you didn't stop her? How do you justify such a crime?" I lash out, my voice rising with my anger and fear.

"I did no such thing. I tried to stop her. I knew that what she believed would happen was only a lie but you led her to believe I was the one to fear. She wouldn't listen to me. If it makes you feel better to blame me then go right ahead. But it doesn't change the facts Tate. You did this to her!" He bellows, his voice commanding and powerful.

"If you had only listened, you could have prevented all of this. She doesn't belong in this world Tate, not yet." He says, glancing down to where her body lay, her soul hanging by a thread that I can feel wearing thin.

"Won't be long now." He chimes out, the anger melting away, replaced by amusement and satisfaction.

The realization of this takes hold and I turn my attention back to Cally. Kneeling before her, I place my palm against her chest.

Channeling all the power my mind can possess, I focus it all on her, willing her heart to continue beating.

"You're wasting your time, even you don't hold that kind of power. We can't save the dead." He says casually, leaning against the stone wall.

"But we can save the living." I plead. "Maybe I can't help her.... But we can. It's not too late to fix this, to make it right. Please....... help me."

He doesn't respond immediately and for just a moment, I feel like he is considering it but then his expression turns dark.

"No." He says casually, without remorse. "This is your mess.... Now you must live with it."

"She's dying......" I plead out once more. Pulling her body into mine, I stand, cradling her like an infant.

"You're an angel. You can't turn your back on this. You are bound by the heavens. Now help her." I demand more confidently.

"And then what? You think you two will just walk away hand in hand and that this will all be behind you.... I am bound by nothing but protecting those who choose the right path."

"What wrong path has she chosen? This was all me and you know it. You can't stand back and watch a mortal die at the influence of a Traveler anymore than you could hand a child to a demon. It is not in our nature to allow those to suffer that do not warrant suffering. You know this as well as I. She is an innocent, only drawn to this fate by my selfishness."

"You understand that either way you lose her forever." He snaps, his black eyes staring holes into mine.

"She will never be able to live knowing of our existence. She will never know you..... If I help you, you walk away."

"I love her." I breathe out, admitting defeat. I can't live without her but I can no longer compromise her mortal life, her safety, for my own selfish need.

I know I have to let her go.... But I don't know how to do that.

I tighten my grip around her and nuzzle my

head into her neck. Breathing in the intoxicating scent that will forever haunt my existence. She deserves more than this. I should have never let it go this far.

She loves me as much as I do her, that much is clear. There is no way she will give up on me, on us. I know this to be true without any doubt.

"She won't remember anything?" I ask, looking at Braize, his features blank, unreadable.

"Your presence will remain with her. Mortals tend to hold to their memories with everything they have, freeing her from them will not be easy but it can be done. She will think of you only as a dream, something she can't explain, holding no real meaning or truth." He says, his tone lighter, his dark eyes softening.

He takes two long strides forward until he is standing directly in front of me. Placing his hand across Cally's abdomen, he takes control, gently lifting her from my arms and laying her back to the earth. I follow her down, grasping her hand in mine.

Braize speaks but his voice is so low, I can not make out his words. The lanterns that light the room erupt into large bursts of flames that then morph from orange and red to white and blue. The heat that so quickly surged through the space dies out instantly.

I can sense her slipping, her soul disconnecting from her mortal body. The fear, the panic, the grief that surges through me is more powerful than ever before. The blue flames dance shadows across her beautiful pale skin.

Braize retrieves the amulet from the ground and slips it into his pocket before standing and taking a couple steps backwards.

The power that had exploded in the room just moments before has now settled into an eery calmness.

"I have given her the ability to find her way back, but she must choose that path. If she chooses differently, her fate will be her own. No fault will rest on our world."

"So what now?" I ask, as he backs away into the shadows.

For a moment, I don't think the answer will ever come but then his voice rings clear.

"She must choose." He says, and then he's gone and I am left alone to face the agony of losing Cally forever.

For no matter what choice she makes, I do not belong in her world. I am only a spectator in this form.

Somehow I have to find a way to let her go. But how does one let go of something that is more powerful than heaven and earth?

What we are is so much bigger, so much more than anyone could ever comprehend, including me. Holding a power over me that I will never understand but have always embraced.

I have never doubted that she was the part of myself that I never found in my human existence. The missing piece to a life that I could never fit together.

I reach down and trail the back of my hand along her cheek. She is everything in this world that is pure and true. She is everything that I have ever wanted, the other half of my soul.

Existence without her seems an impossible choice but then what else can I do?

Right now all I can do is wait. If she chooses to stay here, her soul will reconnect with her body and her memories of me will be gone.

If she chooses to cross over, she will be stuck in the in between existence that lies between the worlds and the heavens.

The amulet is darkness and therefore damns one to such a life. Any existence bound to that life has only two options. To stay, forever existing between two worlds with no connection to either. Only able to watch from the outside. Or to join the darkness and exist again without any recollection of the person you once were.

I have to have faith that she will make the right choice. That she will find her way back to the light.

Gently I pull her into my arms once more. I take the time to appreciate the way I respond to her, the way she feels against me.

Knowing it may be the last time I ever hold her......

****

I can feel the darkness lifting, the heavy weight vanishing, giving me the ability to breathe.

When I open my eyes, I am sitting in a cemetery. In front of me sits the headstones of my mother, my father, and my baby sister.

All three headstones are arranged side by side. Each one large marble cut in the shape of an oval sitting on top of a rectangle base.

Sarah Lenora Price

May 13, 1969 – July 16, 2009

Steven Roy Price

February 6, 1968 – July 16, 2009

Myra Dawn Price

September 24, 1997 – July 16, 2009

All beautifully scrawled across each individual stone. I reach up to the headstone directly in front of me, tracing my mother's name with my finger tips.

I don't know how I got here or if this is even real. Each and every moment seems stranger than the last and I am having trouble processing the events that seem to keep happening in front of me.

The way my scenery seems to just melt into the next like watching a movie, only I am in it. Experiencing each moment.

"Callista…" My mom calls from behind me. I recognize the angelic quality of her voice immediately but don't move from my position on the ground.

I can hear the shuffle of the grass below her feet as she sighs, taking a seat next to me.

It is only then that I glance in her direction. I gasp when the full magnitude of the situation takes grasp.

Sitting only inches from me is my mother. Beautiful as ever, her long blonde hair flowing freely down her back. When her blue eyes touch mine, there is so much warmth and understanding in them that I find it nearly impossible not to give into the sob working it's way up my throat.

"Mom...." I manage to croak out, just above a whisper.

She's dressed in a white flowing dress that gives her a heavenly quality causing me to reach out and touch her arm just to prove to myself that she really is here.

When my hand finds the solid smoothness of her arm, I can hold back the tears no longer. A sob bursts from my throat as my mom puts her arm around me and pulls me to her side.

I rest my head on her shoulder and breathe deeply. She smells exactly as I remember. Vanilla and Lavender. Pure heaven.

"It's okay Cally, it's me.... I'm here." She croons out, with such a soothing quality, I can't help but wonder how I have ever survived a day without her here to comfort me.

She leans into me, resting her chin on the top of my head. I make no attempt to move or even breathe for that matter. Afraid that any movement will shift the moment and I will lose her again.

I can't bare the thought of this, not while having her here with me. Being able to see her, hear her voice call my name.

Eventually curiosity wins and I know that this moment won't last forever, no matter how much I wish it would.

"Mom, is this real?" I ask, not caring how ridiculous I sound.

"Of course it is baby. As real as the sun shining above us." She says, gesturing upwards to the sky.

My mom drops her arm from my shoulder and takes my hand turning it upwards. I straighten my position looking down to meet her gaze upon the palm of my hand.

There in the center, burned clear as day, is the outline of the amulet, but no other signs of the burns that covered my hand from the fire where the necklace was located.

My mom traces the scarred skin with her finger before closing my hand in hers.

"I'm scared Mom." I choke out, not able to keep my emotions in check.

It's all too overwhelming. Having my mom sitting next to me when I had long since given up the hope that I would ever see her again.

"I know..... I know." She says, shifting her position so that she is sitting directly in front of me, taking both of my hands in hers.

"You are in a world that you do not belong in my darling. You must go back." She says, her blue eyes burning fiercely into mine.

"I have to find Tate." I blurt out.

Just saying his name makes my skin prickle and my heart beat quicken.

"I love him Mom."

"I know you do. All I have ever dreamed for you is that you would find someone who loves you the way you deserve to be loved. To find the person that is not just right for you but makes you a better version of yourself. Your other half."

"I found him..... The part of me that I never knew existed. But he's different...." I trail off, not really sure how to explain it myself.

"He's a Traveler." She finishes my sentence.

"How did you......" I start to ask but stop myself, remembering that my mother is no longer of the living, therefore exists in Tate's world in some form.

"I need him Mom. How can this ever work?"

"You have to fight for what you want most in this world Callista. I tried to always show you that. Nothing comes easy, especially the life altering things."

"I can't say what your future holds my beautiful daughter, but I can tell you that the love you share with this man is unlike anything we have ever seen. Some will fight to keep you apart, others will help you." She pauses.

"Whatever you do, don't let go..." She says, reaching up and tucking my hair behind my ear.

"Am I dead?" I ask, not really sure why this is the first time I am thinking of it.

It all makes sense now. I must be dead, the amulet must have worked.

"Your body still lives, as does your mortal souls attachment to it, if that is what you choose."

"I have a choice? What if I choose this? Can I stay here with you?" I ask so quickly the questions seem to run together.

"No...... I am afraid we are destined to take different paths. But I am always with you Callista." She says, pulling me into her arms and embracing me as the tears appear from no where and are steadily streaming down my face again.

"Make your choice, but make the one that is right for you honey. All other things will fall into place in their own time. I love you my darling." She whispers in my ear.

Just like that, she disappears. I scramble to my feet, turning in every direction trying to find her but she's no where to be found.

"Mom!" I cry out. But the only answer is my voice echoing back to me.

"Please don't leave me." I sob, crashing to my knees in front of her headstone.

Footsteps behind me make me suddenly

alert and my body hyper aware. I shoot up to my feet and scramble to find their owner.

For whatever reason, I feel the overwhelming sense of fear and am expecting to see someone that has come to harm me.

Instead, I am shocked to find that not three feet in front of me stands a young, thin, girl with tight golden curls and a very mischievous smile.

"Myra!" I cry out, stepping forward and wrapping her in my arms.

"You must come with me." She says, so serious that it causes me to drop my grip on her.

She takes my hand, guiding me through the graveyard. She moves with such ease and grace that I am too preoccupied watching her to take in where we are heading.

Eventually she slows, stopping at the edge of the cemetery in front of a small light stoned headstone that barely sticks up from the earth. I breathe in a shaky breath and lower myself into a squatting position as to get a better look at it.

Tate Jonathan Harper

January 3, 1968 – September 2, 1995.

I stand there so long my legs begin to

tremble and I am forced to lower myself to my knees.

My mind is going a hundred miles a minute. He died the day I was born.....

"Myra what does this mean?" I look up to find my sister standing patiently by my side.

"It is unknown why his immortal soul is connected to your mortal one. I have been waiting for you to come here. I needed to show you, give you a sign. There is more to this than any of us understand."

"It can't be just a coincidence. The fact that he died the very day I was born...." I manage to get out, searching my sister's face for any sign that I am headed in the right direction.

"There are no coincidences. Things don't just happen. We are all destined for something. Everything has a point, a purpose. There are no minor moments in our existence." She speaks wise beyond the twelve year old body she possesses.

"But I can't tell you the purpose behind this. I don't know what is binding you two together, only that something is."

"But I don't know what to do." I bow my

head in defeat, feeling overwhelmed and unable to process anymore information.

Everything makes sense but then no sense at all at the same time. I don't know what is real and what's not anymore.

"When the time comes you will know your path." Her voice seems to fade into the background.

And before I know it, she's gone and once again I am alone.

****

I wonder aimlessly for hours with no real destination. While I recognize the city that surrounds me, I feel more lost than ever.

If this is some crazy dream, I just wish I would wake up already.

I function as though this is my reality but I know deep down that it is anything but. I am stuck, somewhere in the middle of my existence and all others.

I can feel the loneliness blanketing me. I

pass people on the streets but no one looks my way. When they do, it's like they are staring right through me, as if I don't even exist.

"Where am I?" I scream out for anyone to hear, but no one even turns their heads.

"Someone please.................... Anyone? Can anyone hear me?" I raise my voice loud enough that I can feel the strain in my throat and yet still nothing.

An alleyway to my left catches my attention for some unknown reason and I veer into it. It's dark and cold and gives off a very creepy vibe.

This is a place I would surely avoid if I felt like any of this were real. But it is here, in my mind, where I feel nothing can harm me and therefore I don't fear my surroundings.

The further down the alley I go, the harder it becomes to see. The lights from the city fading into the background, leaving only a dull streetlamp a few yards away to offer any means of light. Suddenly, I feel the familiar pull that tells me he's not far away.

"Tate!" I scream out, not really expecting any answer, so I am not surprised when one doesn't come.

I can still feel the pull. The electricity that sparks when our two souls come together, completing the other.

I close my eyes and let that feeling alone guide me. Myra said I would know the right path when the time came and something is telling me that this is that time.

Reaching the end of the alley, I have two options.

One path is brightly lined and has a clear exit. The sure fire winner to any person with half a brain.

But I am not just any person. I am a soul tied to another and without a second thought I veer to the right, taking the path that is shrouded in darkness but holds no fear.

My surroundings vanish around me until I am basked in nothingness. That is when I hear it.

My name. Softly at first and then more urgently. I hear it again and again until the voice becomes clear. Tate..........................

MELISSA TOPPEN

Chapter Fourteen

I can feel the sun on my face. The light pulling me from sleep. I struggle to open my eyes but they feel like they have been glued shut.

A cool breeze whips past me and finally my eyes flutter open. I am staring at the bright blue sky, cloudless and beautiful.

I stretch, my body feeling tight and sore. Realizing I am outside with no recollection as to how I got here, I shoot up, startling Sasha, who until moments ago, was lounging lazily next to me. She grumbles to her feet causing me to roll quickly to avoid being stepped on.

"I'm sorry girl." I look up at her, noticing how much my abrupt movements must have startled her.

"How did we get out here?" I ask her, knowing she can't give me an answer but needing to ask it anyways.

I am in the middle of the freshly harvested field, just a few hundred feet from my grandparent's farm house. I wish I could remember falling asleep. I don't even remember getting Sasha out of the barn but am not surprised that I would do so.

Standing, I reach out and run my fingers through her long white mane. She dips her head into my touch.

"Come on girl, we should get back." I say, grabbing the leather strap around her shoulders and leading her back towards the barn.

Once I have her secured and have said my goodbyes, I make my way up the house, wishing I had some sense of time.

I have no idea how long I have been out here but based on the position of the sun, I would guess it to be late morning, so it couldn't have been too long.

"Callista, is that you?" My grandmother calls out, appearing in the doorway of the kitchen.

"Hi grandma." I say, leaning in and placing a

kiss on her cheek.

"I'm starving. What time is it?"

"Just after eleven. When did you get home?" She asks, leaning on the door frame as I make my way into the kitchen to rummage the refrigerator.

"Just got in, though I don't remember taking Sasha out. Guess I dozed off." I turn to see the confusion written all over her face.

"What?" I question her wearily.

"How was Chicago?" She eyes me quizzically.

"How would I know? I haven't been back there since......" I trail off, not liking the sickness that spreads through me at the thought of it all.

"Where have you been then?" She asks confused. Rubbing her forehead as if she has missed something.

"I told you, I fell asleep in the field. You feeling okay?" I ask her, a little worried that maybe she is suffering from early signs of Alzheimer's or something.

"For six days?" She lets the question hang there without further explanation.

"Six days, grandma what are you talking about?"

"Six days ago you left for Chicago. You said you were going to visit the cemetery. You left on a bus, grandpa drove you to the station." She breathes out, completely thrown off by my lack of knowledge on the matter.

I can't contain the laugh that escapes my throat but quickly regret it when my grandma's eyes meet mine.

"Really, I have no idea what you are talking about." I say, closing the fridge.

Suddenly my appetite has subsided and I am more than a little confused by what is going on.

"Tate came here looking for you." She states, making her way into the kitchen to stand next to me.

She studies me for a moment. "Have you spoken to him?"

"Who's Tate?" I ask, confused and not sure why she thinks I would know anyone outside of her and my grandpa. I never leave the farm.

"He's your friend, the one you met in

Chicago. Honestly Cally, are you trying to play some kind of prank on me? This really isn't funny." She says, her voice becoming stern.

Something about the name doesn't sit right with me but I can't pinpoint anyone I have ever known by that name.

"Grandma I'm sorry. I really have no idea what you are talking about."

"Get your things!" She exclaims, grabbing her purse off the back of the kitchen chair and ushering me towards the front door.

"We are going to pay Dr. Peterson a visit." She says, causing me to stop in my tracks and stare at her in disbelief.

"What! Why?" I cry out, confused and honestly a bit angry.

"I'm doing good, look at me...." I say gesturing to myself.

Though I am sure my appearance has seen better days than today, dressed in black yoga pants and a long sleeve white t-shirt, my hair tied in a knot. But she understands my statement.

"I am looking at you Callista and you want to know what I see?" She asks, stepping closer and taking my hand in hers.

"I see a young, beautiful woman who suffered a horrific tragedy and since then has been hiding out on a farm afraid to make any connection to the outside world. I see a girl who has been acting very strange for weeks with no real explanation. I see a girl that six days ago left on a bus to visit the graves of her family only to return and have no idea that she ever left. I see a girl that seemed to be very fond of a man that she now has no recollection of." She streams out, causing me to struggle to keep up with the reality of her words.

"But..... That can't be true. I am right here, I have never left. Grandma please you're scaring me." I plead, feeling the tears well in my eyes, trying my best to force them down.

Don't show weakness Cally, is all I can think. I have to stay strong, put on a brave face.

"Something is wrong sweetheart. You need to come with me." She says, tugging my hand and guiding me out the front door.

****

The drive over is a daze. Dr. Peterson practices in an office about ten miles outside of Nashville and just the trip this close to a city is causing me so much anxiety I have the overwhelming urge to jump out of the car and run like hell.

My grandma pulls into a parking spot relatively close to the office and I am thankful to not have to walk far.

For some reason, my body feels like it has run a marathon and I can't quite seem to get it to work properly. Each step feels weighed down and heavy.

As we make our way up the stone steps leading to the front door, I can't help but feel like the last two years of my life have simply vanished and I am still the broken girl in need of professional help.

The building isn't much. A one story brick building that contains three different offices, all identical. Each one with a glass door with the name of the business printed on the front in white lettering.

My grandma opens the door labeled *Dr. Eleanor Peterson* and ushers me inside.

The waiting area is empty but I feel like I am standing in front of a thousand people. My legs tremble and my stomach is full of knots.

Suddenly very queasy, I find a seat in the farthest corner of the small space while my grandma makes sure they can squeeze us in.

"It's urgent." I hear her tell the pretty red headed receptionist behind the desk.

I pick up a magazine on the end table next to me and lounge back in the hard leather chair, flipping aimlessly through the pages, not really caring what is on them, just simply trying to appear normal, casual.

I'm not crazy, at least I don't feel like I am. But my grandma is acting very out of character and is making me feel very uneasy about this whole thing.

Could I really have simply forgotten the last week? Did I really travel to Chicago by myself and if so, was it more than my mind could handle?

And then there's the friend she talked about, Tate. Could I really have connected with another person and now sit here unable to remember?

I straighten my position and clear my throat

as my grandma takes a seat next to me.

"It shouldn't be long." She says, removing her glasses and rubbing her eyes.

"Grandma... I'm sorry. I don't know what's wrong with me." I say, turning to face her.

"Oh dear, this is not your fault....." She trails off, as if choosing her words carefully.

"We just need to figure out why this is happening and get you the help you need." She takes my hand, her face suddenly becoming more confused and turns my palm up.

"Callista, what is this?" She asks, drawing my attention to my hand laying face up in hers.

I gasp, realizing I have a scar plain as day imprinted on the palm of my hand. It's the shape of a cross. I reach over with my other hand and trace the outline with the tip of my finger.

"I have no idea." I whisper, more to myself than to her.

How could I have not noticed this before? It's a least three inches in length and two in width, taking up a good portion of the flesh that makes up my hand. The middle is rippled and bumpy.

It is then that I realize, my grandma must be

right.

How on earth could something like this happen to me and I have no recollection of it? Certainly whatever caused the scar would have been painful, based on the size and how clear it sticks out, and yet I have no idea what could have caused it or how it could have happened.

More importantly, it appears completely healed. How long has it been there and me not even realized it? That thought alone scares me more than anything.

I close my palm tightly, willing my mind to remember something, anything, but I only draw a blank.

"Callista Price." A young woman dressed in light pink scrubs appears at the door leading into the patient area, pulling me from my thoughts.

She looks about my age and for a moment I don't move. Instead, I just sit there, staring at this beautiful brunette with dark brown eyes and a crooked smile, wishing that I knew what it was like to be normal. To have a job, friends..... a life.

"Cally." My grandma breaks my focus pointing to the girl.

"Go." She mouths, and without another

word, I stand and follow her down a long hall way that leads to Dr. Peterson's office.

    When we approach the door, she gives a light knock and walks in, me trailing behind her.

    Sitting behind a large dark wood desk at the back of the room is Dr. Eleanor Peterson. An older lady, I would guess in her early sixties, with salt and pepper hair tied in a tight bun.

    She stands, nodding to the girl who quickly exits the room, closing the door behind her.

    I take in her appearance, seeing that she hasn't changed much since the last time I saw her. She wears the same stuffy dress suit as always, this one is beige and doesn't do much for her pale complexion.

    "Cally, it's so lovely to see you again dear. How are you?" She asks, taking my hand in hers and giving it a light squeeze.

    I shrug my shoulders, saying without words that I don't know how I am. Obviously not too good, considering after two years I am back here yet again.

    "Please have a seat." She says, leading me to a brown leather couch that sits in the center of the room.

She straightens her skirt before taking her own seat in a matching chair directly across from me. I wiggle into the couch trying to find a comfortable position before finally directing my attention back to her.

I spend the next two hours telling her everything that has happened in the past couple of years. None of which is worth anything.

I have no life to tell about. When I get to the events of this morning her ears seem to perk up, holding onto each word as if it were the key to unlocking some hidden compartment in my mind.

"So you really don't remember anything about what your grandmother was telling you. The trip to Chicago, the friend of yours that visited on your birthday?" She asks, leaning forward and staring at me intently.

"Not a thing." I answer dully, throwing my hands up.

"I've finally lost it, haven't I?" I burst out in defeat.

"No Cally, I don't think you have lost it, but clearly your mind is telling you that your problems are far from over. It's not normal to forget such large gaps of time but I am confident that there is a way to help you."

"You're going to lock me up in some home for crazy people and pump me full of medications aren't you?" I snap defensively.

"Heavens no. You need help, not a mental hospital." She says with a small laugh.

Anger blooms in the pit of my stomach. How simple this must all be for her. She's not the one blanking on periods of her life.

"I am going to recommend a treatment facility though." She says hesitantly.

"A what?" I question her for more explanation.

"They have a ninety day program dedicated for people who have suffered traumatic events in their lives and are having trouble readjusting to the outside world. It's not a hospital." She assures me, seeing the panic rise in my cheeks.

"It's a place where you can share your experiences and sort through the reason your mind is choosing to black out certain events or make you believe that things happen that simply are not true."

"How so?" I eye her curiously.

I can't say I am completely opposed to the idea. Accepting that I do need help is the least of my problems.

I have known that something was not right for a very long time now but the thought of leaving my grandparents, the comfort of the farm, sends a fear through me that I am having trouble swallowing down.

"You will have individualized therapy with a team of doctors, group therapy sessions, and many other activities that are specialized to help you cope with the hand you have been dealt. It won't be a quick fix but I am confident it will get us on the right track." She says with a reassuring smile.

After agreeing that this is my only option, Dr. Peterson makes arrangements while I wait in the office with my grandma.

When she finally reappears she is holding a packet. She reaches over, handing it to my grandmother before turning her attention to me.

"You are all set Cally. You have two days to get your affairs in order before your treatment begins. Your grandmother has all the information and there are some brochures in their for you to read as well. I will stop in each week and check on your progress. Do you have any other questions for me?" She asks.

I shake my head no and after my grandma has said her goodbyes, I follow her numbly to the car, wishing that for once things would just be okay for me.

How many bumps in the road can I possibly hit before all my tires deflate and I am simply immobile?

The day has seemed like such a blur and all the while I have a sinking feeling that something is missing. A crucial piece to the puzzle of my recovery. Something I can't put my finger on but the feeling is there all the same.

I don't join my grandparents for dinner. I'm too depressed to stomach up any type of appetite. I wish I could say that I know that things will get better, that eventually I will learn to let go of the baggage I carry around with me like a dead weight, but the future holds no guarantees. Life has taught me that.

I roll to my back, my bed shifting under my weight, and find my star on the ceiling. It is shining brighter than I remember and doesn't hold it's usual comfort.

The tears begin to flow freely down my cheeks and I turn into my side, curling into a ball, I finally just let go.

I'm crying because I don't want to be sick anymore. I want to be normal, happy. I want to live a real life. One with friends and adventures.

But more importantly, I am crying because I feel like a very big part of myself is missing and for the life of me I can't figure out why.

It's like I have been split into two pieces and my other half is no where to be found. The feeling scares me more than a little and as much as I am dreading leaving my grandparents, a part of me is hopeful that I will find the missing piece of myself again.

It really is the strangest feeling. Missing something that you can't pinpoint. I can feel my eye lids growing heavy as sleep begins to take over my body. I succumb to the exhaustion and let myself slip.

It is then that I see them, bright green eyes burning fiercely back at me, and then I fade into unconsciousness.

THE TRAVELER: THE AMULET OF LIFE

Chapter Fifteen

Six Months Later

"Come on boy." I call to Bennett, who has slowed his pace behind me.

He's not much for the cold but I am rather enjoying the beginning of Spring. At least it's not raining today.

In fact, this is the nicest day we have had in quite some time, which is why I am taking the opportunity to take him out for a walk. I will have to bring Sasha out tomorrow, if the weather holds up.

We take our usual path through the woods. The animals are all out and about, the birds chirping happily from their place in the sky. After such a long cold winter, I am enjoying the warmth, the sounds of nature, the pure beauty of everything that surrounds me.

My dad had once told me to stop and appreciate the little things and that is exactly what I have been trying to do. See each day as a blessing, a new day full of endless possibilities.

I find it easier to wake in the mornings now, feeling like I have something worth waking up for. A life, my life.

Therapy helped me more than I ever thought it would. While being away for three months was hard, I enjoyed the interactions and even made some friends that I have continued to stay in contact with.

It feels good to have people to talk to, someone to relate to my situation. While I wish no one in the world ever had to deal with anything similar to my situation, the sad truth is it happens more than we like to admit.

The first few days of my treatment were pure hell. I was terribly homesick and wasn't yet comfortable really talking to anyone.

Charlie changed all that and has since become one of my favorite people in the world.

He came to the facility a couple of months after he found his mother in the shower. She had died suddenly from a heart attack.

While I could tell he was hurting, he kept a positive outlook. Always talking about god's plan and how everything happens for a reason.

I wish I shared his optimism. It was much harder for me to open up in group therapy than him. He has such an ease about him and was perfectly comfortable talking about his situation, though he showed little emotion when doing so.

It was about halfway through the program when I finally realized just how truly lost he was. It was late and I was out wandering the halls, something I did often when I couldn't sleep. That's when I found him, his stocky body hunched in a corner at the end of a hall, sobbing uncontrollably.

At first I started to back away but then seeing the pain on his face, the hollowness of his deep brown eyes, I couldn't just let him suffer.

Offering him a shoulder to cry on, I think that is the first time he ever really opened up to anyone about how much he was suffering.

I like to think I helped him turn a corner that night. I know he helped me. Seeing that I am not the only person in this world that is grieving, that is lost, gave me some sense of hope that I would get through it eventually and be a better person when I came out the other side.

After that night, Charlie and I were inseparable. Instead of wandering the halls late at night, I would go to Charlie and we would talk.

Some nights we would laugh, others we would cry. Some nights he would just offer me silent comfort and we would lay next to each other staring at the ceiling, which the staff had let us decorate in plastic glow in the dark stars.

He helped me more in that twelve weeks than any trained professional could have done in twelve years and over time I grew to love him. Not in a "I'm in love with you kind of way" but in a brotherly way.

I considered if it could be more at first. After all, he is very attractive. Tall and broad with dark brown hair that always looks a mess, but makes him that much cuter. But it's his smile that got to me more than anything. He has the most amazing smile, one that warms your heart on sight.

I wanted to connect with Charlie on that level. Really, I think I needed to, but for whatever reason, no matter how much he means to me, I just can't.

It feels like a betrayal and that still doesn't sit well with me. Who would I be betraying by letting myself be happy?

Regardless, by the end of our stay, we had both agreed that friends was the best fit for us. Though I could tell he was hoping for more, he would never push it.

I haven't ruled it out all together but deep down I know that there is the right one for me and I don't believe he is it.

Still, we have remained very close over the last couple of months. He calls me several times a week to check in and see how I am doing.

I love that I found someone I can talk to when I am feeling less than optimistic about the future.

He is coming out to stay with us for a couple of days next week. I am so excited to see him and I really hope the weather holds up so I can bring him here, introduce him to my world.

He only lives a couple hours north, so getting together isn't too much of an issue.

Since returning home, I have taken baby steps to re-establish myself into the land of the living. I have even gone as far as to apply to some colleges for the fall.

Charlie is applying as well and hopefully we will decide on the same school. One thing is for sure, I can't just lounge around the farm my whole life and wait until I have no one left in this world.

I have to get out there. Learn how to live again. I'm not okay yet, but I am getting there. I still feel the pain everyday, the absence and grief, but I am not afraid of hurting anymore.

I have learned ways to focus on the things that make me happy. The things I want to accomplish. The first step is my education.

Picking a major was the easy part. I want to study psychology and hopefully one day be able to work with troubled children.

I can't think of a better way to spend my days then helping others based on my own experience. Picking where to go has been a bit more complicated.

I want to go somewhere far enough away that I can be on my own and independent, but not too far that I can't jump in a car and drive back to the farm if I need to.

The thought of leaving the farm is a very scary one but something I know I need to do. I only wish I had done it sooner, maybe then it wouldn't be so hard.

The worst part of all of it is that I feel connected to the farm in a way I can't explain. Like something about this place holds a piece of my soul and I am afraid if I leave I will lose whatever it is.

Bennett freezes up behind me bringing me to an abrupt halt. He retreats a couple steps almost as if he senses something.

"You okay boy?" I ask, running my hand through his dark mane.

A branch snaps somewhere not far from us and I jump. Sensing that we are no longer alone, I do a circle, checking the area around us.

I see nothing out of the ordinary but decide not to take any chances. I don't think I will ever get to the point where my past doesn't make me afraid of anything I am unsure of.

Tugging Bennett, I head back in the direction we came from.

THE TRAVELER: THE AMULET OF LIFE

A cool breeze whips through my hair and causes the trees to moan under the strain. I snuggle deeper into my hooded sweatshirt and quicken my pace. Just as my fear has me jumping at every little noise, a feeling of ease breathes through me, somewhat throwing me off guard.

I stop, glancing behind me. I can't explain it but I feel like someone is watching me.

"Is someone there?" I call out, weaker than I had intended.

I hear a shuffle a few feet away, but for reasons unknown to me, I am not afraid.

I stand rooted to the spot and wait, for what I don't know. Finally after a couple of minutes of nothing, I turn and resume walking back up the path, Bennett growing anxious by my side.

I want to run, feeling like I should be afraid. But my body doesn't respond to my minds demands and I keep a steady pace until we reach the clearing where the woods open up to the back of my grandparent's property.

Once I have secured Bennett in the barn, I make my way back outside just as the sun is setting. I am sad to see the end of such a beautiful day.

Instead of going inside like I should, I take a seat on the ground, just a few feet from the back of the house. The ground is still a little soggy from all the rain and I can feel the dampness seeping through my pant legs causing a chill through my entire body but I don't mind.

Instead, I lay back gazing up at the stars that are becoming clearer in the sky. I see what looks like a ball of fire in the sky.

I arch my neck back trying to get a better look at what it is I am seeing. A red star. I don't know how I know it. I have never heard of a red star before.

A strange sense of deja vu takes over me and I can't help but feel like I have seen this all before. The air seems to shift around me and for the first time since I returned to the farm, I feel a familiar peace seethe through me.

Just as I settle into the feeling, I hear the back door open. I don't shift my position, not sure if I am fully visible to whoever has come outside. I am facing the opposite direction of the house and am not able to see who it is.

"Where is that girl?" I hear my grandpa say.

"Oh Richard, you know how much she loves to wander the land. I am sure she will be home soon. Really dear, you shouldn't worry so much." My grandma says.

"I know. She's so much like her father. Do you remember how he would disappear for hours on end?"

"Like it was yesterday. He was such a free spirit. So much like his own father. She's going to be fine honey, you'll see. She's had a rough few years but she has her father's spirit and her mother's heart. She is bound to accomplish great things." My grandma reassures him.

"Have I told you lately how much I love you?" He asks, causing a giggle to escape my grandma's lips.

"As I love you dear." She answers, as they walk back inside.

I sit up, wiping the tears that are flowing down my cheeks. I didn't even realize I had been crying. Something about the way they talked of my father tears at my heart.

I knew they missed him but what's worse, is that I have only made this harder on them. Causing them to worry about me.

Suddenly I feel very guilty for being so selfish. Always so wrapped up in my own pain that I don't see the pain of the others around me.

I always felt like I was so alone in my hell. Had I taken the time to open my eyes and look around, I would have noticed sooner how badly they were hurting as well.

It warms my heart to know that they see my father in me. I only hope that I can do them proud one day.

I shuffle to my feet and do my best to brush the dirt off my jeans but decide its useless almost immediately. As I step onto the back steps and open the door, I look up to see the red star still burning brightly in the sky.

I wish I could remember where I have seen one before and why it is I feel so strongly about it now.

****

I spend the rest of the evening curled up on the couch with my grandma and grandpa watching reruns of *Bewitched*, a favorite of ours.

THE TRAVELER: THE AMULET OF LIFE

My grandparents decide to call it a night a little past eleven and realizing how exhausted I am, I choose to do the same.

Now as I lay in bed, I am finding it very difficult to rest. My mind is racing, running through all the things I have to look forward to but as always I end up stuck in the past.

The weeks of time that I can't remember still haunts me.

I hold up my hand, barely able to see my scar in the darkness. I can't help but feel like it should really mean something but it doesn't. Just a visible scar to go along with all the internal ones you can't see.

I close my eyes, willing my mind to slow down, trying to force myself to sleep but it doesn't do me any good.

The nightmares come less often now but I still struggle with the memories of them. Then there's the eyes. The ones I see every night just before my mind gives way to sleep. They haunt me, consume me.

They are his, the man who saved my life all those years ago. I will never forget the piercing green, the emotion that rushed through me when they met mine.

I have accepted that this is yet another thing that I will never be able to explain. How is it that I can see someone one time and they forever be burned into my mind and yet I struggle to remember the little things about my family?

The way my mother laughed, my father's soothing voice. I try so hard to remember them but the more time that passes the harder it becomes.

I am afraid I am forgetting them. Losing them all over again. With that comes a guilt that I have yet to learn how to reign in. It's always there in the back of my mind. The family I can't remember, the man I can't forget.

****

"Grandma, he's here!" I screech out from the front door, as I watch Charlie pull up the driveway in a beat up old Oldsmobile that looks to be on it's last leg.

He barely gets the car in park before I open the driver door and dive into his lap. He laughs wrapping his arms tightly around my waist and burying his head in my neck.

"It's good to see you too Cal." He says shifting in his seat.

"Sorry." I say, dropping my grip on him and backing out of the car so he can get out.

I watch him intently, waiting for my moment to pounce. Once he is out of the car and shuts the door behind him, I run into his arms and hug him tightly.

"I'm so glad you're here!" I exclaim, pulling away to look at his face.

He's as handsome as ever, maybe even more so. His face seems brighter, happier. It warms my heart to see that he is doing so well.

He shifts from one foot to the other and I realize that I am staring at him.

"Sorry, I just can't believe you're actually here." I say, and instantly laugh as that beautiful smile stretches across his face.

"Come inside I will introduce you to my grandparents and show you your room." I say, linking my arm with his and leading him up the front steps.

After a quick introduction and a promise to join them for dinner, I show Charlie upstairs to his room. I think it makes him more comfortable to know that he will be staying in the room directly across the hall from mine. I know how he feels. It will bring me a comfort knowing how close he will be.

He drops his suitcase on the twin size bed in the corner. The room is pretty plain. A small bed and dresser are all that makes up the small space.

The bare walls are a pale yellow and have always reminded me of summer. My grandma spent days clearing out all the boxes they kept stored in here to make room for Charlies visit. I make a mental note to myself to make dinner for them one night as a thank you.

I take his hand and lead him across the hall pointing out the bathroom on the right and then stop at the door leading to my room.

He grabs me from behind, spinning me around and wrapping me in another hug, pulling me up into him, my feet coming up off the floor.

Suddenly the space in which we stand feels too small, with my petite body pressed into his large frame.

I wiggle out of his grip and take a step back to look at him. His eyes are bright but his face is unreadable.

"Hey." I say, taking his hand. "Everything okay?"

"It is now. I'm just so happy to see you Cal. You have no idea." He breathes out heavily, as if he's been holding his breath for weeks.

"I know just how you feel. Having you here already makes me feel better, stronger." I admit, only because it is the truth.

"Come on, there's someplace I want to show you." I say, tightening my grip on his hand and pulling him to the door.

"Wait, you didn't show me your room." He protests.

"Oh right." I say, turning and opening the door gesturing inside.

"So this is my room.... Can we go now?" I laugh, seeing the amused look on his face.

"Lead the way angel." He says, letting out a laugh.

Something about that causes me to freeze in the doorway.

"What did you call me?" I ask, trying not to show my confusion.

"Angel.... Why?" He asks, his eyebrows arching up in question.

I shake my head gesturing it's nothing and continue on down the hall. For some reason, hearing those words made my heart skip a beat and my blood rush to my cheeks.

I can't figure out who, but someone used to call me that. Someone I know, deep down, that I loved immensely.

I don't know how I know it but I do. Like something that has been forever burned into my heart but my mind can't quite process.

Shaking off the feeling of knowing something that I can't remember, I try to regain the joy I felt just moments earlier by the fact that he is finally here with me.

We reach the barn within minutes and I squeeze through the door gesturing for him to follow.

Once inside I walk over to Sasha and introduce her and Bennett.

"I know it may seem odd but these are the

only two friends I had... before you." I confide in him, knowing that he will understand why.

My need for solitude, a life away from the real world, from the fear and pain that this world possesses.

We don't linger long, my need to show him everything winning out as I rush him through the fields, stopping to point out my favorite spots to watch the stars and even sharing some of the memories I had here as a child with my family.

He hangs onto each word, seeming very interested in it all. I can't help but think he's acting more interested than he probably is for my sake but I appreciate it all the same.

Once we reach the end of the field, I stop, feeling the need to explain.

"This is my world." I say, gesturing to the woods.

"The only place I have ever found peace. I think you will understand why...." I take his hand, not missing that he makes it more intimate by entwining his fingers with mine.

I would be lying if I said it didn't cause my blood to rush and my heart rate to quicken but that doesn't change the fact that I know, deep down, he and I would never work.

Two broken people, the pain of our past always catching up with us.

I try not to linger too long on the thought and begin making my way through the woods, Charlie at my side.

We stop a couple of times to take in the scenery, the beauty of nature all around us. But it isn't until we reach my favorite spot, the creek, that he seems to understand why I love it so much here.

"Beautiful." He breathes, as we stop at the edge of the water. I look up, only to realize he is looking at me, not the location.

"Sit." I command, taking my familiar spot on the ground and patting the space beside me.

He slides down to join me, resting his hand right above my knee.

"Amazing isn't it?" I ask, closing my eyes and listening to the sounds of the water flowing, the peace of being out in the middle of seemingly nowhere.

"I can see why you love it so much." He says, turning his attention to me.

I can feel his eyes on me and needing to put a little space between us, I reposition myself so that I am facing him, my front to his side. Within seconds he does the same until we are both sitting Indian style across from one another.

"Close your eyes." I say, and I can't help but smile when he does without question.

"Now listen..... Do you feel it?"

"Feel what exactly?" He jokes, peeking one eye open to catch a glimpse of me.

"No peeking." I squeal, giving his arm a playful swat.

He closes his eyes again. "Now focus this time. Just listen to the water, the sound of nature. Focus on nothing but that."

As I instruct him, I do the same and for a few moments I get lost in the moment. The feeling of the wind on my face, blowing my hair behind me.

When I open my eyes again, I am surprised to see his eyes are still closed. His expression is light, his breathing even.

Without thinking, I reach for his hand, and regret it the moment I do, because his eyes dart open and I realize I have pulled him from his thoughts.

"Amazing." He says, giving me his award winning smile.

"This place, everything about it...."

"It's magical." I say, finishing his sentence.

"Exactly." He agrees, giving my hand a tight squeeze.

We get lost in conversation about our pasts, our treatment, and everything that has happened since we parted a few weeks ago.

Before I know it, the sun is beginning to set and remembering the promise I made to my grandparents, decide that we should head back.

Charlie stands, taking my hands in his, he hoists me to my feet, only a little to hard and I stumble into him, my hands coming to a rest on his chest as he pulls me close.

For a moment, I forget why it is we can't be more and snuggle into his embrace. I turn my head towards the creek and for a split second I swear I see someone standing in the shadows on the other side.

I pull away from Charlie and step to the very

edge of the water. He starts to protest but then falls silent.

"Cally what is it?" He asks, but I don't answer. Truth is, I don't know who it was but the feeling searing through my veins is pure fire.

Without thinking, I step into the creek and quickly make my way across. A second later, I am standing in the very spot I could have swore I saw someone, but quickly realize that there is no one here.

"You saw someone didn't you?" I ask, turning to face Charlie, who is still on the other side of the creek bed.

"I thought I did. Shit, I don't know Cal, it's getting dark. Probably just the shadows playing tricks on us. Come on we should get back."

I turn to face the other direction one last time, squinting into the fast coming darkness. I know someone was there. Charlie saw it too. But who could it have been?

More importantly, why did nothing else matter in that moment then reaching who ever it was. Like some unknown force pulling me to them.

Trying to shake the feeling away and

becoming increasingly cold from my soaking pant legs, I rejoin Charlie on the other side of the creek and we quickly make our way out of the woods before we lose all traces of daylight.

When we finally emerge, I am relieved to see that the sun has not set. It always seems so much darker in the woods. The trees blocking out most of the sunlight.

Hopefully my grandparents won't be too upset that we are so late for dinner. Then again, knowing my grandma, she planned for us to be gone a while and hasn't been waiting for too long.

I prove myself right as we walk into the kitchen just as my grandma is setting dinner on the table. She really went all out and I have to remind myself she doesn't get the opportunity to cook for anyone besides me and my grandpa very often and she loves showing off her skills in the kitchen.

I take my usual seat and Charlie sits directly across from me. We enjoy a very delicious meal of homemade chicken and dumplings, followed by my grandma's famous apple pie, one of my favorites.

By the time we are finished, I am stuffed to the brim. It's been a very long time since I have enjoyed a meal so much. Knowing full well it had everything to do with the company and little to do with the food.

We help my grandma clean up before heading upstairs to call it a night. Charlie's only in his room for about five minutes when I hear a light knock on the door.

I prop myself up on my elbows and tell him to come in, thankful that I had chosen to put on a pair of sweats. Usually I only sleep in a long t-shirt but tonight I prepared myself in case I went to him, or in this case, he came to me.

"Hey." I say quietly, as he slips in my room, dressed in only a pair of baggy gym shorts. His abdominal muscles tight and defined.

The sight of his body causes my breath to hitch and I pray that he doesn't take notice. I knew he had a good build but was not prepared for this.

"I can't sleep." He says, reminding me of a small child that has woken from a nightmare.

I peel back the covers and pat the bed, gesturing for him to join me. Two long strides is all it takes and he is curling up in my bed next to me.

I turn away from him and snuggle my back

to his front.

For the life of me I can't figure out why I don't want more with him. He affects me, that much is a given.

He's handsome and sweet, everything I could ever want and yet he's not *who* I want. Problem is, I don't know why.

For the longest time we lay in silence. Eventually, I hear his breathing even out and his body go limp, a telling sign that he is fast asleep. I snuggle deeper into his arms, appreciating the comfort he brings to me.

Just as I feel myself drifting, a whisper comes through the darkness.

"Angel." I hear and for a moment I think that Charlie has woken up but then a light snore from behind me tells me otherwise.

Angel... I can't shake the feeling that someone used to call me angel. Only I don't know who. I sit up disoriented, determined to sort this out. Throwing my legs over the side of the bed, suddenly everything starts making sense.

I can't be with Charlie because I belong to someone else. I know he loves me and I love him, more than I could ever imagine loving someone.

I close my eyes tightly, willing myself to remember. Then I see them, like so many times before. The piercing green eyes that see into my soul. But it's not just the eyes anymore, it's the man behind the eyes. Tall, dark hair, the most beautiful person I have ever seen.

My eyes shoot back open just as everything becomes crystal clear.

"Tate." I whisper into the darkness.

MELISSA TOPPEN

Chapter Sixteen

TATE

Nothing could have prepared me for the battle I would face everyday knowing that Cally exists and that I can't be with her.

I try to reassure myself that she is better off without me, and sometimes I even think it to be true. But it's when she is her most vulnerable that I can see how lost she is without me.

While I promised to keep my distance from her and let her live her life, it is utterly impossible not to be near her. I keep a close eye on her, sometimes venturing a little too close and risking being seen.

But like all the years before, the closer I get to her, the less will power I have to resist the *invisible rope that seems to be pulling me to her.*

Today has been the most challenging day, watching her across the creek. A place I have spent many days and nights watching her, feeling her, and eventually holding her.

To see her in another man's arms proved to be more than I could take and the need to reveal myself to her became too much to bare.

I know she doesn't remember me, or us, but deep down I feel like she is still connected to me. I can sense that she feels it too, only she doesn't understand it.

Seeing her with him sent a rage through me that I have never felt before. It's times like this that I realize that we are all still human, in some ways.

We never lose our passion, our love. All the emotions that consume us as mortal souls still linger with us in the afterlife, jealousy included.

I know she doesn't love him, at least not in that way, that much I can tell. I have come to know everything about her. How different smiles mean different things and how a light touch to the arm is a more intimate gesture for her than being wrapped in a hug. But most importantly, I can feel her. I can feel the way he affects her. She cares for him, but it's not the same for her.

I want her to be happy. I want her to fall in love and live a long wonderful life. Only I want her to have that with me.

I like to think that if she ever found that, that I would have the strength to bow out and let go of her once and for all but the truth is, I don't know if that would be possible.

I know I am walking a thin line. She saw me today, she knew I was there. I could tell the way her body reacted, that while her mind didn't recognize me, her heart did.

I wanted so badly to run to her, wrap her in my arms and never let her go, but for once this isn't about me. It's about her, her life, her safety, her chance to be happy in this life, in this world. Something she deserves more than all else.

I settle into my usual spot on a tree branch eye level with Cally's room. It's a few feet back so I can be sure no one will see me, but it allows me to be close enough to her to make sure I can keep her safe.

While I think I can trust Braize on his word to let her be, I refuse to take any chances where *she is concerned and because of this I have not ventured more than a short distance away from her over the last few months.*

The unsettling feeling that consumes me when I can't be near her is more than I can bare. If I can't be with her for a lifetime than I will make sure she gets a lifetime to live, safe and out of the way of any harm.

Just as I feel her settle, I close my eyes wishing I could be the one holding her, breathing in her scent, loving her.

"Angel." I whisper out, remembering the feeling of her in my arms.

A sudden shift in the air puts my senses on high alert. Something's not right. I can feel her panic, her confusion. And in one word she alters my existence yet again.

"Tate...." I hear her whisper out into the night.

She remembers me.... But how? Could our love be that strong, that pure, that no amount of interference can erase me from her?

Could it be so consuming that her heart would win out over her mind and refuse to let her forget the love we share, the connection?

I focus on her and within seconds, I am standing inside a dark hallway, her bedroom door the only thing that separates us.

I place my hand on the old chipped wood and focus on nothing but her. She's scared, she's confused, but more than anything, she's hurt.

I can feel it radiating from every cell in her body. She knows that I gave her up, that I walked away. How will I ever be able to make her understand that I did it for her?

That living without her is my hell. Will I ever get the chance?

****

Words simply can not describe the pain that is slowly consuming every fiber of my being. I have tried desperately to piece together where everything changed but nothing makes sense.

I remember Tate, but it's broken memories and moments that seem more like dreams than reality. Nothing seems to fit together and while I know he left me, I can't connect to the reason why.

To say I have been in a bit of a haze over the last couple of days would be an understatement. Ever since the first night that the memories began to return, I have felt myself slipping.

All the progress I have made over the last few months falling to the way side and anything that isn't Tate seems less and less important.

Charlie could sense the change in me almost immediately but was far too sweet to call me out on it. He stayed with me up until this morning when he finally headed home.

While I was a little less enthusiastic about him being here, it was a welcome distraction from the internal battle that was raging inside me.

I know I need to find Tate. I need to put all this together and feel like for once, I finally know why I have felt so off for months. Why I feel like half a person. Why certain words or places jog memories that I can't place, leaving me feeling lost and confused.

What I need is answers. But what I need more than anything else in this world, is to feel his arms around me again. The intimate moments stand out above all the others. I can remember them the clearest as if each one is forever burned into the deepest depths of my mind.

THE TRAVELER: THE AMULET OF LIFE

Now that Charlie is gone, the only thing standing in my way is me. A part of me is afraid to venture down this path a second time, fearful that finding Tate, only to lose him again, will be more than my heart can bare. But the overwhelming need to be near him, to know why after all the beautiful moments we have shared, that we are not together now.

I wish I could piece it all together, where it makes a little more sense but most things are still gray and while I think I can figure some of it out, I know that I am still missing so much.

Like there is a brick wall dividing my memories. I can feel it shift under my relentless attempts to break through it but it does not give way. Leaving me to only understand half of the story.

I know the answers are there, somewhere in my mind, but I can't connect to them.

Deciding my first step is to reach out, I return to the creek, this time completely alone, which is unusual for me.

I know it was him that Charlie and I saw, so I figure this is the best place to start. Standing in a place that usually holds so much peace for me, I feel anything but.

Every noise makes me jump, my body hyper aware of my surroundings.

"Tate...." I call out. My heart rate quickens with anticipation but I get no response.

"Tate...." I say a little louder this time. Again nothing.

I think a part of me knew going in that this would never work but it doesn't sooth the disappointment that rushes through me. Unable to accept defeat that quickly, I call his name once more, my only response is my own voice echoing off the trees back to me.

He knows I'm here. I don't know how I know, I just do. I can feel it. For whatever reason, he is choosing not to face me and while that doesn't sit well with me, I can't stand out here all day like an idiot demanding a response from someone so hell bent on avoiding me.

Chalking it up to a lost cause, I head back up to the house. Finding it hard to focus on any one thing, my mind a pool of information that I don't understand and broken pieces of memories that are becoming increasingly frustrating.

I barely register my grandfather's voice when I reach the backyard, until he standing directly in front of me, his hands on my shoulders.

"Cally did you hear me?" He says, as if he has been talking to me the whole time and I am just now hearing what he's saying.

"Wait what?" I ask, confused and needing him to repeat himself, my mind not retaining anything he said.

"It's grandma......" He breathes out, his eyes pooling with tears, causing every worst case scenario to flash through my mind.

"What?" I choke out, the fear apparent in my voice.

"I tried to find you. Where did you go? You should have been here." He sobs out, and for the first time in my life, I am witnessing the strongest man I have ever known, breaking in front of my very eyes.

"Is grandma okay?" I plead out, the not knowing almost too much to stand.

"She's in the hospital, heart attack, the doctors don't know if she will make it through the night. We have to hurry." He says, grabbing my forearm and pulling me alongside him.

The car ride over is tense and I am having trouble processing the turn of events that so suddenly have taken place. It all happened while I was out looking for Tate.

I should have been home. I should have been with her. What if I never see her alive again? A life without my grandma's spirit seems impossible to face. I can't lose her. Not after I have lost so much already.

When we finally arrive at the hospital, my grandpa leads me inside. His actions quick, his fear radiating off of him.

I can't imagine what losing my grandma will do to him. He has loved her his entire life, he doesn't know what life is like without her. This thought alone shreds my heart for him.

When he leads me to the third floor, I can't help but once again jump to the worst case scenario.

My grandma's room is in the far left corner of the Intensive Care Unit. The moment I walk through the door, it all hits me. Like a thousand pounds suddenly collapsing on top of me.

Lying in front of me, pale and almost lifeless, is my grandmother. The one and only person in this world that would gladly sacrifice herself for me, for my grandpa. The most selfless caring person I have ever known.

The thought of losing her too, after everything else, is more than I can bare. I stumble to her bedside, no longer feeling like I can support my own weight.

"What happened?" I finally address my grandfather after far too long of silence.

He's leaning against the doorway, his eyes locked firmly on my grandma, as if willing her to be okay. He meets my eyes and I can see the sadness in them, the light that once burned there now but an afterthought.

"I don't know. She went out to feed the chickens, after a while I got worried because she usually doesn't stay out that long. When I went to look for her, I found her unconscious just outside the barn. God, I was so scared." He breathes out, as if it brings him comfort to share the information with another person.

"She's going to be okay. You know she is." I say, more reassuring myself than anything.

I sit on the very edge of her bed, gently taking her hand in mine, careful not to disrupt the cords that are running from her I.V. She has an oxygen mask on and the beeping of her heart monitor gives me a little reprieve from the fear mounting in my stomach.

At least I have this to give me hope, her heart beating, still holding on to life.

****

My grandfather and I spend the remainder of the afternoon at my grandma's side. While we don't talk much, I can feel the comfort my presence gives him, just as his does for me.

The doctors and nurses are in and out frequently, reassuring my grandpa that she's doing well and that tonight will answer a lot of questions on her chances of recovery.

At seven o'clock one of the nurses comes in to inform us that visiting hours are over. Knowing my grandpa will never leave her side, I assure him I will get home safely and to not worry about me.

With a light kiss to her pale sunken cheek, I take one last look at my grandma before exiting the room. Praying to god it won't be the last time I see her alive.

I take a cab home and now standing just inside the front door, I feel a discomfort that doesn't sit well with me.

I flip on the foyer light and take in the quiet that seeps through the house. It's very rare for me to be alone at night, and it is a fear I have yet to overcome.

Standing here, alone, in the realization that no one is coming home, I feel the panic rising like bile in my throat.

I slowly wander the house, checking every door and window twice before making my way up to the second floor, turning on every light as I go.

It's not until I reach my grandparent's room that I realize the fear I have for my grandpa far outweighs the fear I feel for myself.

He will never survive losing my grandma, she is his entire world. Heading across the hall to my room, I collapse on my bed.

I don't bother moving the dresser in front of the door. If someone really wanted to hurt me that wouldn't stop them anyways and honestly right now, I'm not sure that I really care that much.

I am more concerned with my family. The two people that saved my life, that fought for me when I didn't have the strength to fight for myself.

I give into the tears almost immediately. It seems impossible that I had been able to hold them in for so long, determined to stay strong for my grandpa.

Now, I feel anything but strong. I feel lost, alone, and more than anything, I'm afraid.

Afraid of what will happen to my grandma. Afraid that my grandpa will never be the same. Afraid that I am losing the last of my family and that I will forever be cursed to exist in this world alone.

But I'm not alone. I can feel his presence. The soothing calmness that tells me that no matter how bad things get, that he will always be by my side.

"Tate, I need you." I whisper into my tear stained pillow.

Not able to fight exhaustion any longer, I close my eyes and let my mind drift. At first, I think I have slipped into a dream. One where I am laying in this very spot only now I feel safe and loved with his arms wrapped tightly around me.

My eyes flutter open at the electricity surging through my veins, only to find that it's not a dream. He really is here.

"Angel." I hear him whisper, as my eyes close again and I slip into unconsciousness.

MELISSA TOPPEN

Chapter Seventeen

Almost six months have passed since that night on the farm. The night, where for the first time in a long time, everything felt right.

I woke the next morning alone and have not heard from Tate since. It's hard for me to understand why he would show himself to me in my time of need, only to disappear again with no warning and no real explanation as to why he's choosing to stay away from me.

Of course I know the real reason. The more my memory returned, the more sense it all made. I know he is trying to protect me. Only he doesn't realize that in his attempts to do so, he's harming me more than he is helping me.

I would gladly face any danger in exchange for the pain I feel in his absence.

After the health scare with my grandma, I took on a new found independence. Determined to put as little stress as possible on my grandparents.

My grandma was released from the hospital one week after she had been admitted. She is back to her old self now but I can see the toll it has taken on her. At the same time, I can't help but feel like it was all somehow my fault.

As hard as it was for me, I knew that it was time for me to start my life on my own. It's too much for them to have to worry about me on top of everything else.

It was nearly impossible to leave the farm and as uneasy as it still makes me feel, I can't bring myself to regret my decision to do it.

It was time. I think I had known it for quite a while but was imprisoned by my fear.

Nothing could describe the feeling of packing all my belongings and driving away from the farm that day. Of watching the only place that brought me comfort disappear in the distance.

As much as I feared, the hardest part was leaving behind the only memories I had of Tate.

Charlie made the transition easier.

Honestly, I don't know if college would have ever been a possibility without him.

Now I find myself a freshman at Austin State University. I didn't think it was possible but in the few weeks I have been here, I have found a routine, one that provides me with enough comfort that I find myself adjusting in a way I never dreamed.

Charlie and I are housed in the same Co-Ed dorm. I find great comfort in knowing that I can get to him in the matter of two minutes, should I find myself in need of him.

While I have really tried not to rely on him too much, there has been the occasional night where I have gone to his room.

It's always the same. We talk, he will hold me and calm me down from whatever battle I have raging inside. He really is my best friend and I thank god everyday that he came into my life.

Together we have slowly managed to re-enter the real world, and while I love the freedom of being on my own, nothing feels complete without Tate.

I don't want it to be that way. I want to be able to appreciate the love we shared and learn to live a life without him, but that simply is not possible.

To love someone the way I love him. To feel only half a person without him by my side. It's no life worth living. But it's the hope, the dream, that one day we will be reunited again, that gives me my drive to establish my own life.

Deep down, I know he is with me. There is no denying the electricity that pulls me when I sense the other part of my soul is near.

For a while I thought for sure that he would show himself eventually, but as each day passes, I find myself questioning if that will ever really happen.

Glancing at the clock, I realize it's past nine. The study hall is completely empty, with the exception of two professors grouped at a corner table with their noses in books.

Quickly I gather up my books and stuff them into my black cloth backpack. A gift from my grandma.

As I make my way down the stairs, outside of the large brick building where I spend most of my time studying, I feel a shift in the air.

Only it's not the comforting pull that usually

tells me there is nothing to fear. Instead, it's an eery blackness that leaves me feeling chilled and honestly a bit scared.

    I quicken my pace as I reach the sidewalk heading towards my dorm. I usually make it a point to be in my room before dark but tonight I had let my mind drift and lost track of time.

    My schedule is pretty demanding and most of my time is spent with my nose in books. I like it that way though. It provides me with an out, a distraction, from the one person I can't seem to shake.

    I can see the building that houses my dorm in the distance. I immediately feel relief that in a few short moments I will be safe in the confines of my room.

    I pick up the pace, moving at a slight jog but stop dead in my tracks not a hundred feet from my building. Leaning against the wall next to the front door I spot a figure almost completely hidden in the shadows.

    I can't make out who it is and for a moment, I consider turning back, but then again, where would I go?

    Hesitantly, I move forward, my eyes locked

straight ahead of me. I don't look at the person as I punch in my code. For a minute, I think that I am home free.

"Where is it Callista?" A familiar voice rasps behind me, so close to my ear that I can feel his breath on the back of my neck, his thick Australian accent giving him away immediately.

Fear roots me to the spot. As much as I want to scream, to run, I can produce no such actions. My body not responding to my minds demands.

I turn to find myself standing directly in front of Nicholas. For a moment, I can't breathe. I'm in shock. I remember him of course, but up to this point had no real proof, other than an unreliable memory, that he really existed.

Only he's not the same person I remember. His eyes are dark and there is an impatience in his stance.

"Answer me." He demands, blocking my escape as I attempt to side step around him.

"Nicholas...." I manage to get out, my mind finally able to produce a sentence.

"What are you doing here?" I try my best to maintain a casual tone, even though I am screaming on the inside.

"Don't play coy with me Callista. I know you have it. You bare the mark." He says, holding up my hand and examining the scar that is so clearly burned into my palm.

"Where is the amulet?"

His request catches me off guard and I can't help but be utterly confused. Why would he want the amulet? Better yet, why would he think I would have it?

Truth is, I haven't thought much about what happened to it after that night.

"I'm sorry. I.... I don't know what you're talking about." I manage to stammer out.

"You really think I would believe that love?" He croons out, with a bit of amusement in his voice.

"You know exactly what I am talking about."

"I mean, I don't know where it is." I struggle to keep the quiver from my voice.

"Emily Bennett gave you the map and key. Clearly you found it." He says, gesturing to my hand.

"So where is it now?"

"Honestly Nicholas, I don't know."

"Bull shit." He spits out, just inches from my face. He straightens his shoulders, towering over me.

"I swear." I say, stumbling a couple steps backwards, attempting to put a little distance between us with no real way of escaping.

"I was holding it.... That is the last thing I remember." I answer truthfully.

"Well it didn't just get up and walk away now did it? So tell me Callista.... Who has the amulet now?" He asks, stepping towards me until I am trapped between him and the glass door behind me.

"I don't know and honestly I don't care!" I spit back at him, regaining some sense of self preservation.

"I lost everything because of that amulet. Hell, I nearly lost my life. So, no Nicholas, I don't know who has it, nor do I want to know."

I can see the anger surge through him, his nostrils flaring. He's losing patience with each passing second and yet there is nothing I can do about it. I don't know what he will do if I don't give him the information he wants and yet I don't have it.

"Either you get me the amulet or......" He stops just as the door opens behind me and I practically fall through the threshold.

"Whoa Cal, you okay?" Charlie asks as I stumble into him.

I glance to his face, which is masked in confusion, and then look back to the place where Nicholas was just standing. Only he's not there.

"Where did he go?" I ask confused.

"Where did who go Cal?" Charlie asks, stepping forward to stand next to me and peer out through the open door.

"You didn't see the man I was talking to?" I ask, turning to face him.

"What man?" He eyes me questionably, causing the uneasiness to spread.

"Nothing, never mind." I mumble out before turning and making my way down the hall.

My mind is racing and as much as I want to tell Charlie everything, I can't. Telling him even a small portion could put him in danger. Not to mention what the fall out could be for me and Tate if I shared his secret with another living soul.

"Hey, you okay?" Charlie asks as he approaches me from behind.

"Yeah, I'm fine. Just tired." I blow him off as I unlock my door and push my way inside.

"Thanks Charlie. I will see you tomorrow okay?"

"Yeah okay." He says, throwing up one hand in a half wave just as I close the door.

I feel awful for blowing him off but I simply cannot get into this with him. Not to mention the fact that I am so utterly confused and honestly a bit scared about what just happened.

Gone is the sweet playboy Nicholas that I met just months ago in New York. Replaced by a man that I do not recognize. A dark man, one that I feared instantly.

Why is he after the amulet? Why does he think I would have it? I don't know why but until now, I never wondered about where the amulet had ended up once I had retrieved it from the flames.

Now, I am more than a little curious as to

why Nicholas helped me find the amulet, only to show up months later demanding to know its whereabouts.

A sick feeling settles into the pit of my stomach as I realize that maybe, just maybe, things are not as black and white as they once had seemed.

I can't shake the feeling that there is so much more surrounding this entire situation than I realized.

Had I simply been some type of pawn? If the amulet is what he is seeking, then why not just get it himself. Why send me? And why, just as I am beginning to establish a sense of normalcy for myself, does he show up demanding the amulet?

Something is not right, and it is up to me to figure this out.

Tate is nowhere to be found and if Nicholas is as serious as he seemed, this will not be the last time I hear from him.

MELISSA TOPPEN

Chapter Eighteen

"You ready to go Cal?" I hear Charlie call through my door, after giving it a light knock.

I roll to my side and look at the clock, eight forty-five. My English class starts in fifteen minutes and while I know I need to get out of bed, I have not been able to will myself to do so.

"I'm not going to class today, go on without me." I shout back, not sure how well he can hear me.

He knocks again. "Cal! Open up!"

Not wanting to move, I hesitate but then make myself climb out of bed and stumble to the door. The last thing I need is Charlie worrying about me.

I open the door to see my bright eyed

handsome best friend holding two cups of coffee, a very impatient look plastered across his face.

"What the hell? Get dressed we're gonna be late."

"I'm not going today." I manage to get out through a yawn.

Impatience quickly turns to worry. "Is everything okay? Are you sick?"

"No, I'm good, just really tired. Go on without me okay?"

"You sure? I can stay with you if you want."

"No, there's no reason for you to fall behind too. Take notes for me and we will catch up later."

He holds out my cup of coffee to me before nodding goodbye.

"Call me if you need me." He calls out just as I close the door.

Making my way back to my bed, I sit on the edge and replay the events of last night in my head.

I still can't make sense of why Nicholas showed up outside of my dorm demanding that I give him the amulet. More importantly, I can't understand why he would help me find it in the first place, if he wanted it for himself so badly.

    Looking around my small room, I notice my roommate has already left for the day. Bridget is not much of an early riser and from what I know, all her classes are scheduled after eleven in the morning. It's not like her to be out this early.

    She's a pretty good roommate to have all in all. We haven't spent much time getting to know each other, but she's not home a lot either.

    I am usually asleep before she gets in at night and I typically leave for class before she gets up. That being our schedule five days a week, it leaves very little time to really connect to her. But she's quiet and keeps the room clean and for that I am thankful.

    Our room isn't much. A small square space with white walls and two twin beds on each side. Neither one of us has really done much in the way of decorating and my space is typically cluttered with books.

    I am about to crawl back in bed and stay there the rest of the day when something on my nightstand catches my eye. A silver chain and locket coiled on top of a white folded piece of paper.

Hesitantly I pick up the chain and run it through my fingers, watching the charm spin as I do. I flip open the locket to find the silhouette of a man and a woman. This is the locket that led me to the amulet, but how?

I grab the paper that sits beneath it and with shaky hands unfold it. In perfect cursive writing it reads:

Meet me at Sycamore Park.

Follow the bike trail to the bridge.

I turn the note over but there is no more information.

My heart rate picks up speed, what if it's Tate? The thought of seeing him again, talking to him, has me feeling like I could crawl out of my own skin.

But then of course, there is the fear. What if it isn't Tate?

None of that matters as I dress quickly in jeans and a sweatshirt. My mind is going a million miles a minute with only one focal point.... Tate.

****

THE TRAVELER: THE AMULET OF LIFE

Sycamore Park is a public area not far from campus and one that I frequent often. It only takes me about twenty minutes to walk there and by the time I arrive, I am a ball of nerves.

One thing is certain, who ever is meeting me here knows about the amulet and my connection to it.

I don't know at what point I lost the locket. Everything surrounding that night is such a blur and each moment seems to overlap.

With the necklace in my pocket, I quickly make my way down the bike trail. There are tons of people around. Walking, riding bikes, playing with their children on the playground. This fact helps to calm my nerves but only a small amount.

Eventually I reach the duck pond where a three foot wide bridge crosses to the other side. I spot Tate almost instantly. Standing on the bridge, leaning against one of the white rails that reach up over the sides, dressed in a hooded sweatshirt and ball cap, his arms crossed in front of his chest.

He doesn't look up but I know it is him. The calm, the fullness that surrounds us is blinding and I have to fight back the urge to run to him.

He must sense my presence but does not

acknowledge it as he turns and makes his way across the bridge to the other side. I follow him, making sure to keep a good distance between us.

I know the dangers of being with him, the last thing I want to do is to make this harder on either of us. Eventually he slows, taking a seat on a white bench that overlooks the pond.

Slowly I make my way over to him and sit on the other side of the bench. He doesn't say anything at first and for a moment, I am simply enjoying the feeling of being near him, of the peace that it brings.

"Cally." He says, and instantly every nerve ending stands to attention.

It has been so long since I have heard his beautiful voice.

Hesitantly I look to my left. As soon as his eyes meet mine, I am hit with so many raw emotions. I can't contain the rush, the surge of intense passion that courses through me.

A man I know only in distant memory and yet one that I am bound to for all eternity.

Tears are streaming down my face before I can speak and once I manage to get words out they are shaky.

"I was starting to believe this day would never come."

"I'm so sorry angel." He says, his pain etched across his beautiful features.

"I never wanted this for you, for us. We must be quick Cally. I don't know how much time we have."

"Why did you ask me to meet you here?" I ask, not so much caring the real reason.

All that matters is that right here, right now, he is with me.

"Nicholas." He says. One word that answers me without further explanation.

"He wants the amulet Tate. But I don't have it." I reply, trying to keep my voice as low as possible to not be over heard.

"I know angel. I know. Did he say why he is looking for it?"

"No. He just kept insisting that I must know where it is and..... Tate, he scared me. There is something dark about him. Something I didn't see the first time."

"I know, I just can't figure out his play. It doesn't make any sense. Did he say anything to you the night he took you to Emily, anything at all that would explain why he is looking for the amulet?"

"No." I admit, not being able to pin point anything that seemed relevant.

"And I have no idea where the amulet is Tate."

"I do." He says surprising me.

"When I found you that night. Braize was still there. I was pleading with him to help you, save you. At one point the amulet slipped from your hand. He took it. I didn't question it at the time, I was too focused on you. Now, I can't help but think that he is somehow tied into you finding the amulet in the first place."

"But why would an angel want the amulet? It's dark magic, I could feel it in my bones."

"You're right it is and why is a very good question. One that I will find the answer to. But Cally, you must not let this derail you. Continue on with your daily routine as if nothing has happened. Anything out of the ordinary will make anyone watching you suspicious. Keep the locket with you. I don't know how or why but I am positive it is part of the puzzle. Stay close to

Charlie and whatever you do, do not look for me. When it's safe I will find you."

He stands to leave and I can feel my heart breaking all over again.

"Please don't leave me." I whisper, not really expecting him to hear.

He kneels down directly in front of me. His eyes burn fiercely into mine and my body ignites.

"I am with you always Callista. Where you are, I will be, remember?" He says, before leaning in and placing the briefest kiss across my mouth.

The feeling of his lips on mine is so exquisite I can feel it to my toes, but it is short lived.

When I open my eyes, he's gone. The tears are back but this time I have hope. He's still here, he's with me. That has to stand for something. I have to hold on to the possibility that one day we will be as one.

I will do as Tate asks. But if he thinks I am going to just sit around while he tries to figure this all out on his own, he doesn't know me as well as I thought.

Information, that's where I can help him. I am in the center of all of this. Surely there is someway for me to figure out why. Someone who can help me.

Now that I know where the amulet is, maybe that will buy me a little leverage with Nicholas. It at least gives me something to bargain with.

Then there's Braize. I still can't fathom why an angel would want the amulet, unless of course it's to keep it out of the wrong hands.

None of this makes sense. If they wanted the amulet, why not just take it? Braize was right there. He could have taken the amulet before I even arrived, made it so I never found it, but he didn't. Why?

There has to be an explanation. There has to be someone who can help me. One thing is clear, when it comes to Tate, there is no distance I won't travel, no bridge I won't cross, to get to spend eternity by his side.

If it kills me, I will find answers. I will find a way.

THE TRAVELER: THE AMULET OF LIFE

Chapter Nineteen

As much as it pains me, I have done as Tate asked. I can't help but blame myself for the way things have turned out.

Had I listened to him the first time, back at the farm, had I stayed there and waited for him, things may have ended up very differently. I can't be sure, but I feel like maybe everything going on right now is a result of that very decision.

"What's with you Cal?" Charlie asks in between bites of his Turkey sandwich.

"I'm sorry." I say, reaching across the round dining table and giving his hand a squeeze.

"I'm just preoccupied, and I'm not sleeping well. Guess I'm just a little out of sorts."

"Do you want to talk about it? You know

that whatever is going on with you, you can tell me. No judgments." He says, his bright eyes full of worry.

It breaks my heart to keep this from him. He has been my rock these past few months and I can't help but feel like I am deceiving him in some way.

"There's nothing really to talk about. Just lack of sleep taking it's toll. I really should lay off the coffee. I'm sure that's what is causing it." I lie.

"Do you want a refill?" He asks, gesturing to my Diet Coke sitting in front of me.

I nod, handing him my cup, and watch him walk the distance of the cafeteria to the fountain soda machine.

As much as I want to go back to my room and disappear for a while, my Angelology class starts in about a half hour. Out of all the classes I am taking, it is my favorite class and I selected it for obvious reasons.

It focuses on the study of angels, which gives me more insight into the world that I have been thrown into.

"You ready?" Charlie asks, returning with my soda.

"Yeah, I want to get to class a little early today. I need to talk to my professor." I say, grabbing my bag from the floor and resting it on my shoulder.

We walk the length of the grounds in silence. Charlie has learned not to push me for too much and for that I will always be grateful to have him as a friend.

"Meet you here after class?" He asks as we reach the building that houses his next class.

"Actually I have a lot of studying to do tonight. You are welcome to join me."

"Nah, you know me. Not much for that scene." He laughs, giving me a wave.

I walk the rest of the way by myself. Lost in my thoughts, per usual. When I finally reach my class, I am relieved to see my professor is already here and no other students have arrived.

I take a seat in the front row and contemplate whether or not I want to ask him anything regarding my situation.

If anyone can tell me anything, certainly he can. If nothing more than to give me a little more insight into what would drive an angel into darkness or a traveler for that matter.

I clear my throat and he looks up, eying my curiously. So much for subtlety.

He's an older man. I would guess him in his late fifties. He's short and stocky and always wears a sweater vest, even when it's eighty degrees outside.

"Um Professor, can I ask you a question?" I finally get out.

"Ask away dear girl." He says, rolling his hand in the air.

"Well I was just wondering, have you ever heard of an angel choosing a different course?"

"I have, why do you ask?"

"I was reading about Travelers... And I was wondering. If everything is centered around heaven. Why would someone choose a different life?"

"Well that's hard to say. I would think, just as in this life, not one thing is for everyone." He says, taking off his glasses and rubbing his eyes.

He leans back in his chair and studies me intently.

"So just as good people can go bad, do you believe angels are capable of the same?" I ask, trying to keep my questions as simple as possible.

"It's not common but perhaps, yes."

"What do you know of dark magic?" I ask.

I can't help but notice the surprised look that crosses his face. His thick black eyebrows arching up in question.

"I have done some studies, nothing concrete of course, but I know basic information. What are wanting to know?"

"I was just wondering, hypothetically of course, that if something existed that could alter god's plan, wouldn't god have the power to destroy it?"

"I suppose that depends. God is but one being and is said to trust his angels as equals. If one were to turn on him, it's not clear whether or not he would know immediately. I would assume that if he did in fact know, then yes to answer your question, he would. Where is all this coming from?"

"I was just curious." I lie and hope that it doesn't show through.

"Well the library in my office contains books and studies on many different things, including magical beings and objects. You are more than welcome to borrow any that you so desire."

"I would appreciate that very much sir, thank you."

"Meet me after class. We can discuss this further then." He says, taking note that students have begun filing into the classroom.

With that, he slides his glasses back on and takes his place center stage.

****

An hour and a half later, I find myself standing in a small office, piled with more books than I have seen anywhere outside of an actual library.

Professor Greyson was kind enough to pull out a few books he thought would interest me.

"These are on loan of course." He says, piling three large books into my arms. Keep them as long as you like but please make sure I have them back before the end of term." He says, turning towards his desk and taking a seat behind it.

"Is there anything else?" He asks.

"No, thank you again professor." I say, turning to leave.

"Miss Price." He calls from behind me. I turn meeting his eyes.

"Should you find yourself with more questions, you know where to find me." With that, I nod and hurry out of the office.

There are a million things I would like to ask him but unfortunately I don't think he would have the answers for me.

Before anything, I need to read through the books he loaned me and see if I can find any of my answers there.

My plan was to go to the library. It's usually the quietest place and it's easier for me to concentrate. But for whatever reason, I have the overwhelming urge to return to my dorm. I can't help but think it has everything to do with what happened the last time I went there.

That was the night Nicholas appeared, and while I want to see him again, I want to be better prepared as to what it is I need to ask him when I do.

With that, I head in the direction of my dorm. It only takes me about fifteen minutes to walk there and honestly, the fresh air clears my head.

With fall in full swing, the weather is amazing. I love the turning of the leaves, the colors, the smells. A small part of me wishes I could be back on the farm, spending time with Sasha and Bennett, finding peace at the creek.

"Cally." I hear someone call from behind me just as I approach the door to my building.

Hesitantly I turn, only to find my roommate jogging towards me.

"Oh hey! What's up?" I ask, my relief apparent in my voice.

Bridget is a pretty girl. About the same height as me. Curvy with blonde hair that hangs to her butt. Her usual kept appearance is anything but. She's in sweats, her hair tied in a knot, no makeup. Not something I am used to seeing.

"Someone broke into our room." She says breathless, once she reaches me.

"What?" I question her shocked.

Why would anyone want to break into a

dorm room that has practically nothing in it?

"It doesn't look like they took anything but whoever it was, they were looking for something. They completely trashed the whole room. It will take us days to sort through everything. Campus police already checked it out. They said it's safe for us to stay but they changed the key code. Here." She says, handing me a card with 1221 scribbled on the back.

I shove the card in my pocket and notice that the locket is still there. The locket, that's it. It makes sense. Neither me nor Bridget ever have anyone over. Tate said to keep it with me. He must have known that someone would come looking for it. Which means only one thing.

It is, as he said, part of the puzzle. Why else would they go through the trouble of trying to find it?

I pull the locket out and slip it around my neck before following Bridget into the building. Once we enter the room, I stand glued, in absolute shock. It looks like a tornado went through the tiny space. Leaving nothing unturned.

"Do you have any idea who would have done this?" I ask, hoping that maybe I'm just jumping to worst case scenario.

"No, but apparently Josie, next door, saw a man leaving our room earlier today."

"Did she say what he looked like?"

"She didn't see his face directly but from what she told campus police, he was young and had white hair. Strange isn't it?" She asks, seeing the look of shock on my face.

"Yes, very strange." I admit, already knowing full well that our intruder was none other than Braize himself.

We spend the next two hours trying to clean up the destruction he left behind. All the while I search for clues, anything that he may have left behind.

To my disappointment, I find nothing. Bridget seemed satisfied with the fact that the door code had been changed. I, however, know that no lock or code would keep Braize out if he chooses to return again.

As I lay in bed, staring at my glow in the dark star that I brought with me from the farm, I am sure of only one thing. Whoever has the amulet must need to possess the locket and the ring as well. As long as I have the locket, I know that this is only the beginning.

MELISSA TOPPEN

Chapter Twenty

I have spent days searching the massive books loaned to me by my professor. Pages upon pages about angels, demons, and everything in between.

So much of what is documented is legend, with no real proof of the truth it holds.

It wasn't until last night that I stumbled across a section in one of the books that covered black magic.

Most of the information was basic and things I had already known. Black magic is the use of supernatural powers or magic for evil or selfish purposes. That much I understood.

There was no mention of the Amulet, nor any other magical object of it's kind. Leading me to believe that my search for information needs to go beyond what I can find in the everyday book.

Deciding that my best option would be to talk to my professor again, I shelved the books and tried to focus on my studies.

Living my life as normal as possible is a lot harder than one would expect. You just go about your daily routine right?

Well not when you are in the middle of a battle of supernatural beings. With each day that passes I can feel myself becoming more and more withdrawn.

Charlie gets the brunt of it and for that I feel awful. He is the one person I open up to, above all others, with the exception of Tate, of course. He's only going to believe my 'I'm just tired' routine for so long, if he even believed it to begin with.

"Penny for your thoughts?" Charlie says, leaning down and placing a kiss to my forehead before taking a seat across from me.

He agreed to meet me for dinner and a movie, my way of trying to make up for what an awful friend I have been to him recently.

For dinner, we go with our usual, Mickels. A small little pizza place not far from the theater. It's the perfect place to grab a quick bite to eat.

They typically are not overly busy and the restaurant tends to be on the quiet side. It's a small place, only about twenty tables making up the diner style set up. Each wall lined with red booths, a few tables scattered through out the middle of the floor.

"I already ordered, I hope that's okay." I say, smiling brightly at him.

Just being in his presence makes me feel better, normal even.

"You know what I like." He jokes, giving me a wink.

Good old Charlie, he always knows just what to say to make my heart do a little flip flop.

We make small talk as we eat. I do my best to keep the conversation light and casual. By the time we exit the restaurant thirty minutes later, I feel better about where we stand.

Charlie seems to have dismissed whatever it was that he thought was bothering me and for the first time in over a week, things actually feel normal.

We walk to the theater arm in arm. I can't

help but wish that things could be different for Charlie and I.

He's a good guy, sweet, cute, everything a sane girl would want in a man. I know that I could be happy with him, that is if Tate never existed.

Tate owns my heart, he's a part of me. I belong to only him, body, mind, and soul. Even though we have been forced apart, I know deep down that we will find a way to be together again... Someday.

Charlie decides on the latest comedy release and leaves to go get popcorn as I make my way inside the theater to find us seats.

Per usual on a Friday night, the theater is packed full. I finally find two empty seats a little closer to the screen than I would like and make myself comfortable.

Charlie joins me just as the lights dim and the previews start. I kick back and do my best to relax and just enjoy this glimpse into a normal life. We laugh at all the upcoming new movies and then fall silent as the feature begins.

I lose myself in the story and find that I am enjoying myself more than I would have thought possible. I wish life really were as simple as it seems right now.

Sometimes I even forget about all the bad things that consume my past. Moments where my fear just seems to slip away and for once, I just feel like an average nineteen year old college student. It's these moments I treasure the most. The simplicity of it all.

About half way through the movie, I feel my body tense and my pulse quicken. I don't know what's causing it but I feel like I am going to crawl out of my skin.

I glance around, suddenly panicked. The theater is dark and I can't make out faces. What was fun and enjoyable just moments ago, is now unbearable and the need to get the hell out of here takes over.

"Restroom." I whisper to Charlie. He nods not paying much attention as I get up and begin making my way out of the theater.

The panic continues to rise and by the time I enter the brightly lit lobby, I am in near hysterics.

I veer to the left, in the direction of the bathrooms. I just need a moment to compose myself. More than anything, I am terrified by what has brought this on.

Did something happen? Is someone here? I stand in front of the sink and look in the mirror. My cheeks are flushed and honestly, I look a bit feverish.

Taking deep breaths, I splash my face with cold water and try to calm myself. Nothing works. Exiting the bathroom, I head straight for the door leading outside. The moment the night air hits my face, I feel slightly better, but not much.

I don't want to just abandon Charlie, especially since things are finally getting back to normal with us. But for whatever reason, I can't bring myself to care.

Every fiber inside of me is telling me to run like hell and yet I have no idea what I am running from.

Deciding that I just need to move, I start walking down the strip where tons of shops and restaurants line the sidewalk. I don't get far before the panic becomes overwhelming. I stop, ducking into the nearest alleyway and collapse to my knees.

Suddenly, a blinding noise is coursing through my ears. So high and intense I feel like my head is going to explode at any second. I crouch over, holding my ears, silently praying for it to stop. Just seconds later, the noise fades out and is replaced by a woman's screams.

It doesn't take me long to realize that I am the one screaming.

"Cally, Cally....." I hear a voice penetrate through the white cloud that has fogged my mind, just as everything goes black.

****

I wake in darkness. It takes me a second to recognize my surroundings and realize that I am in my dorm room.

I shoot up, disoriented and confused. How did I get here?

I look around the room and jump when I spot someone sitting in a chair in the corner of the room, quickly realizing it's Charlie.

"Charlie." I whisper out, not sure if he is sleeping.

Without a word he stands, slowly making his way towards me. Something about his movements, the way his body seems to be operating on strings, puts me on high alert.

"Charlie?" I say a little louder.

Again nothing. His lack of response gives him away. Charlie would never intentionally scare me, especially knowing my past.

Eventually he comes to stop at the foot of my bed and hovers for a moment.

He opens his mouth to speak but all that comes out is the same blinding noise I heard earlier.

His mouth contorts and his eyes roll back in his head. I struggle to keep sight of him through the pain in my ears, pounding through my head.

Suddenly the veil falls away and I quickly realize it's not Charlie at all. In fact, it's not even a man.

"Emily." I stammer out, scooting backwards in bed, trying to put as much distance between us as possible.

My mind struggles to keep up with what my eyes are seeing.

"The soul of the pure." Her voice cuts through my head as the noise fades into the background.

She's speaking through my mind. How is that possible?

I make no attempt to respond. Something tells me she doesn't need me to respond. She's in my head, surely any response can be collected from there.

"Braize." She echos through me, followed by a high pitched laugh that makes every hair on my body stand up.

I can't process what is happening. Nothing makes sense……

I shoot up once again disoriented and confused. My room is dark, quiet. Was it really just a dream? It felt so real.

I glance around making sure that I am alone and instantly relax when I realize the only other person here is my sleeping roommate.

I lay back down and try to regulate my breathing. How did I get home? Where's Charlie?

My mind is clouded and while I know I need to figure this out, I can't will myself to do so. I feel exhaustion winning out and eventually it takes me under.

****

"Wake up angel." I hear Tate whisper.

I can feel his presence. The overwhelming feeling of peace, of love. I try to open my eyes but they feel like they are glued shut. I feel Tate run his fingers through my hair.

"Cally, you have to wake up." He says again.

I so badly want to open my eyes and look at the beautiful man I am so completely in love with but I can't do it.

I try to reach out to him but like my eyes, my arms feel glued in place. It's like my mind is awake but my body isn't responding to my minds demands.

I feel his lips brush my forehead. I can smell his wonderful familiar scent and all the emotions that smell stirs inside of me.

"Come back to me angel." He breathes against my cheek and finally I can feel the weight lift.

My eye lids flutter open and I quickly shut

them again as the brightness of the room makes it difficult for them to adjust.

I try again, managing to keep my eyes open long enough this time to catch sight of Tate hovering over me.

"How are you feeling?" He asks, relief flooding through his voice.

"I.... I don't know." I stutter out, hardly recognizing my own voice.

"Water." I manage to get out, realizing how dry my mouth and throat feel.

Tate retrieves a bottle of water from my night stand and unscrews the cap. I prop myself up on my elbow as he brings the bottle to my lips so that I can take a drink.

"Cally I need you to tell me what happened?" He says, replacing the cap on the bottle and returning it to my night stand.

"I don't know." I admit, laying back down and shifting onto my back.

"I was at the movies with Charlie...... Tate, where's Charlie?" I shoot up, suddenly remembering that I left him at the theater alone.

"Shhh, it's okay angel. Charlie is fine.

Worried about you, that's for sure."

"You talked to him?" I ask, laying back down.

"I did." He says, running his fingers through my hair.

"He came by to see you a couple of times. He really cares for you. I'm glad you have a friend like him."

"A couple of times? How long have I been asleep?" I ask confused.

"I brought you here two days ago." He pauses and then quickly resumes as he catches my reaction.

"I found you in the alley, screaming your head off. Just as I reached you, you lost consciousness. Cally, I was terrified. I had no idea what had happened to you, if someone had harmed you."

I reach up and run my fingers down his jaw line. "I love you." I whisper to him, realizing it has been months since I could say those words to him.

"And I you, my angel." He says, leaning down and placing a brief kiss across my lips.

My entire body seems to come to life under his touch and everything is instantly ignited. But it's short lived, as he pulls back to study my face.

"I need you to tell me everything you remember."

"I went to the movies with Charlie. I started having what I can only describe as some sort of panic attack. I went outside, tried to walk it off but at one point it became so overwhelming I couldn't even stand on my own two feet. Then there was the noise..."

"What noise Cally?" He questions me as I struggle to remember.

"I don't know how to describe it. It was loud, so loud I felt like my head was going to explode. Like a screeching noise, only in my head." I shudder at the memory.

"White noise." He says, rubbing his forehead.

"White noise?" I eye him questionably.

"A noise created by a supernatural being to overtake someone's mind. It blinds you, makes you incapable of defending yourself. Was there anything strange that happened before that, anything you can think of at all?"

"No.... Tate what does this mean?" I ask honestly a bit frightened by the whole situation.

"It means that it is no longer safe for you. It means someone is trying to weaken you, to overpower your mind. It means from now on, I am going to keep you very close."

"But what about Braize, what about everything..... I know he made a deal with you. I remember everything only it seems like a dream. You promised you would stay away from me. Is it safe for you, for us?"

"It's not safe Cally. But either way you are in danger. At least if I am with you, then I can protect you. I should have never left your side in the first place and for that I am truly sorry." He says, placing a small kiss to palm of my hand.

The hand that bares the mark of the amulet.

"I did this to you... All of it. I should have stayed with you on the farm. We should have faced this together. Instead I doubted your ability to take care of yourself. I didn't think that you were strong enough to face my world. I'm just sorry I didn't see how truly amazing and brave you are sooner. This could all be so very different."

"This isn't your fault. If anything it's mine.

You specifically asked something of me and I disregarded it." I rush out, so quickly the words blend together.

"None of that matters now. There is something much bigger than the both of us happening here. Something not even I can understand. But we are going to figure this out Cally.... Together."

I sit up and pull him to me. Wrapping my arms around his neck, I squeeze him tightly.

"I have missed you so much." I sob out, the fear and love blending together in an array of emotions that I don't understand.

He responds, wrapping his arms around my waist and holding me tightly.

"I know.... Trust me, I know. These last few months have been pure hell. The only thing that got me through each and every day was knowing that you were alive, safe. I couldn't brave this existence without you angel. You are a part of me."

My heart rate kicks into overdrive at his words. Knowing that he feels the same way. That this has been as hard on him as it has on me, maybe harder. It makes it all worth while.

I release him and lean back slightly to take in his beautiful face. He's even more perfect than I remembered.

I reach up and run my fingers through his dark hair. Studying each strand as it falls from my fingers.

I want to know everything there is to know about this man. I want to memorize every detail down to the smallest parts. And as much as I want to just enjoy this moment, I know that I need to apologize to Charlie, to let him know I am okay.

"I need to see Charlie." I say, lowering my hand from his hair to graze down his cheek.

"I told him I would have you call him as soon as you woke up."

"What did you tell him happened? Who does he think that you are?"

"Charlie came by not too long after I got you home. I told him you passed out and that I found you not far from the theater. He was so worried about you, he didn't really question it, until he came back the second time. I told him I was a friend of yours, he seemed surprised but given the details I knew about you, let it go pretty quickly. Honestly he was too focused on you to really over think it."

"So he doesn't know anything about you?" I ask relieved.

"Of course not angel. The last thing I need is to draw unwanted attention to myself. What I have told him, is all he can know."

"I know. It's just hard. Especially when you are not with me. I have no one to talk to, no one to confide in. I feel like I am lying to him all the time."

"I understand and again I can't apologize enough for everything I have put you through, for what I am still putting you through..."

"Stop! You are not forcing any of this on me. I chose this. I chose you. Nothing else matters." I assure him, pulling his face down to meet mine.

"It's you and me against the world Ace." I say, pressing my lips firmly to his.

In this moment, nothing else really does matter. Only this. The feeling of his lips upon mine. The fire coursing through every inch of my body. The burn reassuring me that I am alive and that I am in love.

As much as I want to spend the day losing myself in his touch, I know that now is not the time or place. He clearly realizes that too, breaking away from my mouth, his breathing labored and raged.

"What now?"

"Now, we live. One day at a time. I will stay close to you, keep you safe. We will find ways to spend time together without drawing too much attention."

"We need to find out what Nicholas is up to. And what happened to me..." I interrupt him.

"And we will. In time, all things will come to light. We will cross that bridge when we get there. Until then, I just want to enjoy being with you. We never know how long it will last."

The thought breaks my heart into a million tiny pieces. I have lost him once before, only the blow was softened by my lack of memory.

Each day I faced without him was torture. I never want to feel that way again. Most importantly, I never want to experience losing him head on. It's a thought I simply can not bare.

"I have a few things I need to take care of. Call Charlie. I'm sure he will be so relieved to know you're awake."

"What do I tell him? It's not normal to faint and be unconscious for two days....."

"Honestly, I think he will buy whatever you tell him. He's going to be so happy you're okay, I really don't think the reason will matter much. I'm sure you will think of something." He says, kissing me playfully on the tip of my nose.

"I will see you soon angel...." He says, standing and turning towards the door.

I watch every movement until he closes the door behind him and then collapse back on my bed.

It's hard to keep up with all the strange things that keep happening to me, on top of the man that consumes my mind and body. It's a lot for one girl to process.

I can't help but worry that it will always be this way. Fear and danger fueling our lives. Brought together only by stolen moments and fragments of time that are cut too short and are never quite enough.

MELISSA TOPPEN

Chapter Twenty-One

"So sleep deprivation, that's all this really was?" Charlie asks, studying me intently.

"I told you I hadn't been sleeping well. When I went to the bathroom I started feeling very faint and went out for some fresh air. I guess I passed out. I'm just lucky Tate was close by."

"Yeah... Um, about that. What's the story with you two? You've never mentioned him before and yet the way he was looking at you, how protective he was of you, it leads me to believe there is quite a history there." He says, stretching his arms above his head with a yawn.

"It's a long story. Let's just leave it at that." I nudge him from my place beside him on the bed.

"So... Look, I know it's really none of my business but I have to ask. Are you two a thing?" His cheeks blush crimson with the question. And I instantly pick up on the hint of jealousy in his voice.

"I wish I knew.... We care for each other deeply but it's hard to say if it will end up working out or not." I admit, knowing that at least part of it is the truth.

I really don't know what the future holds for me and Tate.

"Does he go to college here? Why have you not mentioned him before?" He asks and I can't help but notice the hurt in his voice.

"I'm sorry." I say, resting my hand on his forearm.

"Things with us are, well complicated. Until recently I thought it was over. I was trying to move on... He moved here recently and we ran into each other a few days ago."

"Look, I get it Cal. You don't owe me any explanations. I just want to make sure that you are really okay." He says, giving my hand a squeeze.

"I'm good. Two days of sleep is exactly what I needed. I feel better than I have in a long time." I say, giving him a reassuring smile.

"Good.... That's all that matters. You going to be up for classes tomorrow?"

"Yeah I think so. You want to meet up for lunch?"

"It's a date." He says, giving me a wink as he rises to his feet.

"Get some more rest. Call me if you need anything. And Cal..." He says, turning as he reaches the door.

"I'm really glad you're okay. I don't know what I would do if I lost you."

"I'm not going anywhere Charlie, promise." I say, feeling the tears stinging my eyes.

I fight them back with everything I have. I have to stay strong. It's so hard to lie to my best friend when the truth is I really don't know how all this will end.

What if I can't keep my promise? Where will he be then? The thought tears through me with a force that is indescribable.

He nods and then exits the room. Leaving me with a racing mind and a heavy heart.

****

When I woke up this morning I really didn't feel up to going to class. It took everything I had to drag myself out of bed and pretend like everything was normal.

Having made it through two of my three classes, I was thankful for a little time with Charlie.

We didn't talk much through lunch which is not completely out of the ordinary for us. Sometimes just being around each other is enough to bring us some sense of peace. It's when I am alone that I struggle the most.

I spotted Tate as I walked to my Angelology class just after Charlie and I had parted. He didn't look my way but I knew it was him. I could feel it in the air.

I kept walking, even though it killed me. Nothing can describe how hard it was for me to simply ignore the fact that he was just a few feet from me. Every fiber of me wanted to run to him but I knew that I couldn't.

I have spent the last thirty minutes completely oblivious to my professor's lecture. Lost in my daydream of what life would be like if Tate and I were two normal people. Free to be together in every way possible. Free to love one another and share that love with the rest of the world.

My mind suddenly becomes very foggy and for a moment I feel faint. I bump my desk with my elbow and watch as my pencil slowly rolls across the surface and falls to the floor with a shattering crash.

That's when it happens. I am no longer sitting in class. Instead, I am standing in the middle of a graveyard.

Everything around me seems frozen. There is no wind, no sound, just emptiness. I glance down at the headstone that stands before me and find myself stumbling backwards. Unable to process what my mind is seeing.

The stone reads:

Callista Marie Price

September 2, 1995 – November 24, 2013.

I blink rapidly, confusion and fear mingle together in a lethal combination. That's only a little more than a month away. I close my eyes tightly trying to will myself to reality. I know this is in my mind but I can't shake how real it feels.

A shadow flickers across the headstone causing me to look up. Standing behind my grave site is a figure cloaked in black. I can't tell if it's a man or a woman but I can feel the darkness radiate from their very presence.

"Who are you?" I call out.

"What do you want?" I ask again when I get no response.

"The soul of the pure. You were never meant to exist. The soul of the pure." The person chants out in a voice I can't pin point. Dark and raspy, like no voice I have ever heard before.

Then the white noise returns. Rendering me helpless, I collapse to my knees holding my ears.

"Stop! Please stop!" I scream.

Suddenly the air shifts and the noise dies away. Hesitantly I look up, only to find myself on my knees in the middle of my classroom.

I quickly glance around, seeing at least twenty faces staring at me in what can only be described as shock and horror.

"Miss Price, is everything okay?" Professor Greyson asks from beside me.

I don't know if I should be embarrassed or terrified. Honestly I feel a bit of both.

"All right everyone... Show's over." My professor calls out.

"Class dismissed. I will see you all Wednesday." He says as my classmates start to rise from their seats and exit the classroom.

"I'm so sorry.... I don't know what happened." I stutter out, still feeling the effects of whatever just happened to me.

"Come, let's go to my office." He says, helping me to my feet.

I hold onto his arm for support as we make our way the short distance to his office. My legs feel like jelly and are shaking uncontrollably.

When we reach his office, I collapse in one of the high back black leather chairs that sit across from his desk, thankful to be off my feet.

"You think I'm crazy, don't you?" I ask.

Everyone else probably does.

"No Callista, I don't think you are crazy. But clearly something is not right. You were in here a few days ago asking about dark magic, objects that defy god. Then you go into hysterics in the middle of my lecture. I can't chalk this all up to coincidence. So tell me.... What exactly were you looking for when you spoke to me last week?"

"I'm sorry professor but I really don't know what you're talking about." I stammer out.

"Lying to me will not help you Callista. If you want any chance at overcoming this, you have to tell me the truth. Have you come into contact with an object that has been cursed?"

"Cursed?" I question, having never really looked at it that way.

"It is not uncommon for those who exist in the dark to seek vengeance on the living. It happens everyday. People just simply choose to ignore it."

"How would I know?" I ask.

"Is there anything you have been given, anything you can think of that could have come from someone not of this world?"

Instantly my mind clicks.

"Well there's this." I say, pulling the locket out from under my collar.

"Callista, where did you get that?" He tries to hide the fear in his voice but I pick up on it instantly.

"It was given to me, for safe keeping." I say, tucking it back into my shirt.

"You must let me study that necklace." He says, standing and walking around his desk. He takes a seat in the chair next to me and leans in.

"I'm going to ask you something and it is imperative that you tell me the truth." I nod and he continues.

"When you open the locket what do you see?"

"Well, it changes. The first time I opened it there was a picture of me as a child, the other side was a picture of a little boy. Since then, when I open it, it's just a silhouette of a man and a woman. Why?" I ask, unsure of what he's getting at.

He doesn't answer my question.

"Have you had other.... incidents like today, since you first possessed the locket?" I nod and fear spreads through my belly as his eyes widen.

"Callista you must return it to whoever gave it to you. It's not of this world. The longer you wear it, the worse the episodes will get."

"I need to keep it." I say standing. "I think it's trying to tell me something." For the first time I realize that I really feel this way.

"Only darkness can come from this. Here, let me show you something." He says, making his way to the bookshelves in the corner of the office.

He reaches the end of the far right hand shelf before pulling several books down and then opening a secret cabinet in the shelf.

"This book has been passed down through my family for centuries. My dad used to tell me stories about one of my ancestors, a witch. A very dark witch. She created three magical objects said to be able to return life to the dead. I think you should look at this." He says, laying the thick, old book out across his desk and flipping a few pages in.

"This was her book."

"Look here, the locket…. Said to be the map." He flips a few more pages.

"The fire ring, said to be the key." He flips again.

"And then of course.... The Amulet of Life." He says, running his fingers across the image on the page.

Instinctively I hold up my hand. The picture on the page matches my scar perfectly.

"What does all this mean?" I ask, tucking my hand away before he catches sight of my marred skin.

"It's a triangle. One must acquire all three pieces to complete the puzzle. What happens after that, I'm really not sure. But you must believe me when I say, that necklace was not meant to be worn by a mortal soul. It will bring you only darkness. It will consume you." He says, taking a step back to stand directly next to me.

"I can keep it safe for you, away from anyone who may be looking for it. Not only that, but maybe I can help you. It was this legend that fueled my interest in the area I teach, thus leading to the very reason I am here."

"Thank you for everything professor but I can't. I told you, I am keeping it safe for someone." I say, grabbing my backpack off the floor and throwing it over my shoulder.

"I appreciate the information, really. You have no idea how much you may have helped me." I say, turning and quickly making my way to the door.

"Callista! Wait! You don't understand everything....." He calls after me but I keep walking.

I quicken my strides until I am out in the open air. I breathe deeply trying to cleanse my mind of all the things that have taken place in the last hour.

If what he says is true than that means only one thing. Someone is trying to complete the triangle.

Why, I don't know. But I can feel it in my soul and somehow I am tied right in the middle of all of it.

I don't understand my place in all of this but one thing is certain, I have to keep this information to myself. Telling Tate will only put him in more danger. At least until I have more information, something concrete to go on.

I can only hope that what I find won't be more than I can handle.

THE TRAVELER: THE AMULET OF LIFE

Chapter Twenty-Two

"Show me another... Please." I beg Tate as we sit, legs crossed, facing each other, on the leaf covered ground. It's mid afternoon and the weather could not be more perfect.

"Maybe later angel. We are, after all, in a public park." He says, running his fingers down my jaw line.

He's right of course. We are in a public place. Just a few feet off the bike trail at Sycamore Park, I found a spot in the woods that reminds me of home.

I know it's not the same, someone could stumble across us at any minute. But seeing his memories, it's like traveling through time and getting a real life glimpse into someone's life.

"Just one more." I plead.

"Besides, no one can see us through the trees and if someone gets close, you'll know." I say, pouting my lip out to seal the deal.

"Fine." He breathes, taking my hands once more in his.

"Where to my love?"

"The day you died....." I stare deep into his eyes.

"Not the actual incident, but the hospital. Take me to the hospital."

He eyes me curiously. "Cally, what's this about?"

"Don't pretend that you don't know that I was born on the very day you died. Tell me that doesn't make you the least bit curious."

"I'll admit, I am curious. But angel, I have not visited that place before. I have no idea what actually happens there. Are you sure this is a road you want to travel?"

"I have to know Tate. If your ending and my beginning are some how tied together...."

"It could change everything." He finishes my

sentence.

I nod. Truth is, I want nothing more than to prove it was just pure coincidence that I was born the day he died.

Unfortunately nothing surrounding us is that simple and I find it hard to believe that this will be either.

Tate tightens his grip on my hands and closes his eyes. I do the same. When I reopen them, I am standing in the middle of the hospital emergency room.

I can hardly register my surroundings when a young couple bursts into the emergency room, the woman very pregnant, begging for someone to help. Mom! Dad!

"Please, there's so much blood." The younger version of my dad tells the nurse that approaches him.

My mom is pale and her legs are covered in blood. Within seconds they haul my mother away in a wheel chair, my father following by her side.

"We need some help over here." I hear a woman call as two emergency workers enter through the emergency entrance on the other side of the room.

"Young male, severely beaten, there appears to be massive head trauma. He was touch and go on the ride over." She tells the nurse as the medical team rolls him down the hall.

I know immediately that it's Tate. As much as I don't want to see him, I have to be with him the second he dies. I have to know every detail of this night.

I follow the doctors every move. I watch as they frantically try to stabilize the young man laying on their table.

"His brain swelling is too severe, we have to alleviate some of the pressure." One of the doctors says to another stepping to the left to retrieve something from the table.

That's when I see him. My beautiful Tate. Only I wouldn't know it was him if I didn't already know. His face is swollen, bruised, and blood covered. My stomach lurches and I back away quickly, pressing my back firmly against the wall.

I can't see anymore of this. I can't watch his body fight for life. I slide down the wall and hug my knees to my chest.

I open my eyes to find Tate staring at me intently.

"Let's do it again, only this time, can we follow my parents?" I ask, not even sure if that's a possibility.

"I can only show you my time in that existence. You can follow them but the moment I die, the memory will end."

I nod closing my eyes. Again when I open them I am looking at the same scenery as before, only this time when my parents enter the hospital, I follow them.

I know they can't see me, I'm not actually here, but I still keep a distance. I watch as they prepare my mom for an emergency c-section. I watch my dad stand by her side, so brave and yet I can see the fear in his eyes.

When they finally pull me out, I am lifeless. The doctors scramble around me. I can't tell what they are doing.

"Why isn't she crying?" I hear my mom cry out.

As if somehow being connected to my own memory, I hear the first thud of my heart.....

"Oh god." I breathe out as I open my eyes.

They lock with Tate's immediately and I can

tell he realizes the same thing that I do.

"I was dead....." I choke out.

"You were alive and I was dead. Your heart stopped, the second mine started...." I trail off, still not able to grasp that any of this is actually real.

I stand, shaking my head as if trying to convince myself this is some sort of dream. Tate remains seated as I pace back and forth before finally looking down at him.

"Tate, what does this mean?" I ask, not trying to hide my confusion.

Slowly he stands, his expression blank, unreadable.

"I don't know." He says, meeting my eyes.

"Honestly Cally, I don't know. I mean, I have always known there was some sort of unexplainable connection between us but this..." He says throwing his hands up in defeat.

"I don't know what it all means...."

Fear tremors through me causing me to feel unsteady on my own two legs. There is so much that I don't understand, so many things that can't be explained. I am starting to feel like I don't know anything anymore.

"We should go." Tate says, breaking into my thoughts.

I nod, taking his hand as he leads me back to the bike trail.

The walk back is silent. Both of us lost in our own minds. We take the back way through the trees and behind buildings.

I can feel his uneasiness, a dead give away that this is bothering him much more than he will ever lead on to me.

By the time we reach my dorm, the tension is so thick I feel like I am suffocating. We stand at the back at the building, neither of us wanting to talk about what we just experienced and yet not wanting to say goodbye to one another either.

"Look, let's not over analyze this just yet." He says, lifting my chin with his hand until my eyes meet his.

"I know you are freaked out angel. Honestly, I am a bit myself. But it's not anything that changes us. We knew from the beginning that there was something..... different about us. This just gives us a little more insight into how deep the connection between us is."

"I think of you as the other half of my soul Tate. What if you really are?" I ask, not even knowing if it's possible to be linked to the very existence of ourselves.

"You are my soul, angel." He says, leaning down to gently brush his lips against mine.

The contact is just what I need. The surge of electricity that makes me feel alive. But it's short lived and as usual, only makes me want more.

"You know what I meant." I say, brushing off his attempt to put the subject to rest.

"Yes, I know what you meant. And I meant what I said. I love you Callista, let's not lose sight of what is really important here." He says, pulling me closing to him, our noses almost touching.

"You are all that matters to me. I don't care about the bigger picture, the master plan. As long as you are safe and happy, than I can exist peacefully." He says, bringing his lips to mine once more.

"I love you." I breathe against his mouth before wrapping my arms tightly around him and burying my face in his chest.

"I love you so much."

"And I you." He says, kissing the top of my head.

"It's getting late, you should get inside. Don't worry, I won't be far." He interjects as I start to protest.

I nod and give him one last small kiss to the cheek before turning and making my way around the front of the building. My mind is going a million miles a minute and by the time I make it to my room, I feel like I am going to overheat and shut down.

With all the weird things happening to me lately it's a wonder I have not officially lost it yet. It's difficult enough to try to understand a world I never knew existed, but then throw in all the other strange things that seem to surround me and Tate and it's near impossible to even believe.

In fact, sometimes I even convince myself that this really is all just happening in my head. How else do you explain.... well, everything?

I know Tate is right. I shouldn't over think this. It doesn't change one thing between us. If anything, it only convinces me more that we are meant to be together.

Two souls bound as one. He is my heaven,

my hell, on this world or any other.

There are a million unanswered questions and no doubt there will be a million more along the way. But what does any of it mean, what's it all for if I don't enjoy it?

I want to live, I want to love. I want to stop worrying that every second something is going to rip Tate away from me again.

For once, just once, I want to be able to focus on us. Without the worry of our pasts or our futures. A moment where nothing else matters but the present.

Will that moment ever exist?

MELISSA TOPPEN

Chapter Twenty-Three

"Hello." I choke out in my sleepy haze.

It's not like anyone to call me this early in the morning and honestly if I wasn't curious as to why someone would be, I would have ignored it.

"Cally, it's grandpa." The moment his voice comes across the line I know something is not right.

"I think you should come home."

"What? Why? Grandpa what's going on?" I ask, sitting up in my bed, nervousness eating through me like a cancer.

"It's grandma. Honey, she's very ill. I..... I think." He sobs out, not able to finish his sentence.

"What happened?" I ask, completely blindsided by this.

I just spoke to her not five days ago and she seemed fine, happy.

"It's been going on for a while now. She's been having episodes. It's hard to explain. Over the last week she has gone down hill tremendously. She's so weak."

"I'm on my way." I blurt out without hesitation.

"Be careful honey, and hurry." He says, before I hear the line go dead.

My heart feels like it will beat out of my chest at any moment. How is this happening right now?

I throw on a pair of jeans and a sweater, and stuff a couple additional outfits in a duffel bag. I don't bother with anything else. All that matters right now is that I get to my grandma.... before it's too late.

I tape a note to Charlie's door explaining that I had to return home and that I would contact him as soon as I could. I emailed my professor's explaining the situation. Hopefully I won't miss too much but honestly I can't bring myself to care too much right now. All that matters is my family.

I have no clue where Tate is or how to let him know what is going on. I try not to worry too much about it and quickly ramble off my grandparent's address as I climb into the back of my cab.

It's nearly a two hour drive and while I am sure the ride will cost more than I can spare, money is the least of my worries right now.

The cab driver is an older heavy set man with gray hair. He eyes me in the rear view mirror a couple times before turning his attention to the road.

The cab is clean but has an overwhelming smell of dog that has me half sick within minutes.

I open the window and breathe in the fresh air blowing around my face. Leaning back I close my eyes. Silently praying for my grandma, my grandpa, for myself.

I have never been much on praying but at this point, I am willing to try anything.

I open my eyes to find a cloaked figure sitting next to me. I try to scream but nothing comes out. I push myself firmly against the door of the cab, putting a few more inches between myself and the unknown person next to me.

"Everything comes with a price. You really should have listened to me Callista." A voice that I recognize immediately speaks.

"Professor?" I try to say but again, nothing comes out.

"Wake up. Miss…. We're here." My eyes shoot open and are met by a very impatient cab driver.

I glance beside me, only to find that I am alone in the backseat.

"I'm sorry. I must have fallen asleep." I say, handing the driver my money and making my way out of the cab.

I retrieve my bag from the floorboard before shutting the door. The cab driver nods to me and then drives away. Leaving me standing in front of my grandparent's farm house.

As much as I want to see them, I can't make myself move. I don't know if it's how quickly everything has taken place this morning, or if I am still shaken from the dream, but a cloud of disorientation has my mind foggy and my body reluctant to move.

"You can do this." I hear Tate's voice say.

I turn expecting to see him standing behind me, only he's not there. I take a deep breath and try to regain some sense of what is real. I can do this. I have to do this.

I throw my duffel bag over my shoulder and make my way to the front door. I hesitate only a second, before pulling it open, the familiar creek of the hinges announcing my arrival. Before I even have both feet inside, my grandpa rounds the corner.

"Thank god you're here." He says, wrapping me in his arms. "She's been asking for you."

"She's here?" I ask, pushing myself out of his embrace.

"Grandpa, if she's that sick why isn't she at the hospital?"

"She was. The doctors released her. They said all her test results are normal and that it is probably just some type of virus. It's so strange. Everything says she's okay, only she's not. I have loved this woman my entire life. I know when something is not right.... Come, she's upstairs." He says and I follow him immediately.

My grandpa has never been one to over

play things. If the doctors say it's a virus, he would trust them on their diagnosis and that would be that. Only that's not the case at all, and that alone leaves me with a fear that I can not shake.

He stops just outside the door and turns to face me.

"She's not herself, I must warn you. She's been having these spells where she thinks she's somewhere else. I can't explain it but I want you to be prepared." He says, opening the door.

When we enter my grandparent's room, it takes a moment for my eyes to adjust. The curtains are drawn and all the lights are out.

"Callista... I need to see Callista." I hear my grandma's broken voice say.

"Grandma, I'm here." I say, rushing to her side.

I sit on the edge of her bed and wrap her fragile hand in mine.

"I'm right here." I reassure her.

Her eyes are closed and she doesn't acknowledge my presence.

"I will give you two sometime alone." I hear my grandpa say as he backs out of the room, closing the door behind him.

Adjusting to the darkness of the room, I glance down at my grandma. Her face is hollow, pale. She looks like she has lost at least twenty pounds since the last time I saw her. Which is a lot given her petite figure.

She's laying on her back, three pillows propped under her head. Her body covered by a large thick comforter.

"Grandma?" I say quietly.

I see her eyes flutter open, followed by a look of shock that I don't understand.

"Callista, you're here." She breathes, her voice weak.

"I'm here grandma." I say again, rubbing my thumb over the back of her hand. I feel cold metal brush against the tip of my finger, followed my a slow building burn. Glancing down, I see it. The ring, the key.

"Where did you get this ring?" I blurt out, not trying to disguise my confusion.

"I found it. In the woods." She says. Each word is broken and breathless.

"Grandma... When did you find it?" I ask,

urgency lacing my voice.

"You were in therapy. I don't know. Why does it matter?" She asks, closing her eyes again. "I'm so tired."

"I know you're tired grandma, but I need you to tell me something... Have you been wearing this ring since then?" She nods, not opening her eyes.

I don't know how or why but deep down I know that the ring is somehow tied into my grandma's unexplainable illness. Without really thinking, I lift my grandma's hand and grip the ring between my thumb and index finger. Just as I start to slide it off her hand, her eyes shoot open.

"The soul of the pure." She says, her breathing labored, her voice unrecognizable.

"What did you say?" I ask, dropping her hand in surprise.

"I saw it. They need you. You are the final piece..... He told me..."

"Grandma... What are you talking about? Who told you?"

"Cally." She says, turning her head to face me.

"You're not safe. I needed to see you to tell you........" She breaks off, not able to finish her sentence.

"Tell me what grandma?" I urge her to continue, feeling my self control slipping with every passing second.

I am on the verge of panic, I can feel it rising in me like a tidal wave.

"You were never meant to exist." She whispers out, closing her eyes again.

I sit in silence. I have so many questions, so much I need to know, and yet the words won't come.

Suddenly it all becomes crystal clear. The ring. That must be it. It's clouding her mind, affecting her in some way.

Without hesitation, I pick up her hand again, and this time successfully remove the ring from her middle finger. Immediately, she eases, like a weight has been lifted.

Her sleeping body instantly giving off a sense of peace, her face relaxing, her breathing light and even.

I slip the ring onto my right hand and make

my way over to the window. It feels like just yesterday that I left this place, and yet so very much has happened.

I pull back the curtain just enough to peek outside. The land is just as beautiful as I remember it. Closing the curtain, I sit in the arm chair next to my grandparent's bed.

Watching my grandma, her sleeping body rising and falling with each breath. It reminds me of how much I stand to lose in this life. A life where I have lost so much already.

I don't know for sure if the ring plays any part in her illness. What I do know, is that it has exposed her to the dangers of knowing too much outside of our existence.

Then there's what she said. About how I was never meant to exist. The soul of the pure. What does that even mean?

I've heard it before, only now, hearing it from my grandma, it holds more value somehow. I have tried so hard to handle this on my own but now, I know the time has come. I have to tell Tate everything.

It may be the only chance I have to help my grandma, and to save myself.

****

"Angel." I hear his voice pull me from my sleepy haze.

My eyes flutter open, finding Tate hovering over me. The sight of him alone is enough to restore my faith in the fight that lies ahead.

"Grandma." I choke out, my voice is raspy, my throat raw.

"She's sleeping." Tate answers, crouching down to face me.

His expression tells me everything I need to know without saying a word.

"She's not going to make it, is she?" I ask. A knot forming hard and fast in my throat.

He shakes his head and in seconds the tears are flowing hard and fast.

"What's wrong with her?" I manage to get out through my sobs.

"It's her time." He says, his emotion thick in his voice.

"How long?" I ask, straightening my position in the chair.

He stands, turning to hover over her sleeping body.

"Not long..... I'm so sorry angel." He breathes, taking my hand as I stand next to him. He gives it a little squeeze and then turns to face me.

"How did this happen.... it's so sudden?" I search his face for any give away that he has the answers I am looking for.

"It's hard to say, but Cally......" He says, searching my eyes before continuing. "She's been cursed."

"What?" I choke out, taking a step backwards.

"Where's the ring?" He asks, his tone taking a serious turn.

I hold up my hand, the fire that runs through the ring shining through the darkness of the room.

"She found it, in the woods. I must have lost it there at some point. Oh god, this is my fault." I stumble out, realizing for the first time what my professor said about the pieces being cursed in dark magic.

"I did this to her...."

"Cally look at me." He says, pulling me to face him.

"This is not your fault."

"Yes it is!" I bark out, pushing him away from me.

Every emotion is seething through me. The most potent... Hatred. In this moment, I hate myself and the foolish decisions that I have made since meeting Tate.

"Had I not left, had I not went looking for you..... I never would have been given the ring, she never would have found it. I don't even remember losing it. I don't remember having it past the night I found the amulet. How did it get here?" I eye him intensely, my pain clouding all reason.

"You must have still possessed the ring when I brought you back here. I'm so sorry Cally. I wasn't thinking. I took the locket, I didn't see the ring. Somehow it must have fallen in the woods.... I don't know..." He trails off, losing himself in his mind.

My legs give out, no longer able to support my weight. I crash to my knees next to my grandma's bedside.

"Help her...." I choke out, looking up to meet his eyes.

"Tate, you can help her!" I plead.

"No angel, I can't. I don't possess the power to cure the dying, not when it's meant to be...." He says. His pain etched so clearly across his beautiful face.

"How can this be meant to be?" I bite out harshly, reaching out to hold my grandma's hand in my own.

"Everyone has an end. A moment in time that is meant to be their last. I can't interfere with god's plan." He says, stepping towards me.

"This would have happened with or without her finding the ring Cally. While it may be a contributing factor. It doesn't change her fate."

"Don't." I say, holding my hand up to stop him from coming any closer.

"I should have been here. I should have helped her. Instead...." I glance from my grandma to Tate. "She's going to die...." I break off, no longer able to speak through my sobs.

"Callista." My grandma's voice rings out clear, pulling my attention to her.

"I'm here grandma." I say, squeezing her hand.

I look to Tate, only he's not there. I should have known from the shift in the air that he had left but my emotions are blocking out my senses, my ability to connect to him.

"My dear Callista." My grandma whispers out, her breathing labored.

"My brave, brave girl. I need you to promise me something....."

"Anything." I answer without hesitation. Pulling myself up to sit next to her on the bed.

"Promise me that no matter what happens, you will fight. Fight for what you want. Live, love, be free..." She coughs loudly. I can tell she's fighting for every breath.

"I will grandma... I promise." I say, tears flowing freely down my cheeks.

Just then, the door opens and my grandpa walks in carrying a tray of food. He catches sight of me, of my grandma. The tray slips from his hands and collides with the floor, the dishes shattering on impact. I step to the side and let him take my place next to her side.

"She doesn't have long." I say behind him, turning to leave.

Before I exit the room, I chance one last look at my grandma. My grandpa hovering over her. The sight is unbearable. His heart is literally breaking in front of me and it is more pain than I can bare.

I take off running, down the stairs, out the back door. Before I know it, I am where the fields meet the woods, but I don't stop.

I run until my legs can go no further, until my lungs are protesting. Not really paying attention to my surroundings, I trip on a branch that had fallen from one of the trees, and fall to the earth. My hands break my fall before I finally come to a rest on my side.

I curl into a ball and let go of all the emotion I have been trying so hard to hold in for the last twenty four hours. I feel like my heart is breaking apart into a million pieces and being scattered among the leaves that lay below me.

I hear the crunching of foot steps but I make

no attempt to move. I don't care who it is. I don't care if they have come to hurt me…. Let them.

Right now I wish for pain. At least the physical pain would be a distraction from the emotional pain that is ripping through me like knives.

"Cally…." I hear Tate call out hesitantly. I feel the ground shift as he sits next to me.

"I'm so sorry." He says, his voice laced with concern, pity.

"I know how hard this is." He continues, trying his best to comfort me, only he doesn't comfort me.

No one can. I am lost, alone in a hell that I created. That I caused.

"I just need to be alone." I sob out, turning my face into the leaves.

"I understand." He says, rising to his feet.
"But when you need me, I'll be here." He says.

I listen to each footstep grow fainter as he walks away. Once they have faded out of hearing distance, I relax in the comfort of knowing that I am alone.

****

My head is foggy and my eyes are heavy but I manage to get them open. It takes me a moment to realize that I am still laying on the ground, somewhere in the woods behind my grandparent's house.

The events of earlier in the day come flooding back like a tidal wave leaving me feeling winded and honestly, a bit sick.

I sit up, wiping the leaves from my hair. I don't know how long I have been out here. My grandpa is probably worried sick. Oh god, grandpa.

I was so lost in my own pain, I left him there, alone. What if she's gone? What if he is there grieving with no one to help him?

I stumble to my feet, realizing how weak my limbs feel as I do. I slowly make my way through the woods, looking for my usual signs that I am headed in the right direction. A broken tree to my left tells me I need to go right. Finally I can see the clearing ahead.

I quicken my strides and then come to an immediate halt as someone steps into my line of sight. Blocking my path to the field ahead.

"What now?" I scream out. My frustration taking over.

In this moment, I don't care who this is or what they want. All I want is to get to my grandpa.

"Things are not always as they seem child. Look within yourself. You have the strength. Now fight Callista.....Fight." My grandma's voice sings through the air.

I blink, trying to register what is happening, only to reopen my eyes and find myself alone. It only takes a matter of seconds for me to realize that she is gone.

Not as in gone from the spot she just inhabited, though I am sure that was only in my mind. But gone from this world. Adrenaline courses through me as I take off in a sprint.

Running as fast and hard as my body can allow, until I reach the back porch. I rip open the door and run inside, stopping at the sight of my grandpa sitting at the kitchen table. His head buried in his hands.

"She's gone." He sobs out, shaking. "Oh

god, she's gone." He says again as if trying to convince himself this isn't just some bad dream.

Instantly I am at his side. I wrap my arms around his wide shoulders and rest my chin on the top of his head. My tears are flowing fast but I do my best to keep myself calm. He needs me to be strong for him.

"I know." I whisper, holding him tighter.

After my family died, my heart was shattered. My grandma gave me enough thread to hold it together, but only just enough. Now I can feel the strings unraveling. I can feel the pain, the loss, all over again. Taking me under into the darkness of myself.

She told me to fight. But what am I fighting for?

An existence that has done nothing but bring me pain and sorrow. One, that the very moment I think I find happiness, everything is ripped away from me. I don't want to fight for that life. I don't want that life.

Just as I let the pain in, let the darkness consume me. I feel the warmth and love that only exists in the presence of Tate.

I release my grandpa, turning towards the

doorway of the kitchen. He's there. His head down, leaning into door frame.

I turn away from him and sit next to my grandpa at the table. It's then that he finally looks up at me. His face is tear stained and he looks ten years older in the matter of hours.

I reach out, taking his hand in mine. He manages a small smile before releasing my hand and rising to his feet, making his way from the kitchen.

Tate is behind me in the matter of seconds. I stand, turning to face him and then collapse in his arms. He makes no attempt to comfort me with words, instead he just holds me.

I can feel his sadness radiate from him, as clear as the sun shining in the sky. It is in this moment that I remember, that my pain is his pain, as his is mine. I cling to him tightly, trying to remind myself what all this is for.

MELISSA TOPPEN

Chapter Twenty-Four

TATE

I watch Cally as they lower her grandma into the ground. Watch as the last remaining spark in her dies right in front of my eyes. I know she blames herself for this. A guilt that I fear she is not strong enough to carry.

While she chooses to blame herself, I know that deep down I am to blame for all the things that have gone wrong in her life over the last year.

I knew better than to enter her world. I have brought her nothing but pain, fear, and danger. She deserves so much more than I have the ability to give her.

But walking away from her now is not an option. Not only for my own selfish reasons but because I know it would break her, just as it would me.

I still have not managed to figure out what is going on with her. Something is haunting her. Eating her. I can feel her slipping away from me more and more everyday.

I fear it has something to do with the objects she possesses but she won't tell me anything. I can feel the wall she has put up between our connection.

To make matters worse, I know that something is boiling below the surface. Something or someone is waiting for their chance. I just don't know what they plan to do once they take it.

I have pieced together enough information to know that someone is looking for the locket and ring. I just haven't figured out why.

"Someone has a bad habit of trusting you on your word Harper. And by someone I mean me." I hear Braize before I see him.

He steps next to me and cocks his head to one side. "Did you honestly think I wouldn't find out? That I would just walk away and you two would go on to live happily ever after?"

"I don't know what you're looking at, but do

you see any happy endings in the near future?" I nod my head in the direction of Cally.

"Yes, unfortunate..." He says, stepping directly in front of me. His black eyes locked hard on mine.

"Where is the key and map Tate?" He snaps at me.

"What makes you think I would tell you anything?" I spit back. Unable to contain the anger boiling through me at his timing.

"Because I am the only thing saving her....." He trails off with a smirk.

"What is that supposed to mean? You have done nothing but try to rip us apart. Hell, you nearly let her die!" I bite out, my temper threatening to explode.

"I would have never let her die and you know it. I just like to see you squirm." He throws his head back with a laugh.

Before I know it I have him pinned against the tree I was just leaning on. My hand wrapped firmly around his throat.

"I am done with your games Braize. Tell me what the hell you want." I say, dropping my hold on him.

He rubs his neck and ponders for a moment.

"Such violence." He laughs again.

"You have the amulet. That's what you were after all along. It had nothing to do with me, with Cally. You don't care that we're together. You pushed us apart.... Played us on our emotions. All you wanted was the amulet. That's right, I've done a little digging of my own." I say by the look of surprise that crosses his pale face.

"I know that a living soul must retrieve the amulet from the fire. I saw you take it that night. Clearly that's what you were after. So now what? What is your plan Braize?" I round on him.

"Well, I've got to hand it to you Harper, you don't miss a thing..... I need your help." He says, catching me off guard.

I take a couple steps back and stare at him in utter confusion.

"What makes you think I would help you?"

"Because if you don't, she will face a fate much worse than death. Tell me, what has it been like for you to sit back and watch the curse course through her. You gave her the locket, surely you must know. You want the same thing I do, we both know it. Now give me what I need." He says, his face unreadable.

"And if I don't?"

"Then sit back and watch everything you love be destroyed.... You're right, I used your love against you. It was the only way I could retrieve the locket. I originally thought you would be foolish enough to try to possess it for yourself. Imagine my surprise when Cally shows up, more than willing to sacrifice herself for you. Played right into my hands. What I didn't anticipate however, was that possessing the locket wasn't enough....."

"And what of Nicholas, is he working for you?"

"He helped point you both in the right direction, repaid a debt." He says, shrugging his shoulders and turning to face the direction of where Cally and her grandpa stand.

Everyone has left, the workers are now busy covering the casket with dirt. Cally is hunched over in her grandfather's arms. I shake my head and turn my attention back to Braize.

"If you want my help, you have to tell me

everything. How is Cally involved in all of this?"

"Get me the ring and locket and I will tell you everything you want to know. For now, know this. If the amulet, map, and key end up in the wrong hands, nothing will save her. Get me what I need." He says before disappearing.

Leaving me to decide whether I trust him or not. Either way I risk putting Cally in more danger, danger that even I may not be able to protect her from.

****

Saying goodbye to my grandma was one of the hardest things I have ever done. Watching my grandpa say goodbye was even harder. As much as I want to blame myself for this, I know Tate would never lie to me.

She got sick, people get sick and die everyday. Her body was not strong enough to fight off her illness. What effects the ring had on her, if any, I may never know. But blaming myself won't bring her back, that much I have accepted.

I have dreamed about her every night since

she died. For a week now, it's always the same dream.

I am standing at the creek, she appears and leads me through the woods. She doesn't speak and with each dream we travel further and further.

I don't know what they mean, if anything. But each time I wake up with the overwhelming feeling that I am missing something.

Now as I sit here, at the creek bed, a place I once found peace, all I feel is numbness. I am scheduled to return to school on Monday. I can't imagine leaving my grandpa in just two days time but I know that I have to go back. It's what my grandma would have wanted.

I refuse to let myself become the inverted lonely girl I once was. The girl that existed after my family died. As much as I tell myself I have to be strong, it doesn't make the action of actually doing so any easier.

I have lost so much and yet I can't help but feel a bit of comfort knowing that there is life for them all beyond this one. A place where death and sadness are but an afterthought.

I feel him before I see him. "I wondered if

you were going to ever show yourself." I say aloud.

"As if I could ever stay away." He says, sitting next to me.

I turn to stare at his beautiful face. No matter what happens or how much time passes, he still takes my breath away.

"What took you so long?" I ask, unsure of why it has taken him nearly a week.

"I'm sorry angel. I had some things to take care of. How are you feeling?" He asks.

A desperate attempt to keep our conversation light.

"I'm okay.... I think." I admit.

Knowing that my grandma is okay somewhere out there still doesn't erase the pain of her absence here.

"Come with me." He says, standing. Taking my hands, he pulls me to my feet.

"Where are we going?" I ask, more than a little curious.

"We have a lot to talk about angel. But right now, I just want to remember what it's like to be with you. To love you. Can you give me that?" He asks, his bright eyes burning fiercely into mine.

I nod not able to form words at the affect he has over me. He wraps his arms around me tightly.

"Hold on angel." He says and without warning, I feel us spiraling.

The feeling of being pulled in every direction, like my body is being ripped apart, takes over me and then within seconds is gone.

I open my eyes to find us standing on a mountain top. The same mountain we visited once before, back when things were, well, less complicated.

I had forgotten how beautiful it was here. The countryside laid out before us. Beautiful land and sky for as far as the eye can see.

"I want you to remember. Remember the love we share. The connection. The moments that make everything else worth it. Tell me I haven't lost you." He says, holding me tightly.

I pull back a few inches to stare up at his face.

"You haven't lost me." I say, tears forming

in my eyes.

"I love you." He whispers and then takes my mouth with his.

The passion and love that surge through us is overwhelming and leaves my mind fogged and blinded to anything except his touch.

The electricity, the fire that burns through my very soul.

A place where body, mind, and soul all blur together into one perfect combination that leaves me basking in light. His touch is my heaven, his heart my soul.

No matter what comes our way, it's moments like these that reassure me, it really is all worth it.....

****

"Miss Price! Miss Price!" I hear a voice call to me as I make my way out of the cafeteria.

I turn to find Professor Greyson jogging towards me. I stop and wait for him to catch up.

Once he reaches me, I start walking again as

he slows to a walk next to me.

"Callista, it is imperative that I speak with you." He says between pants.

"You haven't been to my class in two weeks."

"I know professor, I'm sorry. My grandma passed away recently." I say, trying to ignore the pain that is suddenly pounding through my heart.

"I know, I'm so sorry to hear that. I know how difficult these things can be. I lost my wife a few years ago. Cancer." He says, not breaking his stride.

"Anyways, I really need to speak to you privately. Do you have a minute?"

"I'm sorry professor, I'm very busy." I lie. Truth is as curious as I am about what he wants, I am also fearful to learn anymore about the amulet.

"Please Callista, I promise, five minutes." He insists.

I nod and follow him as he veers right towards the building that houses his office.

Within minutes we step inside the dark office. He side steps past me to flip on the lights and makes his away around to his desk.

"Please have a seat." He gestures towards the chairs on the other side of his desk.

Hesitantly I step forward and sit down. The butterflies in my stomach taking off in full flying effect.

"Professor, what's this all about?" I eye him curiously as he digs through one of his desk drawers.

"This." He says, placing a few photocopies in front of me. I reach out and retrieve them.

"After we last spoke I did a little more digging. Call me crazy, but I felt like this is information that may help you in some way."

I skim the first page. Realizing very quickly that this was copied directly from the book he showed me during my last visit to his office.

It's not until I reach the second page that time seems to slow down. There, in front of me, in black and white is the answer to the one question I feared to ask.

"The amulet was created hundreds of years ago but the proper magic was never performed to give the amulet it's true power." Professor

Greyson pipes in as I read the same information in front of me.

"So even if the amulet exists, according to this, it is no more than a dark object. Cursed no doubt, but of no other real magical value to the supernatural world."

"What if the spell was completed later, by someone else. How would anyone know?" I ask, knowing that the amulet does in fact hold the power to take life from the living, having experienced it myself.

"Well I guess that's possible. But I wouldn't have any information to that affect." He says, taking off his glasses and rubbing his eyes.

"Does it say what the spell would consist of?" I ask, skimming another page.

"As a matter of fact, it does." He says, replacing his glasses on his face.

He stands and walks around his desk, taking a seat next to me. "Look here." He says, taking the pages from my hands and flipping through them.

"Here." He says, handing me a single page. "According to this, in order for the spell to be completed, there has to be three objects. The locket, the ring, and the amulet itself. Each one infused by the power of a soul. The amulet, the soul of a witch. The ring, the soul of one who was never meant to die. The locket, the soul of the pure."

"The soul of the pure?" I ask, not able to control the spike in my voice.

"A soul that was never meant to exist in this world." He says, eying me curiously.

"So in order for the triangle to be completed...." I trail off.

"A witch would need to sacrifice her soul for the amulet. Take a life from the living, and give life to someone not meant to live." He breaks in, finishing my thought.

"So then what happens if someone actually uses the amulet?" I ask.

"Well according to the information I have, it possesses the power to return life to the non-living. Only in doing so, it gives the soul the power to be mortal while still possessing the power of the immortal. A lethal combination. If in the wrong hands, it literally could mean hell on earth." He says, handing me back the rest of the papers.

"Can it be destroyed?"

"I would think so, yes. Only from what I gather, it would require the wrong that was done to be undone. Therefore taking the life of the soul that was never meant to exist. That's where it seems to draw it's power from."

"The soul of the pure." I say aloud, more to myself than to him.

"Yes."

"Thank you for this professor. You have no idea how much you may have just helped me." I say, tucking the pages in my backpack before throwing it over my shoulder.

"What do you think would happen to the soul that was never meant to exist? Would they simply disappear?" I ask.

"Every soul has a place. I think that soul would simply go to it's original destination." He says. I nod and make my way out the door.

By the time I step out of the building, every part of my body is shuddering. I shake my hands in front of myself trying to calm their quiver.

It all makes sense. My visions or dreams, whatever you want to call them. The very words that came from my grandmother.

I was never meant to exist, I am the soul of the pure. Tate was never meant to die.....

Suddenly I feel faint. The realization that my entire life was never meant to happen is disorienting.

Not only am I part of all of this but I am the key. I am what powers the amulet. That's why the first time I opened the locket it contained pictures of me and Tate. That's why Myra showed me Tate's grave. She was trying to tell me.

I don't want to think about what will happen should the wrong person choose to use the amulet. But what's worse, what will happen to me if the amulet is destroyed? Stumbling forward, I have only one thought, I have to find Tate.

I feel the earth below me shift. I grab a nearby tree to try to steady myself.

"Cally! Cally!" I hear Charlie call just as everything goes black.

****

"Cally, can you hear me?" I open my eyes to find Charlie hovering over me. Bright lights above make it difficult for me to focus.

"Charlie, where am I?" I croak out, not recognizing my own voice.

"You're in the hospital."

"What!" I shoot up, taking in my surroundings.

I am in a little room, white and sterile. Just as I'm about to ask what the hell I'm doing here, a nurse pulls back the curtain that separates my room from the hall. She steps in, closing the curtain behind her.

"You're awake." She says, giving me a friendly smile. She looks so familiar and yet I can't seem to pinpoint where I have seen her before.

She's thin, dark skinned, and has black hair that hangs to her waist, dressed in pale blue scrubs.

"What am I doing here?" I ask the nurse as she hands me a pill and a small glass of water.

"Motrin, it will help with the headache." She says, urging me to take the medication. I toss it in my mouth and drain the glass of water.

"Good girl." She says, taking my empty cup and throwing it in the trash.

"Well, you're lucky your friend brought you in when he did. The doctor will be in shortly to see you." She says, giving me a nod and exiting through the curtain.

"Charlie, what's going on?" I ask, turning to see his handsome face staring back at me.

"I don't know Cal. You were walking out of Dickson Hall. I ran over to catch up with you, when I reached you, you just fainted. Scared the hell out of me. So I brought you here." He says, apologetic.

"Miss Price." A man says, entering through the curtain wearing green scrubs and a white lab jacket.

"I'm Dr. Sanders." He says, reaching out and shaking my hand.

"So what's the diagnosis doc?" Charlie asks, shifting his position in the chair next to me to face the doctor.

The doctor looks from Charlie to me. "It's okay." I answer, giving him permission to speak in front of Charlie.

He pulls over a machine with a small screen on the front. He clicks a button and an image populates the screen.

"This is an image of a normal brain." He says, pointing at the image.

"This is your brain." He says, flipping to the next picture. "You see the dark shaded areas, here, and here?" He says, circling the areas with his fingers.

I nod not really sure what I am looking at.

"These are areas where brain damage has occurred."

"Brain damage?" I gawk at him, not understanding what he is talking about.

"Have you been experiencing any blackouts?" He asks.

"Yes." Charlie answers before I have a chance to.

"A couple of weeks ago she fainted and was unconscious for two days."

"What's wrong with me?" I ask, completely taken aback by this information.

"I'm not positive on what's causing it yet. If

you look closely right here." He says, pointing to another area.

"There's a small tumor. We are going to need to run some additional tests. We will need to admit you. Until we can pinpoint what's going on, we can't be too careful." He says, standing.

"A nurse will be in shortly to move you to your room. In the mean time if you need anything just hit the nurse's button on the remote next to your bed." With that he pulls the curtain closed.

Tears are instantly streaming down my face.

"Cal, don't cry." Charlie says, sitting on the edge of my bed and wrapping his large arm around my shoulders.

"You're going to be fine, you'll see."

"You're right." I say, taking a deep breath.

I need to keep calm in front of Charlie. I can't let him know that I know differently. I'm not going to be okay. How can I be when I was never even supposed to be here?

"Can you do me a favor?"

"You name it." He says, standing.

"Can you notify my professors and see if

they can give you my assignments? It will give me something to do if I am going to be holed up here for a few days." I say, giving him a small smile.

"No problem. But I don't want to leave until they have you settled in your room." I nod and scoot over in the bed to allow him more room to sit with me. He climbs in and I roll to my side, snuggling into him.

"You are my best friend, you know that?" I say. He kisses my forehead but doesn't respond.

"I just want you to know how much your friendship means to me. And how much I love you."

"Now don't you do that."

"Do what?" I ask.

"Don't start talking like you are going to die or something. Seriously Cal, you're going to be fine." He says, pulling me closer.

"I know. I know. I just wanted to say it aloud." I say, trying to fight back the tears that are threatening to spill over.

"I love you too Callista, more than you will ever know." He says, resting his cheek on the top of my head.

The curtain opens again and a little blonde nurse in pink scrubs walks in.

"Miss Price. I'm here to take you to your room." She says, pulling in a wheel chair behind her.

Charlie helps me out of bed and lowers me into the chair. I hadn't noticed until now how weak I feel.

She rolls me down one long hall and then another before we finally reach the elevator. Once inside, she punches the button that reads fourth floor.

Charlie squeezes my shoulder as if trying to reassure me that everything is fine. When the elevator slows to a stop, the doors slide open revealing another hall identical to the one on the first floor. She turns left and wheels me to a room at the end of the hall.

Once inside, she leaves me to get settled. Charlie helps me into bed and shows me how to work the remote to the television.

My room is small. There is a stand with two drawers next to my bed and a television mounted from the wall. Add on a bathroom and that is all that makes up the tiny space.

"You sure you will be okay if I leave?" Charlie asks, hovering at the end of my bed.

"Yes, I'm good." I say, giving him a reassuring smile.

"Okay, I will be back in a couple of hours. No way I am leaving you here by yourself." He says as I start to protest.

He walks over to my side and gives me a soft kiss to my forehead.

"Love you Cal." He says, turning to exit the room.

"Love you too." I call as he walks out the door.

Now alone, the sheer volume of what is happening to me starts to sink in. I know from the way the doctor was talking that he's concerned. Of course, they are trained to give you a positive spin on anything but I know better.

Then given what I learned earlier today. I hold up my hand expecting to see the ring around my finger, only it's not there. I grab my neck realizing the locket is gone too.

Just as my panic starts to rise, the dark haired nurse from earlier walks in.

"Looking for this?" She asks, holding up a small plastic bag that contains both pieces of jewelry.

"Thank god." I breathe out a sigh of relief.

"God has nothing to do with it." She laughs out, stepping closer to me.

That laugh, the familiarity of her face, doesn't sit right with me. I glance to her name tag.

Emily.

"Emily." I breathe out, fear mixing with disbelief.

Then I see it. The red ring the flares like fire around her irises.

"But how… Why?" I stutter out as everything starts to grow foggy.

"What did you give me?"

"Shhh child, rest now." She says, stepping towards me as my eyelids flutter closed.

THE TRAVELER: THE AMULET OF LIFE

Chapter Twenty-Five

I can hear humming. Not a friendly fun tune but something dark. I struggle to open my eyes but can only get them open just enough to catch a glimpse of my surroundings.

It's dark but light flickers from the fire dancing across the stone walls.

It doesn't take me long to realize that I am chained to a wall. My wrists are bound level with my head. My feet chained to the floor.

I straighten my neck and turn it side to side trying to work out the kink in it. I've been here before. The night I found the amulet. A room, or rather a dungeon. Walls made of stone.

I catch sight of Emily almost immediately. She's standing in front of a fire in the middle of the room. Much like the one that I retrieved the amulet from. Her back to me.

"I was wondering if you were ever going to wake." She rasps out, her tone light.

"What am I doing here?" I croak out. My throat so dry it feels like sandpaper.

"Didn't you know my dear?" She says, turning to face me. Her expression screaming that she is pleased with herself.

She pulls a chain from around her neck and within seconds, I realize it's the locket. She holds it just above the fire and releases her grasp on it. It floats just above the flames in mid-air. She pulls the ring from her finger and repeats the process.

"What do you want from me?" I ask, the quiver in my voice giving away my fear.

She lets out a howling laugh and takes a couple steps towards me.

"You are helping me restore order to this retched world." She says, licking her lips and then smiling widely.

"I have been waiting centuries for this. And now, it's almost complete."

"Why are you doing this?"

"Why have you fought so hard to be with the one you love? What, you think you're the only person that has ever fallen in love with someone they can't have?" She bites at me, catching the surprised look on my face.

"I don't understand." I stammer out. She grins, turning to face the fire. She circles to the other side, now facing me again.

"It's been many lifetimes, but once, I was a girl, much like yourself. I fell in love with someone not of this world. He made so many promises. Promises he never intended to keep. I was foolish, desperate. I sacrificed everything to be with him... Everything." She says, meeting my eyes.

"He said we couldn't be together because of what he was. So I took matters into my own hands.... I took my own life to live in his existence..... You want to know what happened next?"

I nod, already piecing together the story.

"I became trapped. Trapped in the darkness. We couldn't be together because I was mortal. Then, when I took care of that problem, we couldn't be together because he lived in the light, while I lived in the dark. It didn't take me long to figure out that he never meant for us to be together. I was simply a conquest. A pitiful mortal girl that played right into his skilled hands. But who's pitiful now?" She says, letting out a light laugh.

"What does this have to do with me?"

"This has everything to do with you. Demons are weak, weaker than Travelers anyway. While in this form I can't harm him. The light will always out muscle the dark. But once I am in the light again, reborn into the mortal world with all my powers in tact. I will show him how it feels to lose everything...."

She slowly makes her way around the fire. Running her hand along the top of the flames as she does. She takes a few steps forward, now standing just a foot in front of me. The ring around her irises standing out in the dark room.

"You my dear, are the key to my redemption. Unfortunate really, you have so much fight in you, so much spirit. For someone that was never meant to exist, you fit in quite nicely in this world. I watched you for years, waiting for my chance. Imagine my delight when you two found each other. The life and the death. I knew it would happen eventually. But the timing couldn't have been more perfect. I no longer needed to figure out a way to get you to the amulet, I simply needed to point you in the right direction, set the stage and watch you fight for eternal love. It's all come together quite nicely really." She says, stepping forward and running her index finger down my jawline, sending chills to my toes.

"Such a pretty thing. I wonder... how much will he love you when the darkness consumes you? You will no doubt be tossed aside, abandoned."

"Tate would never abandon me. He loves me." I bite back, anger flaring in my belly.

"Stupid girl." She spats, grabbing my chin and squeezing tightly. She leans in until our faces are but inches apart.

"He loves you because he is a part of you... Don't you see? The life you live, the years you have spent on this earth. It's his life, his years. Once your soul leaves this world, the connection will be broken. You really think he is going to care about you after that?"

"It isn't just a connection. It's not about this life or any other. Whether our souls are connected or not. Our hearts will always be as one." I say, mustering all the courage I have.

She releases my face and steps back. A devilish grin crossing her tight prim features.

"Well let's test that theory shall we? Right on time." She says, turning her attention to the other side of the room.

I squint my eyes through the darkness. I can hear footsteps, the giveaway that we are no longer alone, but I can't see who it is. But then he steps into the light of the flames and I lose my breath.

"Braize." I shout out not even realizing I had spoken. "I... I don't understand."

"Still haven't caught on have you?" Braize says, stepping next to Emily in front of the fire. His black eyes not breaking contact with mine.

"Emily gave you the map and key but you had to be the one to retrieve the amulet from the flames and I had to be there to ensure you didn't die. What good is the amulet if it's source of power doesn't exist?" He says, grabbing Emily around the waist and pulling her to him.

He leans down, placing a passionate kiss on her lips before breaking away and turning his attention back to me.

"Unfortunately Harper showed up before I

could do anymore. I was able to retrieve the amulet, but the locket and ring remained with you. Fortunately for us, he too played right into our hands. He took the locket from you ensuring you had no knowledge of the events. Then he returned the locket to you for safe keeping. Then there's dear old grandma. Her death couldn't have come at a better time. Thus reuniting you with the ring that she found in the woods. Once the other two pieces were in your possession, it was simply a matter of getting you here when Tate let his guard down."

"And Nicholas.... Is he in on this too?" I stammer out. My heart beat vibrating through my voice.

He lets out a low deep laugh. "That fool served his purpose. Played right into our hands. He panicked later of course, once he put together the pieces."

"So he's not helping you?"

"Well, he did help us, yes, but unknowingly. That little mistake will cost him dearly." He says, turning back to Emily.

The fire in her eyes grows with her anger and vengeance. Suddenly it all makes sense.

"Nicholas.... He's the traveler you fell in love with." I say aloud before I really think it through.

"Such a clever girl she is." Braize says to Emily.

"So all of this, it's all to get back at someone who broke your heart?" I say in disbelief.

"An added bonus... Can you imagine... A world where angels and demons can walk the earth as mortals? Free from the reign of our creator. Free to rule this world as we see just."

"You will never succeed." I retort, no longer caring to sensor myself. If I am going to die anyways then what does it matter?

"Well too bad you won't be around to enjoy the show." He spits back, a malicious grin distorting his features.

With that he reaches into his pocket and pulls out the amulet. Stepping towards the fire, he reaches up, placing the amulet a few inches above the two pieces already hanging in the flames.

When he pulls his hand away, the amulet remains. Now the three pieces are complete, forming a triangle, suspended in the air.

Emily crouches down and retrieves a book from the ground. She shuffles through a few pages before settling on one. She looks to Braize, who nods, and then redirects her attention to the book.

She begins reading something from the pages. Something I don't understand. I am chained, stuck, forced to look on in absolute horror as my world slowly disappears around me.

"What now?" Braize asks, once Emily has finished reading a section from the book she holds in her hands.

I wish I knew what was going on, what she had read, but it was in a language I don't understand. I struggle to free myself from my bonds but the more I struggle against them, the tighter they become.

Emily begins reading another passage from the book, ignoring Braize. Her eyes are closed and I watch in absolute fear as her features darken.

She tilts her head back and breathes deeply just as a breeze whips through the underground room. I glance around trying to pin point it's origin but I see nothing.

"It is complete." She says, opening her eyes

to look at Braize. A wide evil smile crossing her face.

In an instant she is thrown back against the wall to my left. Golden ropes that seem to have appeared out of no where binding her to the wall. She gasps in shock as Braize strolls towards her, his face dark, his mission clear.

"You never learn do you?" He chimes out, standing just inches from her.

"Did you really believe that I loved you, that I would help you defy the natural order of our worlds? Stupid girl, don't you see? You were blinded by love and you paid the ultimate price. How easily you let love blind you again." He says, reaching out to trail his finger along her lower lip.

"You tricked me!" She shrieks out, her voice echoing off the stone walls.

"I did what I needed to do to ensure that you would not bring harm to this world. I simply approached it the only way I knew how. I needed you to complete the triangle, but not so I could help you seek vengeance, so that I could destroy it."

"You wouldn't!" She spits out. "All of this, years of planning.... You would just throw all that away, waste it?"

"My dear Emily, my years are endless. I would spend many more if it meant righting this world of demons like you. You are dark, not because you took your own life, but because you have darkness inside of you. It has always been there."

"I suppose Nicholas sensed it pretty early on. You don't become a demon unless your heart is shrouded in hate. You have no remorse, no compassion. You care for no one but yourself. That is why you live in the dark. You don't belong in our world, or in this world." He says, turning his attention back to the triangle still floating above the flames.

"You won't get away with this!" Emily screams from behind him. "I will destroy you!"

Braize lets out a light laugh. "In case you have forgotten..." He says, taking his place next to the fire.

"I am more powerful than you could ever dream of becoming." Without glancing in her direction, he closes his eyes.

The ropes that hold her in place begin to snake around her neck, her waist, tightening as they coil.

Emily falls silent. Her red eyes burning fire but her body no longer able to fight. A white fog clouding around her mouth making her incapable of speaking.

"Braize." Nicholas steps forward from the stairwell to stand next to Braize by the fire.

"I can't believe it actually worked mate." He says, giving him a rough pat on the shoulder.

"Would someone care to tell me what the hell is going on?" I finally shout out. My frustration taking hold.

"She doesn't know?" Nicholas gapes at Braize in disbelief.

"Don't look at me like that." He snaps, his black eyes not leaving the fire.

"Don't know what?" I shout. Mentally willing them to look at me. To explain what is going on, what they aren't telling me?

"Before the end of the night, the amulet and all connecting pieces will be destroyed." Braize again speaks into the fire.

The fear that had momentarily subsided returns with full force. Unknown to them, but I know what fate waits for me once the amulet is destroyed. I will no longer walk this earth. This life is not my own, and will never be again.

I have accepted the things that I can not change. I knew my time of sacrifice would come eventually. Once the amulet is gone, I will be gone also.

"There has to be another way." I hear Tate's voice, before I see him.

He steps from the shadows, the light flickering across his beautiful face.

"You know what will happen to her if you do this."

"It is already done. You know I can't change this." Braize says, finally looking up to meet Tate's gaze.

"It's my life, I want her to have it. There has to be a way around this." He says, turning to meet my eyes.

The sadness, the fear, it bleeds through him and thus through me. I want so badly to wrap him in my arms, to tell him that it's okay, that I know, and that everything will be alright. But I can't produce the words, the actions to make it believable.

"It's not possible mate." Nicholas chimes in to Tate's right.

"It must be done." Braize says, closing his eyes. Within seconds the fire vanishes and then instantly reignites, only this time the flames are white and blue.

"Noooo!" I hear Tate scream. I search desperately for his face, the light from the flames is nearly blinding and I struggle to see anything at all.

Suddenly the chains holding me in place vanish and I crumble to the floor. Tate's arms are around me instantly, holding me tightly against his chest.

I can feel my body weaken. I know whatever Braize is doing to destroy the amulet is nearly complete. I can feel the life, the light, slipping into the distance.

I look up searching Tate's eyes. The beautiful eyes that have consumed my very existence from the moment they met mine.

"It's okay." I whisper. "I'm not afraid." I reassure him.

Truth is I am terrified, but my body and mind seem to no longer react to the emotion.

"I love you." I whisper, feeling my eye lids growing heavy.

I try so hard to fight against the pull. I'm not ready yet. I'm not ready to leave this life. I need to say goodbye, to my grandpa, to Charlie. I want to spend one more day in Tate's arms. One more day to feel alive.

I want so much and yet I know that I can't change this. I can't fight against it. Tate presses his forehead to mine.

"I love you angel." He sobs out just as everything fades away.

****

A beeping noise pulls me to consciousness. I open my eyes to a tired looking Charlie at my side. I flex my hand causing him to jump.

"Cal." He breathes out in relief.

I glance around and realize that I am back in my hospital room. The beeping noise caused by a heart monitor to the right of my bed.

I'm alive? I don't understand. I could feel

myself slipping away. I was so sure that my final moments had passed. So how is it that I am here, alive, Charlie by my side?

"What happened?" I eye Charlie questionably as he slides onto the side of my bed to sit next to me. Cupping my hands in his.

"What do you mean?" He responds, a little confused.

"How did I get here?" I choke out. My throat so dry it's nearly unbearable.

"Here." Charlie says, handing me a cup of water from my bedside table before I even have a chance to ask.

"I brought you here yesterday remember? They admitted you to do some additional testing." He studies me curiously.

Realizing quickly that he has no idea what I am talking about, I don't push for anymore.

"Do they know anything yet?"

"The nurse came in a while ago. Said that they had your results in and that the doctor would be in shortly." He says, worry blurring his handsome features.

"Everything will be okay." I reassure him,

giving his hand a squeeze. A knock at the door causes me to jump.

"Come in." I call across the room.

The door slowly pushes open revealing an old gray man. His eyes tired, his face sunken.

"Grandpa!" I shriek, as he closes the door behind him.

He quickly rushes to my side. Charlie stands, giving him room to sit next to me in the bed. He leans down giving me a half hug before taking a seat next to me.

"What are you doing here?" I ask, unable to hide my shock.

"Charlie called me. I was so worried." He sighs, taking my hand in his.

"Have you heard from the doctor yet?" He asks. I shake my head no just as another knock sounds through the room, followed by the arrival of a doctor I don't know.

"Miss Price. I'm Dr. Hickman." He says, stepping towards me.

"Hello." I respond, reaching out to shake his hand.

My grandpa stands and joins Charlie at the foot of my bed.

"How are you feeling?" He asks, checking the monitor to my side.

"I'm really tired, but other than that, I feel okay."

"Excellent." He responds, flipping through my chart before placing it on my bedside table.

"I have spent the last five hours studying your scans and blood work. I don't know how to describe it but the dark spots and the mass that we originally found on the MRI are gone."

"What?" I question him, shocked.

My heart rate kicks up speed. Could it be possible? Could I really be okay?

"It must have been a defect with the imaging. We did another round of tests and they all came back clear. Your blood work is clean. We want to do one more MRI before we release you, but as long as everything checks out, you should be good to go home a little later today." He smiles, retrieving my chart.

"The nurse will be in to get you in a few minutes." He says, exiting my room.

The room echos with sighs of relief.

"Oh thank god." My grandpa breathes out, leaning over to support himself on the edge of the bed.

Charlie gives him a pat on the shoulder and then finds my eyes, giving me a wink.

Relief floods through me. The tension and fear that has been eating at me has just fallen away. I don't know how all this is happening. I still don't understand how I even got back here.

One minute I am laying in Tate's arms, preparing myself to never again walk this earth as a mortal. The next, I am in my hospital room with Charlie and grandpa by my side and the doctors are telling me that I'm going to be okay.

I can't chalk this up to coincidence. I don't think it was a defect with the imaging either. Somehow something changed. Somehow I am still alive and what's more, I'm not sick.

The complete one eighty has my head spinning and honestly has me feeling a bit woozy. I let out a large yawn trying to fight back the heaviness in my eyes.

"Come on Charlie, let's let her get some sleep. I'll buy you lunch." My grandpa says, making his way over to me.

"We won't be far. Get some rest and we will be back in a little bit." He says, giving my hand a squeeze.

Charlie gives me a little wave as he follows my grandpa into the hallway. It takes only seconds for the loneliness to swallow me whole. The empty feeling that consumes me in Tate's absence.

What happened to him? How am I still alive? I roll to my side and close my eyes. Trying hard to calm my thoughts.

I hear the door open and close behind me. Assuming my grandpa or Charlie probably forgot something, I make no attempt to roll over and see who it is. My body is still so weak from everything I have been through over the last few days.

"Angel." I hear him whisper behind me. I turn quickly to find his beautiful face staring down at me. His eyes bright, his features soft.

Words fail me. So many questions, so many things I want to say. And yet in this moment, nothing. The love I feel for this man ties me up inside but something isn't right.

He seems okay, nothing screams that things

have changed. But I can feel it.

I no longer feel his presence. He's standing just inches from me and yet I feel nothing. Nothing that ties me to him. I search his face, looking for any sign that he notices it too.

He gives me a sweet smile and leans forward to place a small kiss to my forehead.

"You always were such a bright girl." He breathes against my hair.

"Nothing will ever change the way I feel about you." He places a gentle kiss across my lips.

The fire immediately ignites, coursing through my veins. The confirmation that I am most definitely alive.

"I don't understand." I breathe against his lips.

He pulls back and studies me intently before speaking.

"I thought I lost you.... I don't want to over analyze this or try to explain everything that has happened in the last forty eight hours. Right now, all I want to do is hold you in my arms and never let you go." He says, taking my mouth once more.

I can feel the break in connection. The bond

that ties Tate's emotions to mine seems to have vanished. But the passion, the love, the fire coursing through every inch of me is only confirmation that what we share runs so much deeper than I ever thought possible.

MELISSA TOPPEN

Chapter Twenty-Six

As I sit here at the creek bed, I am reminded of so many things. My parents, my sister, my grandma, but most importantly Tate.

This place holds a piece of all of them, it holds a piece of me. I didn't expect to find myself back here again, not so soon anyways, but my grandpa had insisted that I come home for a couple of weeks to recuperate once the doctors had cleared me for release.

As much as I didn't want to abandon my schooling so close to the end of term, I couldn't deny myself the opportunity to step away from all the things that have surrounded me lately.

I needed this. The peace that comes from being in the one place that has always been my escape.

The ground shifts beside me as Tate sits down next to me. He doesn't look at me at first. Instead he looks out over the flowing creek water.

It takes me a few seconds to realize that he really is here. His appearance is not something I expected but couldn't be more welcome.

"How am I alive?" I ask, meeting his gaze on the water.

He shifts but doesn't look in my direction.

"I was so sure that once the amulet was destroyed that you would be gone forever. While I may not be of this world, I understand it so much more than my own. While you weren't meant to exist you still did. In doing so you claimed your place in this world. Once the amulet was destroyed, you still remained. I didn't understand it at first."

I turn to find him staring at me intently.

"How is that possible?"

"I have spent the last week trying to answer that question myself. Among other things." He sighs, brushing his hand against mine. The contact causing my skin to buzz.

"What did you find?" I stammer out, losing

my focus the moment his flesh touches mine.

"I knew Nicholas was tied into this somehow but I couldn't connect the pieces. It took me months to figure out his play in all of this. When he approached you about the amulet, I was so sure he was working with Emily. Turns out he was working against her."

"And Braize... Why did he break into my room looking for the locket?"

"Originally he thought they only needed the pieces, turns out they needed you as well. Once he realized this, they waited until you had the final components to complete the triangle. They knew I would never trust them so they had to find a way to get to you when I wasn't around. Charlie provided that opportunity when he took you to the hospital."

"I still don't understand... Why did they need Emily?" I ask, searching his face.

"The spell is bound by dark magic. They needed her to release the spell of the amulet in order to destroy it."

"So they played her, just like Nicholas did when she was alive?" I can't hide the disgust in my voice.

"They did." He sighs, running his hand through his hair.

"I'm not saying the way they went about this was right, but Emily was dark, even as a mortal. Nicholas was just being, well, Nicholas. It wasn't until she set her plan in motion that she sealed her own fate. Nicholas helped Braize but later feared that he was in fact working with Emily and began trying to collect the pieces for himself. Eventually he realized they were fighting the same battle."

"So you are telling me that for nineteen years she has been planning this, all the while they have been planning to stop her?" Even saying it aloud, it doesn't make sense.

"To you, it seems like a lifetime. To us, time is limitless. Braize would have followed her for a thousand years if that's how long it took to seize his opportunity to destroy the amulet. She set this in motion, they simply waited until she made her move."

"Why now? Why at this moment?"

"I wish I knew." He says, shrugging.

"How did you figure it out? How did you find me?"

"I have been piecing it together for months now. It wasn't until Braize found me that things finally started to make sense. He was going to destroy the amulet, and if he couldn't do that, he was going to destroy it's source of power..."

"Me." I finish his sentence.

"I enlisted some help after you disappeared. Your professor is a very interesting man." He says, giving me a small smile.

"That he is." I agree, still not fully understanding the events that led us here.

"I was too late. The veil had already been dropped by the time I got to you. I thought I had lost you. That I had failed you."

"After you lost consciousness, I held you in my arms, waiting for the moment your heart would stop... But it never did. Destroying the amulet only destroyed the connection between your soul and mine. It destroyed the part of my soul that fueled your existence in this world."

"But I was never meant to exist, so how is it that I do?"

"Like I said before, you claimed your place in this world. You may not have belonged here in the beginning but this is where you belong now."

"And my illness? How did it appear and then disappear so quickly?"

"The curse that you carried with you everyday was taking it's toll. I should have seen the effect it was having on you. But it's the underlying that makes me wonder."

"You were given my years, so in turn, when my years expired so would you. That time must have been coming to a close, but once the connection was broken, your life was no longer bound by mine. I'm sorry, I should have protected you from this."

"You did protect me, can't you see that. You gave me a reason to live when I was never meant to." I say, standing.

Taking a couple of steps towards the water, I breathe in the fresh air.

"Where's Emily now?"

"I don't know. But I do know that wherever she is, she will never be able to harm you again." He says, taking a step forward to stand next to me.

"She said once the connection was broken that you wouldn't love me anymore." I say, noticing the quiver that runs through my body at the thought.

"She only wanted you to believe that. Look at me." He says, tipping up my chin. The moment his eyes meet mine I lose my breath.

"You are my only reason for existing. How that began no longer matters. What matters is that we are here now." He says, leaning down to place a soft kiss across my lips.

"Where do we go from here? So much is uncertain. You're a traveler. I'm human. How will this ever work? Look at what we have been through already. Could we survive anymore?" I ask, tears forming quickly at the thought of losing Tate now.

"One day at a time angel." He breathes, pulling me into his arms.

I wrap myself in his embrace. The feeling of his arms around me, the beating of my heart beneath his touch. I cannot imagine that there would ever be a better feeling in this world. One of safety, of love, of passion.

He loosens his grip on me to look into my eyes once more.

"I know that you have been through so much angel. Even though I know existence without you would never be possible, I would walk away, if it's what you wanted."

"That's the last thing I want Tate. I don't care about the danger or the fear. As long as you are by my side, I can face anything."

"It won't be easy. There will be forces fighting against us. Love between two existences has never be permitted, but life without you is worse than anything they could ever do to me."

"I love you." I say, my eyes locked hard on his. The electrical current flowing through me makes me want to climb out of my own skin.

"And I you." He says, wrapping his arm around my shoulder and turning us to face the water.

It's hard to accept the things I don't understand. It's hard to believe the things that seem unreal.

I have questioned my sanity on numerous occasions but only this reassures me that it is in fact my reality.

The feeling of his flesh against mine. The way my heart skips a beat at the slightest touch. It makes the unbelievable, believable. It makes the unreal, real. It makes everything that I have been through worth it.

I know that the road that lies ahead will not be easy. I know I will have to fight harder than I have ever fought in my life. But I'm ready. I'm strong. Tate gives me my strength, my courage, to face anything that may come.

It's so hard to believe that five years ago I was just a normal teenager. I was blissfully unaware of the world around me.

Now, standing here, side by side with Tate, I wonder how I ever lived that existence. One where he wasn't a part of my life, a part of my soul, all of my heart.

"So where to next?" I ask, snuggling into his side.

"Where you are, I will be. That's all that matters." He says, leaning down and placing his lips to mine once more.

MELISSA TOPPEN

ABOUT THE AUTHOR

Melissa is a lover of books and enjoys nothing more than losing herself in a good novel. She has a soft spot for Romance and focuses her writing in that direction but hopes to one day branch off and do something completely original. She loves music and is obsessed with the band Blue October! She has a rock star of a husband who gives it to her straight and two beautiful young children that show her what really matters in this life.

Connect with Melissa Toppen

www.mtoppen.com

www.facebook.com/mtoppenauthor

www.twitter.com/mtoppenauthor

www.goodreads.com/mtoppenauthor

Made in the USA
Charleston, SC
17 October 2014